Something Great

By

M. Clarke

This is a work of fiction. Names, characters, places, and incidents are products of the author's imagination or are used fictitiously and are not to be construed as real. Any resemblance to actual events, locations, organizations, or person, living or dead, is entirely coincidental.

Book Cover: Lindsay Anne Kendal
Editor: Maxine Bringenberg

To my husband,
you're my something great!

Dedication

Janie Iturralde—I don't know what I would do without you. You're the best beta reader. You're always there for me and I want you to know how much I appreciate your support and your friendship.

Jane Soohoo—a million hugs for all your time and energy making sure everything is in perfect state. I can't thank you enough.

Linda Lee—thank you for believing in me and for giving me great advice to make the story even better.

Kitty Bowers—thank you for being an angel in my life and for supporting me in everything I do.

Sam Stettner—thank you for being a wonderful, supportive friend. Your words of couragement have given me the spark I needed to know I've written something great. Love ya lots!

Author Alexandrea Weis—I cherish our friendship. Thank you for all your help and expertise.

Author Jennifer Miller—I love how our friendship started from Crossroads and grew over the years even though we live miles apart.

Author Shelly Crane—you took the time to reply and answer all my questions, and for that, I'm deeply touched and grateful.

Michele Luker—I'm so thankful for our friendship. You always go that extra mile. I'm so blessed that we've become good friends.

Extra thank you to Jennifer Miller and Shelly Crane for allowing my teaser to be placed in their book as well as their teasers in mine. You two are the sweetest.

Extra Extra thanks to Mary's Angels—my street team—extra times a million thanks to the admins, Janie Iturralde, Jacque Talento and Elliot McMahon. Your eagerness to get my books out there is amazing.

Thank you Lady Amber for all you help answering my endless questions, and for being one of the host for Something Great release party.

For my Crossroads fan facebook sites, thank you for supporting me in everything I publish. Love you all to pieces. Angie Edwards-Crossroadsbook, Janie Iturralde-Crossraods Saga Beyond, Make Crossroads A Movie-Mejeani Le Grange, Between & Crossroads Saga Eternity-Venna Dowrick, Crossroads Saga-Amber Hulsey-Lee, Crossroads Saga Fan-Christi Valencia

For my friends who took the time to read and review the ARC, I thank you with all my heart. Gracie, Rosie, Michelle, Holly, Hung, and Kristina. LOVE!

Gianormous thank you to the bloggers below. I can't thank you enough for all your support and for loving my story. Max and Jenna thanks you too…giggles.

Prologue

Entering my apartment, I could not wait for Peter to come over. I was planning a surprise dinner for him. Too excited about making dinner and wanting it to be perfect, I decided to ditch my psychology class. I had never skipped a class before, but I couldn't help myself.

Peter and I had been dating for almost a year. He is perfect in every way...charming, sweet, and very good-looking. He was the type of guy I would usually stay away from—the dangerous bad boy that knew how to smooth talk his way into your pants—but lucky for me, Peter has been gentle, loving, and faithful. He is a great, handsome package. The only problem is the distance.

The loud noise from my roommate's room told me one thing. She was having sex...again. This wouldn't be the first time I'd come home to find her with a guy in her room, but it was a good thing she kept her door closed. Cassandra had a very bad habit of sleeping with boys just for her pleasure. I didn't judge since she didn't have a boyfriend and it was mutual. Who was I to judge or even tell her what to do?

Feeling irritated, I quietly went to my room hoping I'd come home at the tail end of it and that it would be over soon. Trying to distract myself, I took out my textbook and started to read, but it wasn't helping. Instead, they were turning me on. Heat flushed to my face and parts of my body. Oh my god! It was like hearing a porn show, not that I would know what that was like.

Not wanting to be here, I got up and started to head for my bedroom door. Just as I reached for the doorknob, the screaming stopped. Debating whether to bolt out the front door or to stay put, I decided to see what they would do. Trying not to make any sound, I started to tippy toe to my desk. But what I heard next froze me in place and my heart dropped to the floor.

The sound of the door swinging open was what I heard first, then Cassandra's voice. "Peter...you don't have to leave. She'll be here in two hours. She's in class right now."

What did she just say? My heart started thumping in overdrive and I felt the blood drain out of my face. Hoping that I'd misheard her, I walked closer to the door.

"I can't be here when she comes."

"Aww...come on. How about round two?" Cassandra's tone was flirtatious.

Their voices were louder and sounded like it was coming right by my door. And that was definitely Peter's voice. Oh my God! What the hell? I couldn't believe this was happening. It can't be true. Feeling as if someone had just punched my stomach, I wrapped my arms around myself as I tried not to drop to the floor from feeling sick. I couldn't breathe and the room started to spin. I wanted to throw up and the taste of acid filled my mouth.

My body started to tremor with hurt and anger as I listened to their voices again.

"I would love to, but I can't. I need to run a couple of errands and I'll be back. What if she comes home early?"

"It never stopped you before. We've been doing this for a couple of months. She's never come home early. You should know by now how she is—the good girl, follows the rules, the boring type. When are you going to tell her you don't want to see her any more?"

As kissing and pecking sounds filled my ears, I backed up against the wall behind me. Soaking in their words, tears filled my eyes. She was right. I was the good girl kind, the stupid good girl who should be mad as hell and bolt out of my room, and give them a piece of my mind, but I couldn't. I hated being confrontational and I would rather run and pretend it never happened than face them.

Peter was the ideal boyfriend. How wrong I was about him. I took a chance on a person who had a reputation of being a player, thinking that I could prove everyone wrong and show them good-looking guys like him could have a serious, long lasting relationship. How wrong I was.

As my body shook and tears streamed down my face, I had to make a decision—stay here and wait for Peter to leave or face them now. When I heard the sound of a door closing and no voices after that, I decided to run out the front door and get away from everything that had happened. Wiping my tears, I quietly walked out of my bedroom door to find Peter by the sofa just standing there. Our eyes locked, both of our faces mirroring the same shocked look. And the dagger that was already in my heart, twisted painfully more, cutting deeper just seeing him face to face.

"Jenna." He cleared his throat. I could tell he'd figured out I was home since he was standing next to my backpack.

"How long—" he stammered.

"No. You don't get to ask me anything." My quivering lips were just as bad as my hands. I wanted to take my backpack with me, but I didn't want to be anywhere near him so I paced sideways to the front door.

"Jenna…please let me explain."

I didn't want to hear all the lies he would feed my mind. "How could you do this to us? You were my first. I gave you all of me…everything!"

Surprisingly, he looked apologetic, but I didn't care.

"Stop!" I yelled when he started to approach me. "I don't ever want to see you again. There is nothing you can do to fix this. We are done." Uncontrollable tears poured down my face. I hated that I was crying in front of him. Crying showed that he meant something to me. Crying showed that I was hurting. Crying showed that it would be difficult for me to trust someone like him ever again.

"Jenna, it's not what you think!"

I huffed a heavy sigh. Did he think I was that stupid? "I hate you! I don't ever want to see you again!" I yelled.

Peter crushed my heart and shattered it into a million little pieces. He broke me that day. Broke me to the point that it would change me forever. Trust would never come easily ever again. From now on, I would guard my heart and always take the safe road.

Without looking back, I ran out the door. That was the last time I saw Peter. As for Cassandra, we were never that close. Knowing what type of girl she was, I never cared to get close to her, but I never thought she would be this low. I learned a hard lesson that day. Some girls will do anything to get what they want, even if it meant hurting other people.

Chapter 1

"You're staring," I said to Becky, who was sitting across from me.

"I can't help it." Becky continued to smile at a stranger, flirtatiously batting her eyelashes, pulling a strand of her light brown hair behind her ear. "He's kind of cute, and he's looking right at me."

Oh…she is good. "But you think a lot of guys are cute," I mumbled lightly.

"It's probably the alcohol talking." She took a drink of her martini.

Becky and I had been roommates since my senior year in college. Our living arrangement transferred after graduation, which was pretty cool considering the expenses that went with living in an apartment near the beach. I had to say, it was an added benefit having your best friend live with you…sometimes.

Though Becky and I lived together, at times it was difficult when our schedules got busy. Sometimes we hardly saw each other, so it was nice to go out to dinner together even though it was in the middle of the week. We were both tired, but our friendship meant more than a little rest.

Becky looked behind her, then turned back to face me. "Twelve o'clock on your time. You see him?"

Trying not to make it obvious, especially since he'd caught my eyes after Becky turned around, I took a quick peek again. "He's okay." I shrugged my shoulders.

1

"You have such high standards. It's no wonder…wait a minute. I don't get you. Not to be mean about it, but you know you can do so much better than what's his face."

"You've told me that like, millions of times."

"Oh…is that all? And I still can't get it through your thick skull," she giggled.

"He's not that bad," I pouted, circling the rim of the glass with my index finger.

Becky's eyes moved again, starting from the back of the room, and stopped right behind me. "Oh my…talk about eye candy. Now…you can't say he isn't good-looking, because he just bumped the others out of the ocean. I think I need to cool off. Perhaps he should cool me off."

"Yeah, yeah, yeah," I said, thinking, here she goes again.

"Look behind you," she ordered, taking another sip of her martini.

"No."

"Why not? Afraid you may like what you see?"

"Becky, it doesn't matter if he's cute or whatever. I'm not a cheater. I'm not here to look for men. I'm here to be with you, to keep you company, to help you find someone. Just because you're not happy, don't think I'm not."

Then I saw the look in her eyes, the look that said I'd gone too far. My mom used to say, "Think before you speak, because words can really hurt, and you can't take back what you said, because the damage is already done." I didn't mean to hurt her. In fact, it had just slipped out from annoyance. Since the day I started seeing Luke, she'd told me nonstop how much he didn't deserve me.

Sure, I understood. She cared for me like a sister, but enough was enough. I was an adult. I was allowed to, and could, make my own decisions. Even my parents didn't tell me who or who not to date. "I'm sorry. I didn't mean to say that. It's not what I meant."

"If you're sorry, then look behind you."

"What?"

Becky crossed her arms. "I won't ever ask you to look after this."

With a heavy sigh, I turned. With perfect timing his eyes caught mine, and they stayed locked for what seemed like an eternity. As if he had somehow spellbound me, I couldn't move. My heart skipped a beat and I couldn't breathe. Look away, I told myself, but I couldn't. I would have sworn I felt my heart lurch and fall into my stomach. Heat like I'd never known before flushed my face. Dangerous tingles awakened every part of me. I couldn't understand this strange hold he had on me, and I didn't know if I liked the feeling at all.

He was gorgeous, about six feet tall with broad shoulders, wearing dark slacks; I couldn't tell what specific color, but who cared? His pin-striped dress shirt was unbuttoned at the sleeves and rolled neatly about a quarter of the way up his arms. Leaning back against the bar in a cool, relaxed manner, he was eye candy all right. Most likely, he was there to wind down after work.

I finally managed to turn back around and look at my friend, who gave me an "I told you so" look.

"Breeeeathe," she mouthed, curling her lips as far as she could, a huge smile on her face.

"He's cute. I'll admit it. So what?"

"Cute? You used the wrong word. He's hot."

Becky was right, but I didn't want to make it obvious that she was. Taking deep breaths, I turned my attention elsewhere, but my heart continued to beat a mile a minute. Why did he have that affect on me? I had never felt that way before. It was exhilarating and dangerous at the same time.

Peering up at my friend after I felt the heat on my face cool down, I wanted to take a gulp of her drink, but I knew I couldn't—I was allergic to alcohol—so I took a sip of my soda instead. When I did drink, which was rare, I would have a strong urge to urinate, and my whole body, literally from head to toe, would turn red, like I had a bad sunburn. Not to mention it would only take me a few sips to get tipsy. Yup…the alcohol affected me in more ways than one.

"Want me to invite him over here?" Becky offered.

"No," I said quickly. "We don't know him."

"Who cares?"

"If you want to invite him, then that's up to you since you're interested, not me." I felt the rush of heat again. Looking down at my drink, I tried to think of something else besides the hunk standing by the bar, whose face and the way he made me feel from just one look kept invading my mind.

"Darn," Becky said suddenly, looking upset.

Her tone snapped my attention to her again. "What?"

"I think he has a girl friend. A blonde just wrapped her arms around him and kissed him."

Without thinking, I turned quickly to find his back turned toward me, and sure enough, there she was. A feeling of disappointment fell on me. Oh my gosh! What am I thinking? I have a boyfriend. Well, not really a boyfriend; we were dating, though it had only been a month. Feelings of relief and guilt swept through me. I am dating Luke, I kept telling myself.

"He's just one fish in the ocean. There'll be others for you to catch," I muttered, gulping down my beverage. The icy, cool drink helped me temporarily, but the heat kept coming back, so I changed the subject and hoped the hot flashes would disappear. "So, how's work?"

"I just got tons of submissions to read. It's never ending. I'm excited about a few of them, but I also need a break from reading."

"You always say that, but then you drown yourself in the stories."

"I do, don't I?" she giggled. "Books are like picking ice cream flavors. Not everyone likes vanilla. The key is to find the flavor that is currently popular, and that determines which authors I take my chances on."

"You've been doing well so far."

"I have had some hits and a few misses, but I have to admit, I enjoy what I do. So, tell me; how's job hunting?"

"Did I tell you I have an interview next week?"

Becky peered over my head. "No you didn't, but that's great. I know how much you hate that job. I'm so glad we're catching up."

"I don't hate it, but I need something different. I really hope I get this one." I paused, looking at my friend, who seemed to be half listening to me. "What are you doing? Are you staring at them again?"

She ignored my question with a bright beam in her smile. "Look behind you...no...don't look behind you!"

"Are you okay?" I let out a small laugh.

Becky leaned closer toward me, like she was going to tell me a secret. "The blonde walked away. She probably went to the bathroom."

"So...your point being...?"

"He's leaning against the bar, but he's looking right at you. Well...not at *you*, but your back."

I busted out laughing...that was one of the most ridiculous things she'd said in a long while. But just the thought of him looking at me made me tense up. "My back? He could be looking at something, or someone, near me. Why would he be looking at my back? For goodness sake, stop staring."

"You think I'm making this up." She waved to the waitress coming our way. "One more please." She held up her glass. "Thanks, and we'd like the menu too, please...actually, are you ready to order?"

I nodded with a smile. "The same."

"I'll have the fish taco combo and she'll have the chicken salad."

After the waitress repeated the order she walked away.

"I don't know how you have the same thing every time we come here," she added.

"I don't know, I just like it, and that's what I feel like having again. What is it, pick on Jenna day?"

"No...sorry," she said sheepishly. "Anyway, just to prove my point, I dare you to turn around."

"No." I leaned back comfortably with my arms crossed.

"For someone so sweet, who never cusses, who plays by the rules, who orders the same thing every time, you sure can be stubborn."

"Well, I can't be all good," I smirked.

"Turn around before she comes."

"No."

"Ugggh. Okay…if I'm wrong then I owe you a favor, but if you're wrong you owe me one."

That sounded like a risk I was willing to take, because I knew for sure she was wrong. Why would he be staring at my back?

"Fine." I turned. My heart stopped for a second and then pounded in my chest. The familiar warmth flooded all over my body. Becky was right. Our eyes matched perfectly. He raised his bottle of beer and gave me a delicious smile that melted deep into my gut.

I didn't even know if I smiled back, but I somehow managed to turn back around. It didn't matter anyway, because guys like him were trouble…big trouble. Guys like him couldn't be trusted. Why? Because he was too damn good-looking, and his ego was probably as big as the restaurant we were sitting in. I was already judging him and I didn't know him, but it didn't matter. I was dating Luke, even though Becky thought he wasn't good for me. At least he wasn't trouble.

At some point in my rambled thinking, I had to look up to my friend, whose feet were tapping on the wooden floor that my eyes were glued to. "Okay," I said, looking squarely into her eyes. "You win." My left index finger went straight to my mouth, a very bad habit I had when I got nervous.

Becky reached over and took my finger out of my mouth. "You're going to bite your finger off over a guy you don't know?" she giggled. "By the way…I can't wait for you to return the favor." A mischievous grin was smudged on her face.

"Great," I said under my breath. "I can hardly wait."

Chapter 2

A feeling of warmth brushed my face as I stretched my arms to the ceiling. The sun's rays projected into my room, making it appear as though I was in the center of heaven's light. Mesmerized by it, I took in the beauty. Gazing toward the open shutters I had forgotten to close last night, I knew it was going to be a beautiful day. Yesterday had been dark and gloomy, but today the sun was showing who the boss was. It was like that in Los Angeles…even in the fall, sometimes if felt like it was spring.

The thought of the guy I'd seen at the restaurant the previous week had faded, and I couldn't remember what he looked like anymore, only how he'd made me feel. In a way, I had forced him out of my mind, because the guilt from thinking of someone else while I was with Luke felt wrong. I wouldn't want Luke to be thinking of someone else while he was with me, either.

Luke and I had met at a work meeting. His company became one of the clients I managed, so I spoke to him often on the phone. He was the owner of a fabric dying company, and our company bought fabric from companies like his, then sold the fabrics to clothing companies or designers. Basically, our company was the middleman, and I did all the negotiating on the prices and made sure everything happened in a timely manner.

Lately I had been bored with my job. I needed more of a challenge, more excitement, and more from my everyday routine life. It was time to move on if I wanted to grow in my areas of expertise…but exactly what did I need? I wasn't sure, but I knew that if I stayed where I was, that's what I would be doing for the rest of my life.

My boss understood. I was good at what I did and he knew it. My salary wasn't great, just enough for me to pay the bills, and I was basically living from paycheck to paycheck. This was another reason why I needed to move on. Thinking about the interview I was excited to have, I continued to lie in bed, when suddenly....

"Aaaahhh," I screamed, bolting out of my bed to look at my cell phone. It was seven in the morning, and my interview was at eight thirty...that day. I couldn't believe I had forgotten to turn on my alarm. I didn't have a clock per se, so my cell phone was my alarm. Strange...it was on, but I must have turned it off and gone back to bed.

Frustrated and mad at myself, I jumped into the shower. After dashing out, I brushed my teeth and pulled my hair into a high ponytail. With just enough makeup on, I got dressed—a dark gray pencil skirt, a white blouse, and a thick gray sweater to match the skirt.

Breakfast was out of the question as I walked out of my bedroom. I noted Becky had already left. She must have had an early meeting or gone to the gym. Surely she would have woken me. Clutching my leatherwork bag, I dashed out the door in world record time.

Just before I opened the double glass doors to enter, I tilted my head back to look up at the tall building in the middle of downtown Los Angeles. Feelings of excitement and nervousness burst through me, giving me tickling tingles from my fingertips to my stomach. *Breathe*, I told myself as I walked in.

Stepping on to the shiny cream polished floor, I felt like I was stepping on gold. I didn't like to compare, but my current place of employment was nothing like this. Gazing around, but continuing my rapid pace due to the time, I noted men dressed in suits and women dressed in pant or dress suits. I couldn't help but wonder which company they were working for, since there were so many in one building. Seeing the elevator sign, that was where I headed.

There were six elevators, three on either side of me. Others were already waiting for the elevators to open. Noting that the button to go up was already pushed, I waited just like everyone else. When the "ding" sounded, I waited patiently until the ones who were waiting before me entered first. It was crowded inside the elevator, but I didn't care. I was happy to be on it so I could get there just in time.

Looking at the buttons, I was surprised to see that there were fifty-four floors. I knew the building was tall, but I hadn't realized there were that many floors. That thought alone made me feel queasy. It was bad enough that my stomach had dropped when the elevator soared. Since the button for my floor was already pushed, I closed my eyes and waited for my turn to exit.

On several occasions I had to step out so the person behind me could exit, but I was glad when I finally exited on the twenty-eighth floor. A lady about my age walked out at the same time I did, trailing behind me. She must have been the one to push the button to this floor. Perhaps she is my competition for the job.

The clear glass window caught my eye first. It covered the entire back wall, the sunlight beaming dimly through it. What a fantastic view of downtown LA! The receptionist, sitting behind a semi-circular desk, peered through her glasses and looked straight at me. She'd obviously heard the embarrassing clicking noise from my heels, which made me feel like an elephant. With her hair tied up, she looked sharp and business like.

"Good morning. How may I help you?"

"I have an 8:30 interview."

"Your name?"

"My name is Jeanella Mefferd, but you can call me Jenna."

She looked down the list. "Ah, yes…there you are." Then she peered up with a smile. "Please have a seat. We are a little behind schedule."

Smiling back, I took a deep breath and eased my shoulders, relaxing for the first time since I stepped inside the building. The fact that they were behind would allow me to give more thought to my answers to the questions I may be asked. "Thank you," I said, turning my back to her and moving toward the empty chairs.

As I waited patiently, I couldn't help but look at my competition from the corner of my eye. Dressed in a black dress suit, she looked confident, and somehow I felt intimidated by her appearance. Perhaps it was from knowing she may have more experience than me, or maybe it was just my own insecurities. Who was I kidding? There must have been tons of interviewees. What made me special? What made me stand out from the rest?

Megan Crawford was the name she gave to the receptionist. Sauntering over to the empty seat next to me, she gave me a quick smile. Suddenly, it wasn't sunny anymore. The air around me, which I hadn't felt before from being too nervous, instantly became cold, and I shivered. I had to stop thinking negative thoughts, or I wouldn't make it through the interview.

Sitting next to a stranger was bad enough, but sitting next to your competition was even worse. She looked calm and collected, whereas I fidgeted like a child in my seat. Feeling antsy, I pulled out my cell phone. There were several texts, one from Becky and others from my friends Kate and Nicole. I clicked Becky's first.

Good luck, and let me know how it went. XO
I texted back. *I will.*
Then Kate's.
Go Jenna!
Haha. Thxs! Hugs!
Then Nicole's.
You'll do great!
Thank you!

Though I was excited to get texts from my friends, there was no text from Luke. Maybe he would call me later?

"Ms. Mefferd," I heard.

My head popped up and my heart raced faster than it ever had, except for the time I saw *him*. Oh God! Why am I thinking of him at a time like this? Funny, though…it actually helped me calm down. Okay. I can do this. "Yes?"

I turned my head to the receptionist to get more direction. She pointed to her right. "They are ready for you. It's the first conference door on your right."

"Thank you," I said, standing up. Not wanting to be rude, I turned to Megan. Before I could say a word, she spoke.

"Good luck," she smiled.

I wasn't sure if it was sincere, but at least she was polite. "Thanks. You too." Then I turned and headed to, hopefully, my future. This interview would make me or break me...well, maybe not break me, but it was a huge opportunity, and I had to do my best.

♥♥

Three pairs of eyes set on me as I paced toward a rectangular table. "Good morning," I smiled, hearing the clicking sound from my heels. Why does it have to click so loud?

"Good morning," they said in accord.

There were two males and one female, and they each had their wooden nameplate in front of them. Feeling a little flushed from anxiety, I tried to take several unnoticeable deep breaths as I sat and placed my workbag next to me on the floor.

"Ms. Mefferd, why don't you tell me a little about yourself?" the lady asked with a smile.

I hated that question. Why do they have to ask this question at every interview? "I was born and raised in Los Angeles. My resume, which you have in front of you, lists the schools and colleges I've attended, along with my extracurricular activities." I paused, thinking I may have given too much random information. Focus! "After graduation, I was hired at Tom Bradley Fabric Company. I'm currently still employed there, but he already knows about the interview today."

"Yes. We've already placed a phone call," Mr. Miles said. "He speaks highly of you. From what I can see on your resume, you've played many roles for that company."

Mr. Miles's words sparked a confidence in me I didn't know was hiding beneath the surface. My face lit up and my tone became different—stronger, with conviction. "Yes. Not only do I work with the clients, I am also the assistant director of the Human Resources Department. Benefits and Workers' Compensation are my specialties, along with customer relations."

"Ms. Mefferd," the other male asked. "We know what we are looking for. The question is…what are you looking for?"

I had never been asked that question before, and I was surprised they had asked it. What did I want? "Mr. Miles, Mr. Cole, and Ms. Simmons." I gazed into their eyes, one person at a time, as I called their names. "I want to work for a company that is fair, where I can learn, grow, and challenge myself to be better. I want to give my all to a company that will treat me as if I were a part of their family."

There was silence. It was so quiet that I could hear the whistle of the wind blowing outside the window. Not one of them looked at me. Had I said something wrong? Had the sun not beamed through the window, I certainly would have been shivering at that moment.

Several more rounds of questions followed about what I did for my current employer, and how long I had worked there. It seemed like I had been at the interview far longer than I had expected. Feeling light headed from not eating breakfast, I just wanted it to be over.

"Ms. Mefferd, we are looking to fill this position as soon as possible," Ms. Simmons said. "We also have a long list of interviewees, so it may take a week. If we feel that your qualifications meet our standards, you'll be hearing from our Human Resources Department. Thank you for your time."

With that, I stood up and shook all three of their hands, gazing at each of them with a smile. "Thank you so much." Then I walked out as softly as I could. Darn these heels!

Chapter 3

Feeling good about the interview, I decided to celebrate alone by feeding myself breakfast. But one never knew about these things. The last time I thought an interview went super well, I never got a phone call. Whatever happened, at least I knew I'd given it my best; but still, if I didn't get this job, I knew I would be very disappointed. Who was I kidding? I would be devastated.

First things first, I needed to eat. My face felt warm and my head was starting to throb, an indication I needed food...quickly. I had been unable to eat much the previous night due to the anxiety building up from the interview, and my body was giving me a warning sign. Recalling a coffee shop I had been to in the area, I decided to head in that direction, since I didn't have to be back to work until after lunch. A warm muffin and coffee would surely hit the spot.

Pacing down the sidewalk, I inhaled a deep, cool breath. Many pedestrians were walking on both sides of me, but I didn't pay attention to them. I was too busy focusing on the location of the coffee shop and the soothing warm sun I wanted to be under for a while longer. As I neared the delicious smell, I peered through the shop windows as I walked by. Then finally, I spotted what I was looking for two buildings down...Café Express.

Entering the double glass door, I quickly noted it was filled with customers, but many of them were leaving; I must have just missed the morning rush. Since the line was short, it put a smile on my face as I stood behind a man. Peering up, I looked at the breakfast menu, and everything sounded delicious. Decisions, decisions...what do I order? I thought to myself as I laced my hair back with my fingers.

The guy in front of me was taking so long that I decided to gaze around the room, looking at the small unique fixtures on the wall. Small paintings and cute little mugs of different sizes and designs added a nice touch to the ambiance.

I was just about done looking at every fixture when I suddenly froze. Heat zapped through my whole body. Sitting under a fixture of a butterfly mug, I saw *him*. I hadn't thought about him for days, and there he was, all dressed up in his work attire of a suit and tie. His eyes were beaming as they pierced through me, but he looked surprised, and radiated an irresistible smile. Surely he wasn't smiling at me, so I glanced behind me; there was no one there, except for the painting I was admiring earlier.

Without thinking I turned back to him. He lifted his cup of coffee at me with a flirty twitch of his eyebrows. I gasped inwardly and took a step to my right, knowing that the man had finished paying, and I suddenly felt something scorching hot and wet, brushing against my hand. My eyes followed my workbag as it fell straight to the floor and landed on top of a pool of brown liquid.

"Watch it, lady!" the man snapped, cursing beneath his breath, brushing off the soon-to-be stain on his light gray suit.

"Oh...I'm so sorry," I apologized sincerely. Without a care for my bag or the rude man, I brushed the wetness that burned my skin. Frowning, I brushed it harder as if I could make the pain go away.

Then I heard a male voice I didn't recognize. It was deep and soothing, and beckoned me to awaken.

"Excuse me, but I think you owe this beautiful lady an apology." His tone was strong and demanding.

I peered up to see *him* standing in front of me, blocking half of my view, as if to protect me with his body. Silence filled the air in the coffee shop; most likely, everyone felt the same tension I felt as we waited for the guy to apologize. If he didn't, what would *he* do? Thank goodness there was no one else behind me in line.

"I'm sorry," the guy said quickly, though not sincerely, and walked out the door.

He turned to me. "Are you okay?"

"I…I'm okay. Thank you, but it really was my fault. I wasn't looking," I said softly. I really wanted to tell him that it was his fault for distracting me, but I didn't.

Surprisingly, he grabbed my hand and examined it. His hands on mine felt light as a feather, but his warmth penetrated through my skin, making me hot all over.

"Ice," he said to the cashier, still holding my hand. At his command, one of the cashiers blinked and went to the back room. "It's not bad, but you should put ice on it just in case."

Feeling myself crumble from his touch, I slowly pulled my hand away and peered up at his beautiful soft brown eyes. I swallowed a nervous lump down my throat. "Umm…thank you, but I'm really fine."

The cashier came back with a bag of ice and placed it in front of him. "Thank you," he said, and without asking for my hand, he snatched it and placed the bag of ice on top of it. Smack in the middle of the shop, there we stood, attracting attention. By now, most of the customers were minding their own business, but I could still see a few looking at us curiously.

Not knowing what else to do, I accepted his help by placing my other hand on top of the ice bag, so he could release my hand. "Thank you. You've been too kind."

He took several napkins and started to wipe the liquid that had clung to the bottom of my workbag, and some that had splashed on the sides. Has he been holding it all this time? He was so sweet, yet I didn't even know him.

"Oh…thank you, but I can do it."

When I leaned toward him to retrieve my bag, my heels slipped on the wet floor that hadn't been cleaned yet. Before I could make a fool out of myself, he caught me with his arms. In his hold, I didn't want to be let go. Seeing his eyes at my eye level, I knew he had bent down somewhat to catch me. As I stared into his eyes, time stood still. The coffee grinder, the cash register, the voices from the conversations people were holding in their small groups, were all muted. I heard nothing but the sound of him breathing, and I felt nothing but his hot breath on my face and my own heart beating erratically.

Then...unwanted...I saw nothing but Luke's face. With a great amount of effort, I released myself from his hold, recaptured my bag, thanked him once more, and strode out of the shop as fast as I could, without looking back. Hunger was no longer on my mind or my stomach. All that echoed inside my head was that he called me beautiful, and his kindness had fed my heart and my stomach.

Chapter 4

"Over here," Becky mouthed, waving her hand.

I saw her from the distance. "My friend is already seated," I explained to the hostess. She gave me a warm smile and gestured for me to go. As I weaved around the tables, I noted that Nicole and Kate were already there, as well. Nicole and Becky wore their work clothes, but Kate was in casual attire since she didn't work in an office.

Excitedly I paced faster. It had been a couple of months since the four of us had gone out together. Days turned into weeks and weeks turned into months as life sped by. We were all busy with our own lives, not like it was when we were in college and it was easier to be under the same umbrella. After hugs and kisses to each of them, I pulled out my chair and sat. Drinks were already on the table.

"Sorry I'm late. I had to catch up since I was out half the day."

"So, how was your interview?" Nicole asked, taking a sip of her water.

"Who knows? I think I did okay, but you never know about these things. I thought I had a terrible interview with my current job, but I got the offer."

"True," Becky muttered.

The conversation stopped when the waitress came by.

"Hello," she smiled at me. "Looks like everyone is here. May I take your order?" After we ordered, she left.

"Anyway, it's not the end of the world if I don't get it," I continued. I gazed at my friends, who were intently listening and giving me the "I know you're lying" look. "Okay…it will be end of my world if I don't get it. I've had my eye on that company for so long." Exhaling a heavy sigh, I plopped my head on my crossed arms.

"It's okay, Jenna. Think positive. There'll be other opportunities if you don't get this one. Everything has its right timing. Everything folds into its place the way it was meant to be at the right time. Geez, I sound like a Hallmark card. Maybe I should write a book," Becky snorted.

I strongly believed what she'd said, but I had needed to hear it from a friend's mouth. With that, I sat tall and enlivened the mood. "So, how was everyone's day?"

"Breast feeding and feeling like a cow," Kate sputtered.

We all broke into laughter, except Becky laughed a little harder. Liquid sprinkled out of her mouth from trying to hold it in. "I'm so sorry," she laughed, dabbing the table with her white linen napkin. Thank goodness dinner hadn't arrived yet.

"It's fine," Katie continued. "I get spit up on by my baby all the time. I'm used to it."

Giggling, we calmed ourselves down. Kate was the first one of our group to get married, and the first one to have a baby. Her being pregnant was one of the reasons why she'd married her college boyfriend. I still remembered her beautiful wedding as if it had happened yesterday. Becky and I were in her wedding party, and Nicole was her maid of honor. Having been placed in a group project together in college had brought our band together.

"That's all I do all day long. Feed, burp, diaper change, and clean spit ups. Don't get me wrong…I love my baby, but I'm so glad I'm out here with all of you. I miss just hanging out," Kate continued. The wetness in her eyes made her eyes twinkle. "We should do this more often."

"We need to set the next date now," Becky suggested, taking out her cell phone. "Cause…." She paused as she clicked away.

"We say that all the time, but it's difficult and time just flies by. Next thing you know, months have gone by."

The rest of us took out our cell phones, punched some keys, and marked the date on our phone calendars. After about fifteen minutes, the waitress came back with our dinners. Becky and I had ordered the same seafood salad, Kate was having seafood linguini, and Nicole had ordered salmon with assorted vegetables.

"Becky told us you're seeing someone," Kate said suddenly. "What's his name, what does he do...give us his history."

I shot my eyes to Becky then shifted my gaze to Nicole and Kate. "His name is Luke, and I met him about a month ago. His company is one of the companies I deal with. He's cute and nice." I didn't have much to say after that.

"Do we get to meet him?" Kate asked, turning her fork, making a ball with the linguini.

"I met him already," Becky blurted. "He's no good for her."

I nudged Becky on the shoulder and gave her a look.

She ignored me. "You need to date around. Don't be exclusive with him. If you don't you won't know what you're missing...like that guy we saw last night. You need to do this while you're young and not officially in a relationship. I know you don't have much experience." She paused. "Hardly," she giggled. "But that's okay. Our little miss innocent here is finally adventuring out."

"Let me ask you this." Kate leaned over. "When you kiss him, do you see stars and fireworks? Do you explode...way down there?"

Becky and Kate giggled, but Nicole was keeping to herself. She had been quiet, which was unusual, but I didn't ask. Instead, I kept one eye on her facial expression, which was pretty much blank. Her fork played with the broccoli, but never entered her mouth. While our plates were already a quarter empty, she had hardly touched her food.

"Well?" Kate twitched her brows, demanding an answer.

I didn't say a word...I didn't have to. My roommate sitting next to me did, since I told her practically everything. "She hasn't kissed him yet," Becky shared.

Kate's brows raised. "Really?"

"You know how Jenna is," Becky reminded. "She's careful. She's safe. She's not like us. I've kissed guys on the first date...hell, I've even had one night stands."

"Well...in my defense, we've only dated like four times. I'm seeing him again on Friday night. Maybe I'll let him kiss me."

"That's like three days away. I want to meet the guy who finally stole Jenna's heart. Can I come?" Kate said out of the blue, teasing.

Becky and I flashed our eyes at her in accord.

"I'm just joking. I'm just so excited for Jenna," Kate said. "It's been so long." Kate paused. Her eyes grew and cringed. "Shoot...my nipples are hard and my breasts feel like water balloons ready to burst." Kate started eating a little bit faster. "I'm going to have to go soon."

"But you just got here," I pouted.

"I know, but when they get really full, they don't feel good, and then I start leaking...the joys of breast feeding."

"Wow. Sounds like something I may not want to do," Becky commented, sticking her fork into her shrimp.

"You say that now, but just wait until you have the little one in your arms," Kate gushed. "It's just the most wonderful feeling you'll ever know...well, next to sex, of course."

With her statement, we started to laugh again. But when Nicole didn't laugh with us, I knew for sure something was wrong. "Nicole, is something wrong?"

Nicole's eyes were focused on the table at first, then tears dotted her cheeks. "Keith broke up with me."

"Oh, sweet Nicole." Kate wrapped her arms around her, making her face disappear into her shirt. Nicole had been dating Keith for about a year after meeting him at work. Actually, he was one of her bosses at a huge insurance company. In a way, I'd had the feeling that it wouldn't last. Keith was not the type of guy to settle down. How did I know this without really knowing him? Because there were two types of guys...the ones that would break your heart, and the ones who would treasure it.

"What happened?" Becky placed her fork down.

Nicole finally took a breather, sat up, and wiped her tears. "Actually, I broke up with him. He didn't ever want to get married, so I left him. I mean…why would he just drag out our relationship if he never wanted more?" Her eyes started to pool with tears again.

I wanted to comfort her, but I was sitting on the opposite side of the table, so I tried my best to comfort her with my facial expressions and with my words.

"It's okay," Kate said softly. "It's better you know now than in another year."

"Okay," Becky said loudly. "Next Saturday, everyone at our place for dinner. We're getting Nicole wasted."

Then that was that. Kate said she didn't have enough milk pumped, so she needed to head back home to feed her daughter of two months. Becky and I stayed to console Nicole.

M. Clarke

Chapter 5

Thank God it was Friday!

When I entered our apartment, Becky was already home. "Hey, Becky," I said out loud.

"Hey, there," she greeted, popping out of the kitchen with an apple in her hand, and then eyed my chest. "I love the delicate ruffles on your cream sweater."

"You can borrow it, if you like."

"I'll let you know," she winked. "So, got any plans tonight?"

I watched her take a bite of the apple. Apples had never looked so good, and my mouth was salivating. I guessed I was hungry and didn't know it. "Got another one?"

She went back to the kitchen and tossed one to me. "Thanks." With the first bite, the juice streamed down my throat. With a crunch my teeth pulled the meat off it, and I savored the taste. "Good," I managed to say while I was chewing, and then remembered her question. "Oh…Luke is taking me out. We're going out to dinner."

Taking another bite of her apple, she leaned against the white wall next to the television. It wasn't a big one, but it was big enough for our smallish apartment. Her eyebrows narrowed, most likely trying to think of something to say. "Oh yeah…I forgot. Okay, have a great time, and give me details tomorrow."

My mouth was full, but I spoke anyway. "What details? We're just going out to dinner. I'm not sleeping with him."

"That's fine, but you're gonna kiss him, right?" Her tone sounded muffled from a mouth full of chewed up apple.

"What?" My tone went up a notch. "I'm not making the first move."

Her eyes sparkled. "I had a feeling you were going to say that. I think he will, and when he does, you'll know if you see or feel fireworks."

I was just about to say something when our land phone line rang, but Becky beat me to it and answered it. "Hello...yes...yes. Hold on a minute please." She looked at me with a questioning look. "It's for you."

During the whole week I'd been trying to forget about my interview. I had a strange gut feeling this wasn't a personal call. My family and friends usually called me on my cell phone. Swallowing a nervous lump in my throat, I answered.

"Hello, this is Jeanella Mefferd. Yes...yes...yes...sure...no problem. I can do that. Thank you so much."

I hung up with a frowning face and looked at Becky, who had been staring at me the whole time, as if she knew. Perhaps the speaker had told her what company she was from.

"It's okay," she said softly, pulling me into a hug. "There'll be other jobs, I promise."

I couldn't hold it in any longer. Not only was I a bad liar, I couldn't even fake disappointment that long. "I got the job!" I squealed at the top of my lungs.

Becky pulled back, squinting her eyes, looking surprised. "You...." She socked me lightly on my arm. "Congrats!" She pulled me in again and squeezed me tightly.

"Ahhh...I can't believe it. I thought they would take at least another week to decide."

"So when do you start?"

"They said as soon as possible. I'll have to go in and talk about details." Floating above the ground from the awesome news, I plopped myself on the sofa. Becky went to the kitchen to throw her apple core away, sank down next to me, and narrowed her eyes at my sweater. "You're not wearing that tonight, are you?"

For a second, I had forgotten I had a date, and I stared at my half-eaten apple. "Should I wear something else? I thought you liked my sweater."

As if she had sat on a pin, she jolted up and quickly pulled me along with her to her bedroom. "You need to wear something else if you want him to kiss you."

Becky's room was like mine, very simple. A queen size bed sat in the middle of her room, a tall wooden dresser was placed at the corner, and a small desk was situated on the opposite side of the dresser. One positive thing about our apartment was that we each had our own bathroom, but the down side was that when our guests needed to use one, they had a peek of our rooms.

On top of the desk were a computer and her cell phone, and the top of the dresser was adorned with several Swarovski crystal picture frames I had gifted to her on her birthday. In one of the frames was a picture of us that I had slid inside. Another one held a shot of the four of us—Nicole, Katie, Becky, and I. The third frame held a picture of her family—her parents and her younger sister.

Rummaging through the closet, sliding hanger after hanger, she pulled out a black dress. "Here. This is the perfect dress. He won't be able to resist you with this on."

I was just about to take a bite, but instead I shook my head vigorously. "Noooo way. That thing is way too tight and too low. I don't want to tease him or send him the wrong message."

"Just try it on, and if you don't like it, you can take it off. It doesn't look the way you think it looks."

How could I say no when she gave me the puppy eyes and an alternative? With a sigh, I exchanged the apple for the dress and tossed it on her bed. After I stripped off my sweater and pants, I slipped it on and stood in front of her long closet mirror. To my surprise, I liked it. It transfigured me into an elegant woman. Dipping just enough to show the cleavage of my breasts…but not too much…it fell nicely on the curves of my body.

I felt different, more confident and even beautiful. Turning to face Becky, I knew she would give me an "I told you so" look, and sure enough she did. Shaking her head with a proud gleam, she lit a huge smile. "Love, love, love. See…I always know what's best for you. Come on, let's fix your hair and makeup."

Becky handed my apple back to me, tugged me to the bathroom, and started to fuss with my face and hair. "If only that guy from the restaurant could see you. If you had been dressed like this, he would have come to our table for sure."

"He was with someone, remember? Why are we even talking about him?" I arched my brows. "I'm going out with your favorite person." Rubbing in the word "favorite," I watched her grimacing facial expression.

"Okay…I'll give Luke a chance if you tell me that you like him after you kiss him." She reached over with one hand while holding the curling iron with the other. Placed in front of me were a pair of fake diamond earrings and a pendant necklace. "Here. Save some time, put these on."

"You don't give up, do you? And thanks."

"Nope, not when it has to do with your happiness."

Needing free hands, I bit the apple in my mouth and put them on. They added a touch of flavor to the dress. Then my mind wandered to thoughts of Nicole, and I turned to face Becky as I took the last bite of the apple, but she guided me back to face the mirror. "That was a good idea putting us in a group text," I slurred as I chomped away.

"Now hold still or I'll burn you by accident," she scolded. "And yes…it was a good idea. Glad I thought of it." She giggled proudly with a smirk on her face.

"At least we can be close to each other through texting, since it's difficult to get together. We're still on for tomorrow night, right?"

"Didn't you read the text?"

"That's the problem with group texting; if you don't scroll up, you miss things. I guess somehow I missed it. Nicole seemed fine when I called her last night, but you know how she is. She won't say much."

"Don't worry. If she says she's fine then she is. Just worry about your date tonight." She let go of the strand of hair that she'd just curled. It bounced softly against my cheeks, but it was hot so I turned a bit to the right. I thought about telling her that I had run into *him*, but it didn't matter. The likelihood of running into him again was slim to none. And again, I was dating Luke, not him.

Just as she finished curling the last section of my hair, the doorbell chimed. Looking at my watch, I saw that he was right on time. Startled, I flashed my eyes to Becky.

"I'll open the door. Go get your black heels, sweater, and your purse."

"Thanks." I hugged her, speed walked to the kitchen to throw the apple core away, and headed toward my room.

Taking a peek through the crack of my bedroom door, I could see Luke standing by the door waiting, looking slightly uncomfortable next to Becky. He wore casual black pants and a yellow sweater, bringing out his emerald green eyes. He looked simply "nice." Smiling, I paced toward them, wondering what kind of questions she was drilling him with. She was really good at that. Though at times it was annoying, I knew her heart. Her intentions were always good.

The clicking sound of my high heels caught Luke's attention. When I caught his eye, his eyes popped open with a shy smile. I couldn't read what he was thinking, but I think he liked what he saw.

"Hello," I said nervously. Though the unbuttoned sweater covered the front of the dress somewhat, you could still see a little cleavage. I wasn't used to wearing any type of clothing that even showed a peek of my breasts…except my swimsuit, sort of.

"Hi," he greeted. "You look very nice."

"Thanks, so do you."

Then it was silent. The three of us stood there for an awkward several seconds until I finally spoke. "Shall we?"

Luke nodded and I led him out the door. Just before I closed the door behind me I looked over my shoulder. Of course Becky was right behind me, puckering her lips, making a kissing sound. "I can't wait."

I busted out laughing, but just before it became even louder, I covered my mouth. Shaking my head, I mouthed. "I love you too. Don't wait up for me."

She raised her brows in surprise, but her interpretation of "don't wait up for me" was different than mine.

Chapter 6

Luke wasn't the "perfect gentleman" type of guy. Most men opened the car door for their date, but he never showed that kind of charisma. But what did I know about men, anyway? They were all different, just like us. Was it too much for me to want him to open the door for me?

The restaurant was nice, dimly lit, and not too crowded. White linen tablecloths covered the tables that were adorned with candles on top, giving it a romantic ambiance. I had to give him credit for that. The hostess took us toward the back to a table for two, but the tables were very close together. I had hoped there wouldn't be anyone sitting near us.

The hostess pulled out my chair, and after I sat, she placed the white linen napkin on my lap. "Thank you," I said to her.

"The waiter will be right with you." She smiled and left.

"How was your day?" Luke asked. He had one eye on me and the other eye on the phone. "Sorry…checking an urgent email."

"That's okay. I had a fantastic day actually. I got the job I was talking about." I tried my best to contain my excitement, but he looked at me like he had no idea what I was talking about. I clearly remembered texting him about it the night before. Apparently, he hadn't read the text or had forgotten.

"Yes, of course, I remember," he said slowly and mechanically as his eyes flickered to his phone, then to me. "That's wonderful. What position will you be holding for the company?"

"I'll be going in to talk about that next week."

"I see," he nodded, looking past me, seemingly in deep thought, but not about our conversation.

The waiter came by with the menus. "May I take your orders for your drinks?"

I was just about to ask for a glass of water when Luke broke in. "We'll both have glasses of water, please."

He didn't even ask me what I wanted. I brushed it off, thinking he knew I always ordered water.

"Sure." The waiter left after he told us the specials.

Gazing from top to bottom of the menu, I had a hard time deciding what to order, especially when all I could think of was the need to use the restroom. "Excuse me. I'll be right back. Can you order me the salmon special if the waiter comes back before I do?"

"Sure."

Not knowing exactly where the restroom was, I headed toward the back where restrooms were usually located. This place was like a maze, or I had a very bad sense of direction. Seeing a bar, I thought I'd ask the bartender.

Though there was no one standing behind the bar, I figured the bartender went to get something and would be right back. From where I stood, I could see the waitress and waiters, but I didn't feel like walking in that direction again just to ask a question, so I waited. I could see the pendant on my neck sparkling brilliantly against the mirrored wall. What a great fake diamond!

From the corner of my eye I saw a figure, but dismissed it and shifted my eyes to the right, where they settled on the elusive restroom sign. I was just about to head in that direction when someone spoke to me from behind in a deep, manly voice that sent shivers down my back.

"I'm your prescription. Let me be your new addiction." His words glided like butter, smooth and cool.

Startled, I twitched, and turned my body to his voice. There he was, all six feet of him, peering down on me with that smile that could make me do just about anything. Though there was nothing to laugh about, especially seeing this hottie in front of me, I couldn't help but giggle from his words.

He wore beige casual pants and a black sweater that fit perfectly to the tone of his body. His hair was brushed to the side, showing his nice forehead. Whatever kind of cologne he had on made me want to dive right into his arms...maybe it wasn't the cologne, but just him.

"Pretty cheesy, huh?" he chuckled.

I shyly giggled as I stared down at my shoes. What's wrong with me? Answer him. "Umm...kind of," I smiled as I peered up, only to have him take my breath away again.

"Sorry. I just had to say that. You looked so lost and vulnerable. Did you need some help?"

Great! To him I was just a lost puppy...lost and vulnerable. "I actually found what I was looking for." I was staring into his eyes, melting, feeling myself sinking into him. Snap out of it!

"You certainly did," he said with a playful tone.

Arching my brows in confusion, I thought about what I'd said. From his perspective, my words had been about him.

"We meet again, for the third time."

He was counting?

"You left so abruptly at Café Express, I didn't get to ask you for your name."

"Umm...my name? Oh...my name is Jeanella Mefferd, but you can call me Jenna."

Extending his hand, he waited for me. "I'm Maxwell. But you can call me Max."

Nervously, I placed my hand in his to shake. It was strong, yet gentle...just right, and heat blazed through me from his touch.

"Are you here with someone?"

"Yes." I looked away shyly.

"Are you lost? Do you need some help?"

"Actually, I was looking for the restroom. Since I didn't know where it was I thought I'd ask the bartender, but I guess there isn't one, and I'm on my way to the restroom." I rambled nervously as I slowly pulled my hand back to point in the direction I meant to go.

I had just realized we were holding hands during our short conversation. "So...I'd better go."

"I'll walk you there."

What? "Oh...no need. I'm sure I won't get lost." Feeling the heat on my face again, I turned before he could say another word, but it didn't matter what I had said. His hand was gently placed on my back, guiding me to the women's room. I turned my back to the bathroom door to thank him, but he spoke first.

"I think this is my stop," he muttered, looking straight at me. "I'm not wanted in there. What do you think?" He arched his brows, and his tone held a note of challenge.

Huh? He wants to go in with me? I gasped silently, as I was still lost in his eyes. "I think the women in there will throw themselves at you." I couldn't believe I'd said those words. I couldn't take it back. What was I doing, flirting with him?

He seemed to like what he heard. His arms reached out, his muscles flexing as he placed one on each side of me on the wall. With nowhere to go, I was trapped inside the bubble of his arms. He leaned down toward the left side of my face and brushed my hair with his cheek. "You smell...delicious," he whispered. His hot breath shot tingles to places I hadn't expected them.

Out of nervousness and habit, my left index finger flew inside my mouth. Max gave a crooked, naughty grin and slowly took my hand out of my mouth. "Did you know that biting one's finger is an indication one is sexually deprived?" His words came out slowly, playfully, but hot. "I can fix that for you, if you'd like."

He did not just say that to me! I parted my lips for a good comeback, but I couldn't find one. Feeling my chest rise and fall quickly, I tried to control the heated desire. Sure, he'd helped me once, but that didn't mean we were friends, or flirting buddies, or that I would allow him to fix my sexual deprivation. Oh God...can guys tell if you haven't done it in a very long time? This had to stop or else...oh dear...I wanted to take him with me into the restroom.

Needing to put a stop to the heat, I placed my hand on his chest... big mistake. Touching him made the heat worse, and tingles that were already intensifying burst through every inch of me. I had to push him away.

As if he knew what I meant to do, he pulled back, but his eyes did the talking instead. There was no need for words; I felt his hard stare on my body, as if he was undressing me with his gorgeous eyes. His gaze was powerful, as if his eyes were hands; I felt them all over me, completely unraveling me.

Just when I thought I was going to faint, his eyes shifted to mine again. "It was really nice to meet you, Jenna. I'm sure we'll see each other again, real soon. I better let you go. Your someone must be waiting for you. By the way...." There was a pause as he charmed me with his eyes again. "You...took my breath away. If I were your someone, I wouldn't let you out of my sight for even a second, because someone like me will surely try to whisk you away." He winked and left.

Oh no...don't ever wink again. That wink made me shiver even more, let alone his words. I pushed the door with my behind without thinking. Thank goodness there was no one by the door, or I would have knocked a stranger over with the force of my push. Max was right. How long had I been away, but did Luke even care? Oh no...what if he came to find me and he saw...oh no! I quickly took care of business and headed back toward our table.

Wiping Max and his words out of my head, I had to think of an excuse. What would I say if he saw us? How could I explain? Anxiety was rising to the surface, and so was my blood pressure. Just as I turned the corner to our table, I saw that another couple had been seated next to us. I gazed around the room, a little upset. Why would they seat another couple next to us when there were other empty tables around us? I didn't understand.

"Luke, I'm so sorry," I apologized as I sat. "I got lost and then...."

Oh no...Max was sitting adjacent to me, and his beautiful date was sitting across from him. My face felt hot, but my hands felt cold as the blood drained down to my toes. Max having a date was not the issue. Flirting with me when he was on a date was. How wrong was that? He was trouble for sure. In a way I felt guilty, guilty towards Luke, because I had enjoyed it.

"Are you okay?" Luke asked.

Placing my hands on my cheeks, my cold hands soothed them somewhat. "I think I'm coming down with something," I whispered, trying not to attract Max's attention, but who was I kidding? He was not blind or stupid.

"Would you like to go home?" Luke asked, looking concerned.

"I'll be fine, Luke. Maybe I just need something to eat."

When dinner arrived, our conversation was minimal. A part of me kept quiet because of Max. In a way, I was more interested in their conversation, because his date giggled every so often. From what I could tell, she was tall and her dark hair fell to her shoulders. Was this a personal or a business date? I couldn't tell, but why did I care?

Never once did I look his way, and never once did he look my way. Well, truth be told, I did peek with my peripheral vision. I wasn't sure if Max snuck a glance, but Luke looked their way when Max's date was a little bit too loud.

When Luke excused himself to the restroom after he had finished his dinner, Max's date did the same thing. Though there were more couples around us now, I felt as though this place only existed for the two of us. Feeling uncomfortable, I focused on my plate. With my fork, I swirled around what was left of my mashed potatoes. Suddenly, I gasped and turned. I knew it was Max, but the fact that he'd pulled up his chair and bumped his shoulder into mine startled me.

"Hi, again. Ignoring me, aren't you?" he said casually, as if we were good friends.

I turned to him. His face was way too close for my comfort. I had no choice but to gaze into his hypnotic eyes. "Ignoring you? I hardly know you, and you and I each have a date," I snapped. I didn't know where the angry tone was coming from.

"We can fix that."

"We can?" I asked, dumbfounded.

Instead of answering, he tilted his head, with a look as if he remembered something he wanted to say. "I meant to ask you how your hand was earlier, but I got a little...distracted." Max grabbed my right hand and tenderly rubbed the area where the hot coffee had spilled. He'd even remembered which hand it was.

"It's much better. Thank you for asking," I mumbled, fixated on his index finger, stroking the area on my hand. His touch produced a tingling vibration that was slowly waving throughout my body, and I didn't want him to stop, but I managed to pull back without offending him. If I'd let him continue, I would have dived into his arms, and I didn't want to make a fool out of myself.

"Good. I'm glad, but I think your someone is boring. And he doesn't treat you well."

Now, he was being rude and arrogant. "He's just fine. You don't know him."

"True, I don't know him. Maybe your someone is with my someone, and they're making out in the bathroom."

I didn't know why I thought that was funny, but I laughed, a good hardy laugh, the kind of laugh that gives you tears, and he laughed with me. No, I couldn't see what he'd just planted in my mind, but the thought was hilarious. But why? Because I thought that a sweet, non-dangerous type of guy like Luke wouldn't make out with someone like her. Nah...couldn't picture it.

Wiping the little tears that had settled in the corner of my eyes, I looked at Max. His eyes were soft and kind, and he looked at me with the sweetest smile. Neither one of us looked away, as if we were reaching for something deeper. I felt something that I couldn't describe in his gaze, like I had known him all my life. There was a strong, undeniable connection, like two lost souls finally finding each other. Was it the hot, steamy flirtations we shared, or was it the laughter? I didn't know. Whatever it was, I liked the feeling too much. But at the same time, it frightened me deeply, so I looked away.

Just in the nick of time, Max settled back to his table. Luke showed up first. He didn't ask me if I wanted dessert or if I was finished; he'd already paid the bill, and just asked me if I was ready. As usual, he didn't walk with me. I followed behind him. Was someone like Luke—a readable, easy, non-dangerous type of guy—what I wanted? I wasn't sure, but my eyes were opened that night.

Just before Max was out of my sight, I peered over my shoulder. I figured I was safe to look since his date had come back just as I got up, but I was wrong. His piercing eyes were watching me the whole time as I exited, and just before I turned the corner to disappear, he winked at me, leaving me completely unglued.

Chapter 7

Luke and I walked down the long hallway in silence and stopped at my door.

"I had a nice time," he said. "Are you busy next weekend?"

"I'm not sure yet. I'll be starting my new job, and I don't know how busy I'll be."

He nodded with a smile. "I understand. How about we play it by ear, and you let me know what evening you are free."

"Sure," I agreed as our eyes locked. He leaned closer. This was it...Becky was right. He was going to kiss me. There it was, his lips on mine. While he rubbed my arms, he pressed deeper. I kissed him back, but not for long, and I pulled back shortly after.

"I'll call you later," he said and walked away, leaving me wondering if I'd seen fireworks...and nope. But it was a nice soft kiss. Since I hadn't kissed many guys, I didn't have much to compare it to. If I had to describe it in two words, it was wet and sloppy.

Opening the door with my keys in my hand, I was almost positive Becky would be waiting up for me since it wasn't too late, but she wasn't. Either she was out or she was already sleeping. Not wanting to wake her, I went straight to my room. After I showered and got ready for bed, I snuggled inside my blanket and cuddled up with a book I had started reading.

Young adult romance novels was the genre I loved to read, ever since I'd picked up a book from Target...recommended by Becky, of course. The author was one of her clients. Though I loved books about vampires, angel stories were my favorite. Just as I reached the part where the heroine described how she was feeling about the male she had encountered, my heart did a funny flip. Then a vivid image of Max's face pooled to the forefront of my mind.

Not liking how he was invading my mind, I closed my book and turned off the lamp next to my bed. Why was I thinking of him? I didn't even know him. Sure, we flirted, but it meant nothing. Obviously he got a thrill out of doing it, even though he was with a date. Guys like him were trouble. Luke was safe, and he was nice, the kind of guy that would only date one woman at a time, the kind of guy that would never cheat on his girlfriend. Yes…Max made me open my eyes, but regardless, Luke was safe, and I liked it that way.

I grabbed my cell phone to see if I had any messages. Our group had been texting away while I was on my date. Reading the texts, I chuckled out loud. Apparently, they were betting on whether Luke would kiss me and if I would see fireworks. They all agreed Luke would kiss me, but they disagreed on me seeing fireworks. Kate said I would, but Becky and Nicole disagreed. Then they ended with *see you tomorrow* and *can't wait*. Just like them, I couldn't wait to see my friends.

Oh, how I loved the weekend. Still in my pajamas, I was all smiles to see Becky, but she wasn't around. When I went to the kitchen, a note was on the refrigerator. The note read: Going to the gym, then lunch date. See you when the posse comes around at four. I'll pick up salad and dessert. It's potluck, just in case you missed the text. No need to make anything. See you later. Hugs!

How I loved Becky. She was always looking after me and making my life easier. She was the sister I wished I had. Just because we weren't related by blood didn't mean we couldn't be sisters. Nicole and Kate were like that for me too, but Becky and I were closer, mainly because we had lived together and had been through some hard times together. Through thick and thin, we were always there for each other, and I was blessed to have them all in my life.

Before I forgot again, I placed a phone call to my parents, since I hadn't spoken to them in a couple of days. I tried to call as often as I could since my mom was a worrier. My parents lived in San Francisco. My dad was a dentist and mom was a stay at home mom. Being an only child was lonely at times, so my closest friends had become my family. Of course, people changed and friends changed too, but I was grateful for everyone in my life.

Since I didn't have much to do, I cleaned our apartment, did the laundry, went to the grocery store to stock up the refrigerator, and watched some television. The day had gone by fast, though I felt like I hadn't done much. Lastly, I turned on my laptop to check my email, but instead of doing that, I became so engrossed on *Facebook* that I didn't notice when Becky walked in.

"Hey, Jenna. Where are you?" Becky shouted from the kitchen.

Happy to see her, I followed the sound of the shuffling noises.

"Hi, Becky." I peered into the kitchen. She had placed the salad and the dessert on the counter.

"Looks good," I said, admiring them both. "So…who did you go out to lunch with?"

After folding the recyclable plastic bags, she shoved them under the sink cabinet. "It really wasn't a date. He was an old friend I knew a long time ago. No biggy."

Just when I was about to ask when Nicole and Kate would get here, the doorbell chimed. That answered my question. Opening the door to let them in, Becky and I took turns giving them hugs. Nicole brought pasta salad, and Kate brought some wine.

After we piled food on our plates, we settled around our square wooden dining table for four. Kate took care of the wine for everyone, and even remembered to pour me only a little. Since she was still breastfeeding, she had none.

"How are you, Nicole?" I asked, thinking about her break up, then wondered if I should have brought up the sore topic. When everyone completely froze so that I could hear the sound of my own breathing, I figured I should not have spoken.

Shockingly, Nicole put down her glass of wine, then looked up at us. "After a year, I realized I didn't love him after all, not in the way I wanted to. I think I loved the idea of being with someone, to be loved by someone, but I wasn't in love. You know, that kind of love where you can't be without him? And to be honest, the sex wasn't that great."

Becky had just gulped some wine, but regurgitated it, and it came shooting out of her mouth. She did that once in awhile. "Sorry." She shrugged her shoulders, wiping up the crimson liquid around her plate. Thank goodness she'd spat it out in front of her and not at us.

"I'm not sitting next to you next time," Kate giggled, stabbing her fork into the salad.

"Anyway," Becky turned to Nicole. "Hello…why didn't you tell us that in the first place? It's important, you know. Did he at least make you come?"

"Becky!" I squealed in a scolding tone, though I didn't mean to.

Nicole finished swallowing her mouth full of pasta salad and poured more wine into her glass. "You know…I'm not sure."

"What?" Kate spat. "Are you serious?"

"Do you?" Nicole asked hesitantly.

"Oh yeah." Kate's lips curled into a smile and her eyes radiated with thoughts I could only imagine. "You wanna know something funny? The first time we had sex after the doctor gave us the green light, I squirted milk all over John's face when I came."

We all busted out laughing, and Becky squirted wine out of her mouth again from almost choking, producing a choking laughing sound.

"Oh my God, that is hilarious." Becky coughed relentlessly. "I could just picture it—though I wouldn't want to picture both of you naked—but how funny is that?"

"It was that good. So…." Kate turned to Nicole. "If you were breast feeding, would he make you squirt?"

Nicole pulled her brows together, creating a pinch in the center, seeming to think. "I'm not sure."

"Everything in life has ups and downs. I'm sure that applies to sex too…right?" I asked hesitantly. Did I even really know much about this topic? Not really.

"True, that applies to life in general, but maybe not sex," Nicole replied. "Either he's good at it or not. There is no in between with sex, I guess…I don't know. Anyway, thanks for the phone calls and the group texts. It cheered me up knowing you were all there for me, but I'm sure I'm fine with the break up. I guess it's better to know sooner than later."

"That's what friends are for," Becky said sincerely.

"Cheers to that," Kate said, raising her glass.

"To everlasting friendship," I muttered, raising my glass. After the clinking sound echoed in the room, we all gulped down our liquid.

After dinner was finished, Becky placed the strawberry cheesecake dessert she'd bought on the table. Carefully slicing each piece, she placed them on small paper plates and passed them to us. Shoving the fork through the cream, I scooped up a chunk and placed it in my mouth. "Mmmm…this is so good," I raved. "Good choice for dessert, Becky."

"Knowing it was your favorite, I got it for you," she winked.

"You're the best."

"Don't you forget it. So…I've been patiently waiting all day to ask you a question."

"You mean, *we've* been patiently waiting," Kate broke in, pulling the fork out of her mouth. "This is probably the best strawberry cheesecake I've ever tasted, and I've tasted plenty."

Nicole nodded her head in agreement and looked at me. "We have two questions. One…did he kiss you; and two…did you see fireworks?"

Making them wait for my answer, I took another bite, savoring the sweet creamy taste, but Becky was getting very impatient.

"Well...answer, or I'll have to take that away from you," Becky said playfully, tugging my plate away from me.

"Mine." Sounding like a child, I pulled the plate toward me. Then all of a sudden, I got really shy, but not from the thought of telling them about Luke. It was just from the mere thought of Max. Knowing Becky would get a kick out of what had happened, I had to tell her...maybe that night.

"Yes, Luke kissed me," I said with conviction.

Their eyes lit up as they waited for an answer.

"And...," I continued. "I didn't see fireworks." Before they could say, "I told you so" to each other, I spoke again. "But that doesn't mean I want to stop seeing him. He's cute, and he's really nice."

Nicole looked disappointed. "If you didn't see fireworks, then the likelihood of having great sex isn't there. But...who am I to judge? He could prove otherwise. So, when are you going to—"

"Nicole," Becky barked. "Jenna isn't like you."

"I'm just making sure she doesn't make the same mistake I did, so relax, Mother," she said to Becky, narrowing her eyes at her. Then she turned to me. "You see...think of sex like this creamy, soft cheesecake." She patted it with her fork. "It's good, but how you make it and what you put on it makes it even better. There are many cheesecakes out there, but what makes this one stand out from the rest?"

"The ingredients," Kate added. "How much effort you put in to making it. You can take the short cut, or put more time and add different ingredients to make it even more delicious."

"True," Becky seconded. "You can even spice it up by adding toppings." She lit a sly grin. "And yes, I'm talking about food and other things."

"No you didn't!" Nicole squealed, her voice went up an octave with excitement.

"Yup, whipped cream and all."

Suddenly I felt hot. I'd known when I gulped the wine down that I would feel it right away, but in a way I didn't care. I was at home with my friends.

"Are you okay?" Kate asked me.

"It's the wine. You know how Jenna gets," Becky explained. "She only drank half a glass."

"I wish it only took me half a glass to get buzzed like that," Kate commented.

"I'm okay. I just feel hot all over, and somewhat buzzed," I giggled, taking another bite of the cheesecake, then rubbing my temples and feeling the blaze all over my body.

"I don't blame you," Kate muttered, fanning herself with her hand. "Cheesecake and sex talk is making me leak milk already."

Laughter rang in the dining room from Kate's remark. Looking at the cheesecake and their comparison to it, I knew I'd never experienced what they had, but then again, I had only slept with one man. Raised by extremely strict parents, I didn't get to go out much in high school. Witnessing all the heartaches, drama, and even being a late bloomer myself, I didn't want to go through that. And I didn't want to just make out because I thought some guy was cute, or have meaningless sex I was not mature enough for. Studying so I could get into a good college was my main focus.

Finally, in college I met an amazing guy—at least I thought he was, until he broke my heart by cheating on me with my roommate. I immediately moved out, and lucky for me, Becky was looking for a roommate; the rest was history. I'd dated many guys, but I couldn't make a connection with any of them. My friends had tried setting me up on several dates, and they'd all turned into nothing. It wasn't that I didn't find men attractive. I was just being picky, and no one had ever made me feel the way Max did, and...dear God...I was thinking of him again.

"Who are you thinking of?" Nicole asked. Her hand was tucked underneath her chin, glaring at me with a mischievous smile, like she knew something was up.

Gazing at my friends, I hadn't realized they were staring at me. Was it that obvious?

Becky placed a fork full of cheesecake in her mouth and mumbled. "Surely it's not Luke. Your face never lit up like that before."

I wanted to blame it on the wine and the effects of the alcohol, but I said one word. "Max."

"Who the hell is Max? Are you dating two guys?" Nicole blurted, smiling like she'd never smiled before, giving me that "you go girl" look.

"No...." Then I realized I had just opened up a can of worms. Lacing my fingers through my hair, then down to my face from the heat of the wine, I had no choice but to tell them what had happened. As they listened intently, they all grinned as if it were happening to them. They giggled like schoolgirls and teased me at times, but it was all in fun. I assured them it was nothing, since the likelihood of running into him again was slim, but one never knew about these things.

After dessert, we all cuddled on the sofa with warm blankets around us and with cups of coffee. We sat and talked about love and life, and everything in-between.

Chapter 8

My stomach dropped as the elevator soared up. This was something I would have to get used to, at least five days a week. Excitement tingled through every inch of me as I walked out of my elevator to the first day of my new job. My former boss had already known that there was a possibility I would be resigning as soon as I got the good news, so it was easier to start my new job. Thankfully, he didn't expect me to stay the whole week. He only asked me to stay couple of days to train the girl who took my place. Wearing a brown sweater dress and a scarf around my neck, my workbag by my side, I was as ready as I'd ever be.

Then there went my feet again, but this time it was the heels on my boots, but hearing others pacing by, making the same clinking noise, I didn't feel so bad this time around. As I approached the secretary, she was all smiles. "Ms. Mefferd. I've been expecting you."

From her greeting, I felt warm and cuddly inside, and it gave me a feeling of belonging. "Thank you." I quickly searched for her nameplate and found it on the right corner of her desk—Mrs. Ross.

Mrs. Ross pointed to the left. "Go this way, and the first door on your right is the office to the Human Resource Department. Mrs. Ward will show you to your office, and she'll go over everything with you."

"Thank you," I smiled, and paced myself there. After I knocked, I heard someone tell me to come in.

The door was already ajar so I pushed it just a little bit more until I saw a face smiling back at me. "Mrs. Ward?" I questioned.

"Come in." She stood up. "You must be Ms. Mefferd." Her strong grip shook my hand. "Have a seat."

Pulling out a chair, I settled myself into it as I watched her skim through several pieces of paper in front of her. "Ms. Mefferd, I'm going to go over a few details we discussed over the phone first."

I nodded with a smile. "Sure."

"As you already know, the position you had interviewed for had been filled by someone else we felt was more qualified; however, we believed you would be a strong asset to our team, so we would like to start you off in the Customer Relations department. Our Knight Magazine company takes pride in customer relations, and with your experience and your personality, we feel that you can take it to a whole new level.

"Since our previous manager took a permanent leave of absence a while ago, Lisa, whom you will meet real soon, was doing double duty. We were going to announce the opening of that position after the rep position was filled, but when they interviewed you, they felt you were perfect.

"Customer Relations Manager is your title. We have four employees who will be working in your department under your direction, and you will be following mine," she smiled. "Lisa will be assigned to you, and she will help you with everything you need. Before I take you to your office, let's go over your salary and your benefits."

After the logistics and signing contracts were taken care of, she led me to my office. Gripping tightly on my bag, I could feel the tension in my knuckles, and the palms of my hands were moist. Nervousness and excitement had claimed me. As I inhaled deep breaths, I walked behind Mrs. Ward.

The office was fairly large, but the five of us shared it. My desk was placed next to the large window, and the other desks were place on the either side of the wall. In the center was another table with chairs, perhaps for meetings.

There were two females and two males. The one that approached us first was Lisa, who had light brown hair and soft brown eyes. She looked just as young as me, and seemed friendly. Then I was introduced to Rachel, Dan, and Eric, who were just as welcoming. After the introductions, Mrs. Ward left, and they all sat down and got back to work.

Lisa knew all the ins and outs of the place. She showed me the lists of our clients, and where I could find their information on the computer on my desk. There was so much to learn and so much to do. As I sat, I turned my black leather chair around to face the window. My stomach lurched up to my heart from my fear of heights, so I backed away to marvel at the beauty of my view.

Looking straight down I could see the front entrance, people rushing in and out of the building, and cars whizzing by. I inhaled a deep, thankful breath at the thought that I was given this wonderful opportunity. Though I didn't get the job I'd wanted, things happened for a reason. I hoped it would be a good one.

Before I knew it, it was almost noon. "We usually take our lunch at twelve-thirty to miss the lunch rush. Would you like to go to lunch with us?" Lisa asked, smiling.

Though I should have said yes, I had so much to do, and knowing they would be gone for an hour, I declined. "I'm just going to grab a sandwich and get back to work. How about I join you tomorrow?"

"Sure," Lisa smiled and everyone left, leaving me all alone.

Grabbing my wallet and my cell phone out of my workbag, I headed out of the office, down the elevator, and stepped out into the wind. It had been comfortable that morning…where had the wind come from all of a sudden? Trudging through the heavy wind, I entered Café Express. My heart pounded, wondering if I would see Max again. I did a quick scan of the room and relaxed my shoulders when there was no sign of him.

The line wasn't as long as I had expected it to be, but thinking of Lisa's words, I guessed I was at the tail end of the lunch hour rush. To pass the time, I checked my emails and texts as I stood in line. Becky, Nicole, and Kate had texted to tell me to have an awesome first day. They were so sweet. My parents did the same. There was a missed call from Luke; Becky asking me to find a rich guy for her; Kate telling me to find someone who made me leak; Nicole telling me to find someone who would rock my sex life. I giggled a little bit too loud, and looked up when the cashier said something.

Too engrossed in my texts, I hadn't realized the line had moved fast. "Sorry. I would like to order your turkey sandwich, a bottle of water, and...." Should I or shouldn't I order one? Heck...I deserved one for being good and not having sweets for the past couple of days. "One Rice Krispies Treat, please."

The cashier came back with my stuff and rang up the register. "That will be thirteen fifty."

I opened my wallet and was just about to place a twenty in his hand when a hundred dollar bill crossed my vision. "I'll have what she's having, except for the Rice Krispies Treat; and I'll be paying for both."

I froze. I knew the sound of his voice, his smell, and his warm breath against my face when he reached over. Turning, I peered up to him. "Um...thank you, but it's okay," I said politely.

"Jenna, we meet again. I got this." There was excitement in his tone. He gave a stern look to the cashier, a look that meant, "take it now."

Not wanting to make a big fuss, I turned to him again. "Thank you, but it wasn't necessary."

"It's my pleasure, and since we're friends now we can sit together." He grabbed his change and our lunches, and headed to an empty table toward the back with one of his hands on my back.

Having no choice, I let him lead me. "We're friends?" I cocked my head to the side with a questioning look.

"We've run into each other four times already, and we even had dinner together," he joked, pulling out a chair for me.

After I sat, he pushed it forward. What a gentleman! A part of me felt guilty for sitting there with him, but he was being friendly, and in a way, we were friends. "I didn't really have dinner with you," I corrected.

He opened the cap to the water bottle and placed it in front of me. Then he unwrapped the paper that was tightly hugging my sandwich and placed that in front of me as well, but he held on to the Rice Krispies Treat that was inside a brown paper bag. "Here you go. You must be hungry. But we did. You sat across from me, didn't you?" he winked.

Oh...don't wink. My heart did a funny flip. "Yes, but I was with someone, and you were with someone, so I hardly call that going to dinner together," I giggled, thinking how funny this conversation sounded.

"We can change that. And just so you know, I wasn't stalking you." He smiled that irresistible smile. "I come here to grab a quick bite to eat. Unless you *want* me to stalk you, then I can make that happen."

My eyes grew wide.

"You know I'm joking, right? Someone has to protect you from people who like to accidently bump into you, make it seem like it's your fault, and then be really rude about it," he winked again, opening his mouth to take a bite of his sandwich.

Stop staring. I focused on my sandwich and took a small bite.

"So, what brings you here?" he asked, wiping his mouth with a napkin.

"I just got a new job."

"Congratulations. Where do you work?"

"Today is my first day. I'm the Customer Relations Manager for Knight Fashion Magazine."

His brows and tone lifted high. "Really? And what do you do for them?"

"Basically, I make their clients happy. My team takes orders and makes sure their shipment gets to them on time. There is more to this, but this is my responsibility for right now. Someone else took the position I wanted, but I'm excited to be there. It's a start, and at least I have my foot in the door."

"What position were you interviewing for?"

"I wanted to be one of their reps. Part of the job description was to attend the New York fashion show," I explained, finding myself opening up to this stranger who made me feel so comfortable. Here I was telling him things I hadn't even discussed with Luke or my friends. "I know it's not the reason to get hired for that position, but I wanted to do something exciting. But don't get me wrong. I'm lucky to even have the position I have now. I mean…to work for Knight Magazine is a dream come true."

Max listened intently, nodding, and hadn't taken a bite since I started spilling my guts. I didn't remember much about what we talked about, but I remembered the whole conversation centered on me, which I wasn't used to. Looking at my cell phone without trying to be rude, I noticed the time.

"Max…I'm sorry, but umm…I need to go." I got up, wrapped the half-eaten sandwich, closed the cap on the water bottle, and grabbed my wallet and my cell phone that were on the table. "Thank you so much for the lunch. I…I…." I didn't know what to say or how to end the lunch. My finger laced through my hair, wondering what I should say or do at that point.

Max stood up too. His sandwich was half eaten, like mine.

"I'm so sorry. I was talking away and you didn't get to eat your lunch. But I gotta go," I

rambled. As I was talking, Max reached into the brown bag. "May I?"

"Sure." I had forgotten about the treat. "You can have it. Thanks for lunch again." I turned on my heel and started walking.

Suddenly, Max placed his hand under my elbow. With a slight tug, I was somewhat in his hold. With a light gasp and a wave of heat flushing through me again, I was lost in his eyes. He leaned in. "I had a wonderful time," he whispered. "Thanks for being my lunch buddy." Then he handed me the brown bag. "Lunch buddies share their feelings, stories, and even goodies."

I radiated a huge shy smile and walked away. Needing that Rice Krispies Treat right that moment, I reached inside the bag. What I saw stunned me, and even tugged at my heart. He hadn't broken it in half as I had expected. Instead, he had molded it into the shape of a heart.

After that, I knew…unwillingly…I was making a space for him in my heart. Thinking he would be devouring his sandwich, I looked over my shoulder just as I pushed the door to exit. His eyes were set on me intently, and I got a glimpse of his wink that made me want to dive into his arms. I liked the feeling way too much!

M. Clarke

Chapter 9

Luke went on a business trip to San Francisco. He had asked me to go with him, but I wasn't ready to go away. Going away and sharing one room meant sleeping together, and I wasn't ready for that...at least not yet. Becky was way too happy I didn't go, and not going also meant spending time with her.

"So, you want to catch a movie or stay home tonight?" Becky asked, folding her laundry.

"You w...wear th...at?" I stuttered, looking at what was supposed to be underwear. "It doesn't cover anything. It's...just...do you floss your vagina with that thing?" I cracked a joke.

Becky laughed out loud. "No...it's a G-string. Don't tell me you haven't seen one before?" Becky tossed one to me.

Catching it, I stretched the waist. "Of course I have. I just...don't...have one," I said shyly.

"That's okay. None of my business. You can wear anything you want, but I hope you're not going to wear grandma panties when you start dating Max. Instead of watching a movie or staying home, we need to go shopping for panties."

"What? Max and I are not dating. He's had plenty of chances, but he didn't ask," I huffed, then I was stunned at myself for sounding mad. I calmed down. "I meant...we're friends. He thanked me for being his lunch buddy." My mind went to that moment at Café Express, when time stopped and everything around me was nonexistent. I sighed inwardly, secretly. I had told

Becky about the accidental lunch encounter, but of course she'd insisted that it wasn't a coincidence.

A comfortable silence filled the air while I helped her fold the rest of her clothes. The sound of the doorbell chiming broke the silence, and we flashed our eyes to each other in surprise.

"I'll get it." Becky reached for the door.

Keeping my ears opened to the conversation, I didn't hear much. "Thank you," I heard her say, and then she walked back to the living room. I turned to ask what it was all about, but stopped when I saw a tall glass vase full of red roses, and a box in her hands. I excitedly beamed a smile. "They're beautiful. Who sent them to you? And what's in the box?"

"I don't know. I didn't open it. And they're not for me...they're for you. So the question is, who sent them to you?" She giggled with a smirk on her face, like I already knew who sent them. Becky handed me a card and placed the vase and the box on our dining table.

Leaning against the chair, she waited for me to open the card. They had to be from Luke. Who else could they be from? As my heart pounded from anticipation, I opened and read the note. I was in shock, and my heart beat even faster. Did I somehow misread the sender's name? I read it again and stared at the name.

"Who is it from?" I heard Becky's voice ring in my head. Peering over my shoulder, she read out loud.

Dearest Jenna,
Hope you had a wonderful week at your new job.
Until we meet again.
Lunch buddies share their feelings, stories, and even goodies.
Thinking of you!
Your lunch buddy, Max

"I knew it," Becky squealed. "Luke never sent you flowers. He's not the sending flowers type of guy. Wait...are you not telling me the whole story?"

I turned stoically. "I told you everything." My voice was soft and still unbelieving.

Turning my gaze to the flowers, I couldn't help but smile. They were the most beautiful roses I had ever seen. They must have been expensive, because roses that exquisite were hard to find. Leaning over, I smelled the scent and touched the silk like petals. "They're beautiful."

Then my eyes shifted to the white box and I pulled it to me. An oval sticker on top read Café Express. Using my nail to break the seal, I opened it. Inside were a dozen heart-shaped Rice Krispies Treats.

"Oh my God! This was really sweet of him, but I don't think he thinks of himself as just a lunch buddy. He wants more."

"But I can't," I sighed lightly, feeling confused. "I'm dating someone else."

"True, but did Luke say he wanted to date exclusively?"

"We never talked about that."

"So you're assuming. Maybe he's dating someone else while he's dating you. Have you thought about that?"

Becky was right. It was a possibility. Just because I was a one-man-at-a-time dating type didn't mean he was. "I don't think he would."

Draping her arm around my shoulder, she shook her head. "My inexperienced, innocent friend, who only thinks the best of everyone, you need to figure out what you want. I think you feel safe with Luke, but at the same time, you want to jump into bed with Max."

"Becky!" I said, a bit too loudly.

"Admit it. You've got the hots for Max. Who in their right mind wouldn't? But you're scared that he'll hurt you once you let him in. I understand. I've been there before, and so have you. But Max may turn out to be different."

"First of all, Max hasn't even asked me out. He's just having fun flirting with me, because I'm not giving him the kind of attention he probably gets from other women, like throwing myself at him. He probably sees me as a challenge and nothing more."

Becky released her hold on me. "Don't judge him without getting to know him. To me, he seems like a great package, but...." Both of her hands went up. "I don't know him. And you won't know until you try. You don't ever want to regret, and think of 'what ifs,' because that will eat you alive."

"You sound as though you have a regret of your own," I said, but when I saw the impassive expression on her face, I knew I'd touched a sore topic.

She pulled her lips into a thin line that curled into a quick smile. "Let's not talk about me. If he asks you out, what are you going to do?"

Pulling out the dining chair, I slumped down on it and placed my fist under my chin as I stared at the roses in a dream-like state. "He sent me flowers and my favorite...Rice Krispies Treats. He also shaped my treat into a heart shape when we had lunch together. That was so sweet. What am I going to do?" Then I plopped my head on the table.

Sitting adjacent to me, Becky started laughing lightly. Copying my position, she looked squarely into my eyes, seemingly preparing to give me good advice. "Why don't you sleep with both of them, and see who makes you sing hallelujah?"

Sing hallelujah? My eyes grew. I couldn't hold it any longer, and I spit out a loud laugh. Becky joined me and I pulled her in for a hug. Then she squeezed me tightly and spoke into my ear. "I just want the best for you; you know that, don't you?"

I nodded. "I know. I don't like being confused. We haven't even gone out on a date, and he's invading my thoughts...not to mention my body. I want him out of my mind." I wasn't ready to let Luke go. We were just starting to get to know each other. I had to give him a chance, but what would I do if Max ever asked me out?

"I know. Just follow your heart."

But what if my heart split down the middle? Then I popped the question that was on my mind earlier. "How does he even know where I live?"

Becky released me. "I don't know, but that should tell you he's slowly making his move. He's feeling the water first. He knows you're dating someone, but he's trying to find out how serious your relationship is. And the fact that you had lunch with him gave him the okay sign to send you flowers."

"It did?" I sighed. Extending my arm to reach for a treat, I gave it to Becky. "How do you know so much?"

Becky graciously took it and took a bite. "Experience. Been there, done that."

"Hey…I thought I knew everything about your love life." I grabbed one for me and took a small bite.

"I only met you during our senior year in college. You didn't know me when I was a junior. Let's just say…I had too much fun," she winked. "Now go, get your purse…we're going shopping, but *after* we finished our Rice Krispies Treats. Hmmm…yummy."

"Okay." I had to agree with her. Delicious!

M. Clarke

Chapter 10

Monday mornings were usually a drag and made it hard to get back into the swing of things after a fun weekend, but I was pumped up to go to work. In fact, I was there half an hour early, checking emails and replying to clients. As I continued to stare at my computer, the sound of the door swinging open caught my attention.

"Good morning," I greeted Lisa and everyone that trailed behind her with a smile, coming to work right on schedule. After the greeting, everyone went straight to work. After time had passed, I looked at the clock and noted it was almost noon.

"You have a meeting with Mrs. Ward in five minutes," Lisa reminded.

Lisa was the best. Though she wasn't my personal secretary, there were times when she acted like one. "Thanks, Lisa. I'll be back." Gathering my notebook and pen, I walked out the door. Walking down the hall, a few employees passing by gave me quick smiles. Smiling back, I was just about to enter Mrs. Ward's office when I did a double take.

Keeping my back to him, from the corner of my eye I saw Max talking to the front office secretary. I wanted to look away, but he looked so fine in his suite and tie, I couldn't help myself. Mrs. Ross was all smiles, giggling like a schoolgirl at whatever he'd said to her. What was he doing there? Maybe he was one of our clients? Before he could turn and see me, I walked in.

"Good afternoon, Ms. Mefferd," Mrs. Ward greeted warmly. "Have a seat."

"Please, call me Jenna," I smiled. Pulling the chair out, I sat comfortably and pulled out my pen.

Looking at her computer screen, she glanced at me, and then back to her screen again. "Sorry, I'm reading this email. It's regarding you."

"Oh...." I stiffened. "Is something wrong?"

Still looking at her screen, she spoke. "No. You can put your pen down. You won't be taking any notes." Then she shifted her eyes to me with a smile. "Traveling was not part of your job description, but how do you feel about traveling?"

"It depends where I'm going," I joked, to be funny and to make her smile. But before she had a chance to reply, I spoke again, since I didn't get the smile I'd anticipated. "I'm just joking. Sure. I don't mind." As long as it wasn't like every week or very often, then I was okay with it. There was an excitement about traveling by myself, and since I hadn't been to...well...I hadn't traveled much, the thought alone was exhilarating.

"Good. You'll be leaving this Thursday for New York. I'll email your flight information and have an agenda ready for you by this Wednesday morning at the latest. This is all so sudden. I need to get this ready for you."

"Thank you, but I was wondering why I am going, and if I am going by myself?"

She paused and looked at her email again. Her nose crinkled, looking confused. Turning her eyes at me, she clicked her pen. "Um...I believe you'll be representing our company at the New York fashion show."

My eyes grew wide and I was in complete shock. Never in my wildest dreams did I ever think that I would be attending the New York fashion show. "Are you sure it's me? I mean, I wasn't hired for that position." I didn't mean to sound as though she had made a mistake, but this was too good to be true.

"No. The email said Jeanella Mefferd will be attending. You won't be going alone. Megan Crawford and Jake, the photographer, along with his team, will be joining you. You might want to introduce yourself to them before you go," she suggested with a smile.

"Do you think I was asked to go because Ms. Crawford needs an assistant? I did interview for that position." I was so curious as to how this could have happened that I was trying to draw out any information from her, but it was to no avail.

"I'm sorry, Jenna. I don't have any more information. I got this email straight from Mr. Knight's secretary." She leaned closer. "If I were you, I wouldn't ask any questions, and just enjoy this opportunity paid for by the company. It's like taking a mini vacation, and you get to go to the fashion show."

I nodded with a smile. She was right. Why was I asking all these questions? Who cared? "Thank you. I will be looking for your email."

"Great. Have a good day."

"Thank you," I said. Standing up, pushing the chair back into its position, I left, hovering off the ground. Excitement infused through every part of me. I couldn't believe my luck. Walking back to my office, I gazed straight ahead to the glass window and looked at the sun seeping through. What a beautiful day it was, despite the gray clouds. How wonderful my job was, despite the fact that I didn't get the position I wanted. It didn't matter what the reason was for me going to New York. I couldn't wait!

Heading to my desk to get my wallet out of my workbag to grab some lunch, I spotted a wrapped sandwich, a heart shaped Rice Krispies Treat, a water bottle, and a note on my desk. The note read:

Dearest Jenna,
Thought you might be hungry.
Hope you liked the flowers and the box of goodies.
Lunch buddies share their feelings, stories, and even goodies.
Thinking of you!
Your lunch buddy, Max

Putting the note back down, I ran out the door. Looking to my left and right, I didn't see anyone. I must have missed him. Noting how he was there earlier, my mind started reeling. Did he hand deliver the sandwich himself? Most likely Mrs. Ross wouldn't have let him in, but the way she was googling eyes at him, it could be a possibility. I bet he could talk himself through anything with his looks and charm.

Sitting back down in my chair, I ate from hunger. I didn't have his phone number so I had no way to thank him. In fact, I only knew his first name; not that knowing his last name would help me find him. The only way I could thank him was to go to the Café Express and hope that he would show up.

When Lisa, Rachel, and the rest of the staff walked in, I had only finished half of my sandwich. Quickly folding the wrapper around the sandwich, I dumped it into the trash. I didn't mean to. I could've saved it for later, but my face flushed red, thinking that somehow they knew who'd placed it there. The rest of the day went by quickly, and I was eager to go home to tell Becky, but since I couldn't wait, I texted on the group text.

Turning the key and pushing, I walked into my apartment. "Becky," I called, seeing light from the kitchen. The smell of spaghetti churned in my stomach. I hadn't realized I was starving until I smelled the aroma of the ground beef and tomato sauce.

"I'm here." Becky was draining the hot, boiling water from the pasta into a strainer.

"You made dinner?" I squealed, happily.

"You and I need to celebrate. Congrats on going to New York. This is your dream…well…one of your dreams."

"I know…right? I can't believe it." My tone filled with excitement. Opening the cabinet, I pulled out two large plates and set them on the counter. Becky dumped some pasta on each plate and poured sauce on top of each. Taking the plates, I set them on the dining table. My eyes set on the beautiful roses that continuously filled the air with their sweet scent, reminding me of Max.

"When do you leave for New York?" Becky asked, breaking me out of my stare, sitting across from me, handing me a fork and a glass of water.

"This Thursday," I replied, winding the noodles around the fork. "I'll be back Saturday night."

"You should ask Max to come along."

I blanked out from the thought of the surprise lunch on my desk. "What?" I giggled. "I don't even know his last name. In fact, I don't know him at all."

"I was just kidding, but I could tell from your stalling that you thought about it." Becky took a bite. "I'm sorry, but the flowers reminded me of him. Not that I'm interested...don't get me wrong."

With my mouth full, I spoke anyway. "I know what you mean."

During the dinner conversation, we talked about what happened during my lunch hour. We discussed her job and her dateless nights. After dinner, I called my parents. I thought about calling Luke, but I couldn't. Going to New York was a great escape. Perhaps it would help me with my decision; continue dating Luke and make it work, or let him go.

M. Clarke

Chapter 11

The next day at work, Lisa, Rachel, and the team got the news that I was headed to New York. Lisa was most thrilled. Being a New Yorker herself, she was suggesting restaurants I should try if I had the time. Being that it was Tuesday, Lisa informed me that most employees were going to Café Express for lunch. Thinking that I may run into the photographer and Megan, I agreed to go.

A part of me was hesitant, afraid that I would run into Max again, but I couldn't refuse since I had turned them down several times before…or so I told myself to make myself feel better. There was no way around this. One thing for sure…he worked nearby, and we were bound to run into each other one way or another. I had to stop being timid, hold my head up high, and face whatever came my way.

The group of us walked to Café Express. When we entered, waves of hands greeted us. Though I didn't know who they were, the group I was with in line did. Instead of waving back like everyone else, I just gave a heartfelt smile.

It seemed as though the company's employees occupied most of the space, and there was hardly room left for the other customers. After we ordered and got our lunches, I followed Lisa to join the people that waved at us. Lisa introduced me to a bunch of people, but I quickly forgot their names except for Jake, the photographer, since Mrs. Ward had already talked about him. Megan wasn't there.

Jake gave me the warmest smile. His hair was slightly long, but he had a nice smile and he was cute. He had a friendly aura about him, the kind that showed he made friends easily. After arranging chairs, we sat.

"Are we on the same flight?" Jake asked me out of the blue, after swallowing a spoon full of soup. He had ordered sour dough bread filled with clam chowder soup.

"I'm not sure. All I know is that I'll be flying Thursday."

"I'm flying Wednesday, tomorrow, with Megan," he informed me. "I wonder why we're not flying together? Have you been to New York before?"

"No, it's my first time," I said, looking at Lisa and a few other ladies sitting next to her, who were sitting up straight, smiling, looking past me.

"He's so handsome," one of the ladies said. "Too bad he doesn't sit with us. I could just stare at him ordering food and watch him walk out."

Out of curiosity, I wanted to turn to see who they were talking about, but I thought better of it. Since I had just met them, I didn't want to be a part of their drooling session. It was really none of my business.

"He looks so delicious in his suit and tie. I'm wondering what he looks like without it," the brunette with short hair said.

"I heard he dates a lot of women and never stays with one. I wonder why that is?" another asked.

"Guys like him like to fool around," Jake said. "And why not? Nice car, beautiful women. Women throw themselves at him all the time. He's loaded. He can do what ever he wants. Yup, I'm jealous."

"If he'll take me, I'll throw myself at him," one giggled.

As the sound of footsteps approached us, Lisa and her friends' eyes grew even bigger. "Oh my God, I think he's heading our way," one said.

"Hello, Mr. Knight. Would you like to join us?" Lisa asked sweetly.

Mr. Knight! I stiffened. I was about to meet the person behind the company I worked for.

"May I?" the voice said.

Great. Why next to me? Then I froze. I knew that voice, as if it were the sound of my own heart beating. Peering up, Max stood right above me. Mr. Knight? Surely I'd misheard, but how would Max know all these people?

Max pulled out the chair next to me and sat way too close for comfort. I gasped inwardly as an electrifying feeling sparked from his knee touching mine. When I moved it away slightly so they would not touch, he moved closer to me without trying to make it obvious underneath the table.

"Please, eat your lunch. I hope everyone is having a great day."

"Yes we are, Mr. Knight," one blonde said, a little too bubbly.

There was that word again. The word Mr. Knight rang in my head. Surely it couldn't be *the* Mr. Knight?

Max turned to me, and I felt the heat from his gaze fixated on me. "We meet again. How's Knight treating you so far?"

Gazing at him with mixed emotions, my mind started reeling. I had told him I started my new job at Knight. If he was the president or even worked there, why didn't he tell me? Now it was all clear. He must have gotten my address to send the flowers. He looked into my profile...grrr! I didn't know how to feel about this. He hadn't been honest with me from the start. It was a very bad sign.

"Fine, thank you. I enjoy working with my team," I said flatly, turning my eyes from him. For reasons unknown, the heat was now brewing inside me as anger. What if I had told him things I shouldn't have? I had opened myself up to this no good, good-looking stranger who wanted to have lunch with me and I was swept away. Not any more.

The muscles of my shoulders were tight as I looked straight ahead. The ladies giggled when Max said a few words that I didn't recall from tuning out of their conversation. My mind was not there. It was at our last lunch conversation. Suddenly, not meaning to, my body twitched from the warmth of his hand on my lap underneath the table where no one could see.

"Ms. Mefferd, I'll see you at the department meeting in your office at six." Then he lifted his hand away, while turning his attention to the rest of the group. "Have a good rest of the day. Thank you for allowing me to join you. I have a meeting to attend in ten minutes." He stood up, lighting up that irresistible smile he did so well, and left.

"Oh…look at that fine man go," one whispered, making her friends giggle around her.

Watching him walk out the door was not my cup of tea, especially when all I could think was that I was unaware I had a meeting at six. I looked at Lisa. "Did I miss something?"

"I'll check for you, Jenna. Sometimes it happens. Maybe you missed an email."

This wasn't good. I would've almost missed a meeting had Max not spoken about it. Then my worries turned into stress. Confirming a meeting clearly stated that he did work for Knight. What was even worse was that he was my boss. But what was most upsetting was the fact that he was not honest with me from the beginning.

I didn't understand why I was feeling that way, but I felt betrayed, lost, and confused. My heart felt as though he had twisted a dagger into it. He had already hurt me, and we hadn't even gone out.

"Thanks," I said with a smile, trying to hide whatever it was that I was feeling.

After lunch, we all got up and walked back to our office building.

♥♥

At five thirty Lisa, Rachel, and the rest of the team left for the day. Sitting behind my desk, I waited for the meeting that was supposed to happen in my office as I searched the email frantically. Though I had already searched for it when I arrived back from lunch and couldn't find it, I didn't want to spend the rest of the afternoon looking for it.

Not wanting to look unprofessional, I told Lisa that I had just gotten the email when we got back from lunch, and that I hadn't checked my messages before we left. By ten minutes past six, no one had showed up. Had I misheard him from being so distraught to find that he worked there?

Staring at the computer, searching again for the meeting email I might have missed, I heard the door close. Stealthily, footsteps came toward me. Then I heard the sound of a chair rolling quietly as if he or she was purposely trying to keep the noise level down. I guessed the meeting was about to start.

Somewhat irritated that I couldn't find the email, I closed the computer to sleep and stood up to see who had come in first. My heart did a somersault and I jerked back from seeing Max, nearly stumbling out of my chair and almost falling flat on my bottom as the rolling chair behind me pushed away from me. He stood up swiftly, seemingly to help me, but luckily I broke the fall.

Totally unexpected, I got a glimpse of his radiating smile, the kind of smile that made me lose my breath and voice.

Max comfortably sat back down. "Hello, lunch buddy."

I glared at him and didn't say a word as I stood there with my fist on my desk.

His happy grin disappeared, now looking impassive. He sat up straight. "I'm sorry. I should've told you, but—"

"Yes, you should've," I snapped. Oh God! I am being rude to my boss. Wait. Is he even my boss, or my boss's son? Suddenly remembering the meeting, I managed to calm down.

"I was swept away by you, so it didn't cross my mind. I wanted to get to know you. I didn't want to talk about me," he stated.

What did he just say? I think I dropped my jaw as my gaze on him continued to linger, unable to say anything. Finally, I blinked, ran my hand through my hair, and changed the subject. "I think we should get ready for the meeting."

He didn't respond. Instead, he stood up and held my gaze as he paced to me. My mind told my body to move, but I couldn't move my legs. Approaching me the way he did put me in a trance, and I gasped lightly when his body was just inches away from mine. "This is *our* meeting, Ms. Mefferd."

Oh, no, he didn't! It was no wonder I couldn't find the email, because there was no meeting. I didn't know whether to be furious or to be flattered. Regardless, what he did was not professional. "What are we meeting about, Mr. Knight? And I think you're standing way too close for a meeting; or are all of your meetings this way?"

He looked amused, and curled the corner of his lips into a sly smile. "Only with you. I'm not adjourning this meeting until you agree to have dinner with me."

Dinner? He is asking me out? Thrilled that he had finally asked, I almost smiled, but suppressed it instead. Too overwhelmed with his proximity, I wanted to sit back down in my chair, but I didn't, just to prove I was not affected by him. Instead, I extended my hand to his chest to push him back, but that was a mistake. A funny tingle ran through my inside from simply touching him. Unexpectedly, Max grasped both of my hands and held them tenderly.

"I can't go out to dinner with you," I said sharply, yanking my hands away.

"And why not?" he asked softy.

"I don't do my boss." That didn't come out right. I was hoping he would overlook it.

His brows arched. "Do? So you're thinking of going to bed with me already?"

"No!" I squealed. "I had no such thoughts." My face flushed, remembering the dreams I'd had about him once or twice…or way too many times. It is way too hot in here.

"Really? It didn't even cross your mind?" His body pressed closer, making me step to the side, and I accidently sat on my desk. "Even the roses didn't remind you of me?"

Suddenly I felt bad for being rude, and cleared my throat. "Oh, umm, by the way, thank you for the beautiful roses, the Rice Krispies Treats, and the surprise lunch on my desk. You really didn't have to." My tone became soft.

"I know, but I wanted to. So, will you allow me to take you out to dinner?"

"No," I whispered, shivering from his face being way too close to mine. His eyes shifted from my eyes to my lips. Don't kiss me. I won't be strong enough to resist you. My index finger headed toward my mouth, then stopped on my lips, recalling what Max had said to me the last time. Seeing that smirking expression plastered on his face, I dropped my hand immediately.

"Why not? Is it because of Duke?" His hands were resting on my desk, on both sides of my grips. I was locked, unable to move. When he spoke, I could feel his breath on my lips.

How did he know Luke's name, though he had called him Duke. It was close enough. I assumed he had overheard me call Luke's name over dinner when Max sat at the table next to us. He must have had ears on our conversation...or the lack of it. "His name is Luke," I corrected.

"I don't care what his name is. And since you don't have a ring on your finger, and since it didn't seem like you were into him during dinner, I can ask you out."

Staring at his luscious lips as he spoke, I wanted to pull him in for a kiss, but I dared not. Instead, with all the will power in me, I pushed him slightly away, just enough to give me room to slide out and move quickly to the other side of the desk. "It doesn't matter. You're my boss, and we shouldn't be having this conversation or this meeting."

He beamed a playful smile. "I met you before you started working here. We've been running into each other a lot lately. I believe it's a sign. Have you heard of serendipity? If it will change your mind, I can fire myself."

He was cute, I had to admit it. It took every ounce of my will power to keep from smiling, but I wasn't going to give in just because my body wanted to.

"Anyway," he continued. "I'm not your boss. Mrs. Ward is your boss."

My head cocked slightly to the left in confusion. "Are you *the* Mr. Knight?"

"No, my dad is *the* Mr. Knight," he said, emphasizing the word "the" as he slowly advanced toward me, making me nervous, making my heart thump faster. "So technically, I'm not your boss." Now he was standing right in front of me, his energy holding me, cuddling me, making me melt without even a touch. Then he backed away, giving me space. "So lunch buddy, what do you say?"

Frazzled, I stood there just putting the pieces of his words together, trying to register all that he had said. He was asking me out, and I was screaming inside saying yes, but my mind repeatedly said no. Oh God…how badly I wanted to say yes. "I shouldn't…I mean, I can't…I…."

"You mean, you're scared," he suggested. "All I'm asking is for one night." He approached me again. "I promise you won't regret it." His fingers slowly brushed through my hair, holding on to the last bit of the strand. I stood there frozen, hypnotized by his words, by his touch. His hands moved to my face, gently cupping it as if he was holding a wounded dove, and idly stroking his thumb over my cheeks. "Women blush around me all the time. But the women who throw themselves at me don't. I like how I can make your cheeks turn red. It's different…sweet, yet sexy at the same time…somewhat innocent."

Oooh…he was just being arrogant now. The office wasn't big enough to fill the size of his ego. Sure, my body said yes, but my mind said no.

He continued. "And…somehow…you make me blush…and I've never blushed before. I think I like how that feels…too much." His words were slow in coming, and every word made me wither in his deep sensual gaze, reeling me in.

I made him blush? Blinking, I reluctantly broke out of the hold he had on me, went to my desk, grabbed my workbag, and started heading out the door. "This meeting is adjourned, Mr. Knight," I stammered.

Letting out an amused light chuckle, his eyes followed me storming out the door. But just before I left, I heard him mutter, "All right, you leave me no choice."

What did he mean by that?

M. Clarke

Chapter 12

"How was work?" Becky asked when I entered.

"Awful. Just awful." Pouting, I went straight to my room, dropped my bag, changed into sweats, and sat on my bed. Sitting cross-legged on the edge of my bed, I ran my hair back and let out a heavy confused sigh.

Becky peered through the door that was already ajar. "What happened?"

I inhaled another deep sigh. "I'm in big trouble," I said softly, without making eye contact.

I didn't even hear Becky come into the room until I saw her slippers as she sat next to me, shifting me a little from her weight on my bed. "Whatever it is, I'm sure you can fix it."

Looking into her eyes, I saw my sweet friend who was always so positive, always knowing the right words to say to me, but this wasn't an easy fix. "I can't fix this unless I move out of state," I mumbled.

"Spit it out," she said sternly. "Now I'm really worried. What happened?"

"Max happened," I groaned, making a funny sound I couldn't believe came out of my mouth.

Becky smiled, the kind of smile that surged a certain energy that was contagious, so I reflected the same smile back. "Tell me, tell me," she said, way too excitedly.

As I explained the details of Max being my boss's son and what had happened in the office, every emotion I had in me was

75

portrayed through my tone, body gestures, and the speedy beats of my heart. Becky didn't say a word as she listened, but her facial expression said it all. She was just as excited as I was.

"I'm in so much trouble," I said at the end of my explaining. "I don't know what to do."

"I've been telling you to go for Max, but clearly if you are this distraught, you must care about Luke more than I thought you did. This is one decision you'll have to make on your own, because this is your life. I can listen and tell you what I think, but I can't feel what you feel since I'm not in your shoes."

"Luke isn't the ideal, prince charming type of guy. But he's safe. He'd probably be the good husband that I could trust. But Max...he makes me feel things I've never felt before. When I'm with him, I spark alive. This wanting, needing, desire burns through me. Not only is he intelligent, but he can be a real gentleman, the protector, the romancer, the thoughtful guy. But...but...is he the faithful, family type of man? I don't want to hurt Luke, but I don't want to let Max slip through my fingers. What do I do?"

"Oh, Jenna, Jenna, Jenna; always thinking about other people's feelings over your own. Don't worry about hurting Luke. This is about you, and what you want. I wish I could tell you what to do, but this is going to have to come from you. Follow your heart...that is all I can say. You know I'm going to give you my two cents worth," she giggled, draping her arm around my shoulder. "Taking the safe road is good, but sometimes, you may miss what could be better. I'd rather love hard and get hurt then not really love at all. Well, it's a good thing you'll be gone for several days. Maybe it will help you clear your head, and you can decide what you want when you come back."

"I hope so." I reached over and pulled Becky in for a hug. She was my comfort, my voice, my friend, and my sister. "Thanks," I whispered.

"Always," she said, releasing my hold. "I'm starving. You must be too. Let's make dinner, and you need to start packing soon. Are you excited?"

"Beyond words," I said cheerfully, as my eyes twinkled with elation. "I'll send you pictures through my phone."

"Make sure to send me pictures of hot male models," she said, pacing to exit my room. "Come on, let's make dinner."

"Max made me sing hallelujah," I blurted before she was out of my sight.

Becky swung around, arching her brows in bewilderment without a word. But I knew that look that was plastered on her face, so I spoke before she could ask.

"No. I didn't sleep with him. But when he stood in front of me, looking like he wanted me, I could almost feel his naked body on mine." I giggled shyly.

Motionless, Becky's eyes lit up. She parted her lips as if she wanted to say something, but didn't.

"It took every once of my will power to walk away from him," I continued. "I've never felt that with Luke...ever, or with any other guys before."

"I think you know what you need to do. Singing hallelujah doesn't come that easily." Becky gripped my hand and tugged me out the door. "I'm starving, and we need to talk some more." Then she started to belt out "Hallelujah" by The Canadian Tenors, making me sing right along with her.

♥♥

Becky offered to take me to the airport, but I declined. Driving to the airport was bad enough, but I didn't want her to get stuck in traffic both ways, coming and going. After checking in my bag and going through the security gate, which was hell, I sat comfortably while I waited to board.

Thumbing through my texts, I saw that Luke had arrived home late the previous night. I had texted him earlier that I was going to New York for work during the weekend, so he had called me early that morning wishing me a safe trip, and said that he would take me out when I got back.

I didn't know why I felt so bad, as if I had cheated on him; we were just dating, right? Sure, Max was invading my mind even more so after our so-called meeting, but we hadn't gone out.

Feeling a little antsy, I got up when a whiff of coffee tickled my nostrils, so I headed to Starbucks. After I ordered my favorite, hazelnut latte, I headed next door as I savored the sweet taste.

Peacefully walking by myself, I took the moment of solitude to simply enjoy being by myself; no friends, no Luke, and especially no Max, so I could try to clear my head. As I looked through the magazines, I decided to buy a few and stuffed them inside my oversized bag. Looking at my watch, I noted the time and started panicking. Was it time to board already?

Grabbing my ticket out of the bag, I ran to the back of the line. Thank goodness I hadn't wandered that far. What was I thinking? The lady collecting the tickets cut a section off my paper ticket that I had confirmed on line and gave it back to me with a smile. Following in line, I walked through what looked like a tunnel and stepped onto the plane.

"Can I help you find your seat?" the stewardess asked.

"Sure, thank you," I said. After I handed her the ticket, I turned to the coach seats.

"Ma'am, you're going the wrong way."

I turned, giving her a confused expression, and headed back to her. Looking at my ticket, she pointed at my seat number.

"You're in business class," she smiled.

"Oh, sorry." I let out a nervous giggle and followed behind her. Wow! I didn't know. Well…I guess I should have checked. I naturally assumed I would be flying in economy class.

Passing through a split curtain, I felt like I was in a different plane. There were fewer seats per row, and only about twelve of them in total. A few people were already seated, but it was pretty much empty, while the other side of the curtain was pretty full. I could understand why…it was double the price, which most people couldn't afford—like me.

"This is your seat, Ms. Mefferd. If you need anything, please let me know. I'll be serving cocktails and lunch soon after we take flight."

"Thank you," I smiled, taking off my overcoat. Normally, I would have to scoot side ways to get to the window seat, but I walked right to it. Talk about luxury. Sinking onto the plush leather cushion, I buckled the seatbelt, placed my overcoat over me like a blanket, and closed my eyes. Feeling the stress of starting a new job and then the men in my life, I guessed I was simply tired.

When I heard the sound of someone sitting next to me, I opened my eyes. I didn't want to make it obvious by turning my head, so I just waited for the opportunity to open up. But I didn't have to wait too long.

"It's good to see you again, Ms. Mefferd."

There it was, that heat spreading through my body again, and that voice that did crazy things to my insides. Slowly, I turned to him and shrank as far into my seat as was possible.

"Mr. Knight? What are you doing here? I mean...are you...will you...are we going to the same destination?"

"I believe so. You're part of my team. Didn't Mrs. Ward inform you?"

I didn't want to get her in trouble, so I played along. "Yes, she did, but she didn't tell me who was on the team. All I knew was that Megan and Jake and his team left yesterday."

"I see," he nodded and reached over. Pulling my seatbelt to make sure it wouldn't unbuckle, he pulled his too.

As I watched him being so kind to care for my safety, I continued with my questions. "Exactly who is on our team?"

"I'm not sure. I just go. I guess we'll find out at dinner tonight."

What he said didn't make sense, but I wasn't going to question him.

"Are you comfortable? Would you like a pillow and a blanket?"

Letting out a short giggle, I arched my brows at him. "Do you want me to take a nap?"

Max let out a small chuckle. "You don't have to if you don't want to. But when I arrived, you had your eyes closed, so I assumed you were tired. You'll be out late tonight, so you may want to take a nap. Or maybe you should wait till after lunch, since our flight is five hours long."

"Maybe after lunch then." The words "five hours" rang in my head. I'd be stuck in the same space with Max for that long. I didn't know what we would talk about, but how could I think of sleep when I was sitting next to my boss's son? Come to think of it, how could I even think at all when I would be with him the whole trip? I was hoping to escape from it all, and one of the persons I wanted to escape from was sitting right next to me. My fingers were wiggling, itching, wanting to text Becky, but that would have to wait.

After he nodded, the captain announced we would be taking off and asked us to turn off any electronic devices. Then the stewardess placed the ugly orange floaty on herself and showed us how to use one in case of an emergency as we watched a video on the screen situated in front of us.

It was strange to be sitting next to Max, and silence filled the space between as we waited for the plane to take off. As the plane sped down the runway, getting faster by the second, my heart hammered rapidly against my chest. My jaws were tight and my hands became numb from me holding onto the seat tightly underneath my overcoat so Max couldn't see. It was the way my stomach lurched that I dreaded when flying, the same way I felt everyday on the elevator to my office.

"Are you okay?" Max asked.

Max must had noticed the anxious look on my face. "Yes," I lied as we both leaned back in our seat as the plane jetted off the ground. I knew the plane would steady itself soon, and knowing that was enough for me not to panic.

When it became difficult to hear from my ears being plugged, I looked out the window to see the grandness of Mother Nature. How small the world looked from above, reminding us how vulnerable we were and how precious life was. Ascending higher, the clouds came into view, and I was completely awestruck. Seeing nothing but the vast sea of clouds beneath me, I felt like I had wings, floating into heaven.

"Beautiful view, isn't it?"

Too engulfed in the view, I hadn't realized Max was looking out the window. When I turned to reply, our lips almost touched, and I jerked back just in time to save myself from the embarrassment of what could have been. "Yes, it is," I replied, and looked away.

"Would you like anything to drink, Ms. Mefferd?" the stewardess asked with a bright smile.

"Some water please."

"Make that two," Max said.

Reaching back into her big, rolling, metal tray, she handed me a bottle of water.

"Thanks," I said with a smile.

After I drank, I took out a magazine and started flipping through the pages. Slowly, Max peered over to see what I was reading.

"Interesting stuff?"

"Just something to read to pass the time."

"Hmmm…maybe you should be reading the company policy, where it *doesn't* say you can't go out with anyone you work with."

I couldn't help myself…I giggled softly. He was determined, and he was adorable for saying that; and he also knew how to get a laugh out of me. "That's because…." I paused. There was no policy that said you couldn't go out with people you worked with. It was my own opinion. It would be unprofessional. If something were to ever happen, it could end up being really bad for one or both of them. And having this once in a lifetime opportunity wasn't something I was just going to throw away because I had a crush.

"I see that you don't have an answer, so I must be right. Actually, come to think of it, I'm always right."

Saved by the stewardess again, she came to bring our lunch. I had expected it to be the processed, plastic looking lunch I'd had several times before when flying, but it was nothing like it. It actually looked delicious. A nice looking tray had a bowl of shrimp linguini, an assorted salad, a cup of vegetable soup, a cheesecake for dessert, and even an extra bottle of water.

After lunch had been eaten and cleared, Max asked me if I wanted to watch a movie. I told him any movie was fine, so he set it up to enable us to watch the same movie at the same time. After placing the head set on my ears, I looked straight ahead onto my screen in front of me. I had only gotten maybe five minutes into the movie when my mind and body started to float into a deep slumber. The combination of a full stomach and being tired from not getting enough sleep the night before were catching up with me.

Blinking rapidly, I desperately tried to stay awake. But no matter how hard I fought, no matter how many sips of water I took, and no matter how many times I shifted my body, my eyelids were too heavy and they surrendered to darkness.

Chapter 13

"Jenna," a soothing voice whispered my name. What a wonderful dream I was having. I was hearing Max's voice, and that alone put a smile on my face. I could feel my cheeks pinching and my lips curling upward. Then suddenly it came to me that my eyes were closed as my mind focused into reality.

I knew I was still on the plane, but how I was positioned while I was taking a nap was the question. Slowly, I began to peel my eyelids open when I heard my name again, and the first thing my eyes beheld was Max's gorgeous eyes. His face was so close we were almost nose to nose, but when I realized my head was resting on his shoulder, I jolted right up.

"Hmmm…what time is it?" I asked, feeling embarrassed, shifting back to my seat. Oh God! My head was on his shoulder, but for how long? But he'd let me rest there.

Leaning over, he brushed the corner of my lip with the tip of his index finger. "Drool much?" he chuckled.

Mortified, I ran the back of my hand over where his finger had just been.

"I was just joking," he teased, nudging my shoulder. "I just needed an excuse to touch you." He winked.

My eyes grew wide with an irritated frown, but what could I say after that. Though I was flattered, he was too smooth with his words, and I wondered how many girls' hearts or pants he'd sweet-talked his way into.

"Sorry to wake you, but we're landing," he continued.

"Okay," I nodded and smiled, trying to remain professional, reminding myself why I was there in the first place. New York was three hours ahead so it was already dark. By the time we got to our hotel it would be close to eight. Looking below, I could see the dazzling, colorful city lights in "the city that never sleeps." I could feel the excitement tingling through my stomach, spreading through every part of me.

After we landed, we went to retrieve our bags and got into the same taxi. We were headed to the same hotel, that I knew for sure as I looked at my itinerary and placed it back into my workbag. My heart raced from excitement, and every fiber in my body had awakened as I looked out the window, knowing that I was where I'd always dreamed of being.

Max must have noticed my excitement. Placing his hand on my shoulder, he gave me a warm smile. I gazed back into his eyes, and held them there a little bit longer than I had expected to. I couldn't turn away as he locked me in place. I didn't know if it was just being inside the small space with him or the city, but whatever the reason, my heart tingled with bliss. I wanted to hold onto this feeling just a while longer, until reality settled back in.

Suddenly, the driver honked his horn, cursing out loud as he jerked the car to the left and back to the same lane. "Everyone okay back there?" he shouted.

"Don't you lock your doors?" Max asked, growling in anger. I felt him shudder while I was in his hold.

"Sorry!" The taxi guy yelled.

Had Max not grabbed me, my head would have pounded against the window. Not only that, I had unintentionally pulled the door open by grabbing the door handle, which was the first thing my hand grabbed for when the cab swerved. The seat belt would've held me in place, but half of my body would have hung out the door; the thought alone was terrifying.

Thank goodness Max had fast reflexes. From the gravity of his speedy pull, my breast collided against his firm chest, and my head slid perfectly into the empty space between his head and shoulder.

I sucked in air when I noted how my arms were draped around his neck.

"It's okay. You're safe," he said softly, caressing my back.

Unable to respond, my body shivering was my answer. I was in his hold, and he was in mine. It felt so right, and yet it felt so wrong, but I welcomed it because at that moment I needed to feel safe, and he provided that. When I tried to pull back, he wouldn't let go. Unable to fight his strength, I relaxed and allowed the beat of my heart to become steady again, but it couldn't. Now my heart hammered from our bodies molding together. The truth was, I was happy he didn't let me go.

Since I hadn't moved a muscle, my nose and my lips were still glued to the side of his neck. How manly and sweet he smelled. I fought with all the willpower in me, when what I wanted to do was to open my lips and indulge myself with a taste of him. When he turned his head, I inhaled a deep breath. A bubble of want was building up too fast. I could feel myself losing control, especially when his warm breath tickled the side of my face.

"Are you okay? That was pretty close," he whispered softly, every puff of air when he spoke tantalizing me.

Afraid to part my lips to speak—for they would definitely rub against his soft skin—I nodded.

"We're here," he whispered again, letting out a soft sigh, seemingly fighting something himself.

When his hand gently slid off my back, he directed my body forward. I was afraid to look him in the eyes, afraid of what emotion I would see in them, so I rooted my eyes to my shoes, feeling overcome with several emotions I desperately needed to control. The door swung open and I stepped out with my workbag.

"Thank you," I said to the bellman, but I wasn't sure if my words escaped my mouth. Not only did the icy, cold breeze make me suck in air abruptly, it stung my cheeks and my hands. Next thing I knew, Max's arm was around my shoulders, guiding us through the entrance of The Plaza Hotel.

Though I knew I shouldn't let him hold me that way, my legs were unsteady from what happened in the cab, so I allowed it until we reached the front desk. There we went our separate ways to check in.

"Hello, and welcome to The Plaza Hotel. Do you have a reservation with us?" the lady asked sweetly.

"Yes," I replied, and gave her the information she asked for.

While I waited as she clicked away on her keyboard, I looked over my shoulder and saw Max standing by the sofas nearby, checking his messages on his cell phone. He had already checked in. That was fast. Was he waiting for me? It was totally unfair. Why did he have to be my boss's son? And why did he have to make my heart skip a beat? Apparently I wasn't the only one. He was oblivious to the ladies passing by, smiling and checking him out.

Finally, the desk clerk gave me the key and directions to where I was headed. Trying to forget what had happened ten minutes earlier, I turned toward Max, but he was already right behind me. I retreated a couple of steps from his close proximity.

"Ready?" He smiled.

"Yes." I gave him a quick smile back and turned away.

"I'll lead the way." Even after he pivoted to his right, he waited for me to walk side by side with him.

"Are we headed the same direction?"

"Mrs. Ward tries her best to book our rooms close together."

"Oh." I gulped, but I didn't know why I was panicking.

As I paced toward the elevator, all I could do was gaze around the beautiful, elegant setting of the hotel. With the finest furniture and trimmings, it was surreal to stay in such a luxurious hotel that I could never afford. It was definitely an added bonus to working at one of the hottest fashion magazine companies around.

Standing in front of the elevator, I reached over to push the button at the same time Max did, but his hand was on top of mine. Feeling the warmth of his skin, I pulled back, but Max did too. In the process, his hand caught mine and stayed there longer than it needed to before he let go.

"Sorry," he smiled, and gestured for me to enter first as the elevator door slid open.

Stepping inside, I went straight to the right corner while Max pressed the thirty eighth-floor button. When he turned to me, he arched his brows in bewilderment.

"I don't like elevators," I explained.

"I could make the ride a whole lot better." He twitched his brows playfully and practically cornered me. Luckily the bell saved me, and he stood at my side when an elderly couple entered. We had stopped on the twentieth floor.

"It's going up," the old lady said with a frustrated tone. "See, I told you we got on the wrong elevator. We need to go down."

"What did you say?" the old man asked.

"Never mind. You always pretend not to hear me when I'm right."

"It's no wonder I can't hear at all. You think you're right all the time."

Max and I caught each other's eyes with a huge smile. I could tell he wanted to laugh just as much as I did, but he held it in— barely.

Then silence filled the air as I felt the weight of his stare. When the elevator opened to our floor, Max held the door as he waited for me to exit first. Unexpectedly, he looked over his shoulder to the elderly man. "Sometimes you just have to let it go. It's not worth the fight." Then he let the door close.

"This way." He turned left, and again he slowed his pace to match mine. Such a gentleman, melting my heart with his simple gestures. But how did he know my room number? Perhaps he figured it was close to his.

Strolling down the quiet hallway, I wondered where his room was, but we didn't have to walk that far after my thought.

"I believe this is your room."

Looking at the key card I held in my hand, he was right. Sliding it in, it made a clicking sound, and Max opened the door for me.

"Thank you," I said.

"Your suitcase will be delivered to your room, and I cancelled our meeting tonight. You look pretty tired, and we have a long day tomorrow. You must be starving...I'll order room service. Let me know what you would like to eat, and I'll have it sent to your room."

"Sure, but what is your room number?"

"I'm right next door."

I didn't know why I felt nervous all of a sudden. It wasn't likely that our rooms were joined. After I thanked him again, I entered to set my eyes on the humongous, too big for one person, breathtaking room.

Chapter 14

I woke up to the phone buzzing. "Hello," I answered, rubbing my eyes. Oh! The phone alarm I had set last night. Lying there, I didn't want to get up. The bed, the sheets, the pillows all felt so soft and comfortable. Everything about this room was grand. From the plasma television, to the bathroom that was designed for a queen, to my bedroom that connected to the huge living room…did everyone get a room like this?

Stretching and yawning and enjoying the peace, I plunked my feet to the plush beige carpet and slipped them into the white slippers that were provided. Admiring the room, I headed to the restroom and stopped when I saw a white envelope that was obviously slipped under the front door.

After I picked it up, I opened it to find that it was from Max.

Dearest Lunch Buddy,
Sorry I can't be with you during breakfast or lunch. I have a long meeting. I'll meet you at the fashion show. Inside is your ticket to enter.
Eagerly waiting to see you later,
Your favorite, one and only lunch buddy.

I didn't know what to make of the letter. It wasn't professional, and I knew he was being friendly, but regardless, it put a huge smile on my face. Before I forgot, I took a picture of my room and sent it to my friends. I thought about telling them Max was there too, but I decided to wait and tell them when I saw them. Giggling like a schoolgirl, though I shouldn't, I hit the shower.

♥♥

Catching my breath, the cold, swift breeze disheveled my hair upward, making it look like a mop. Brushing it in place the best I could, I practically ran to the bellman, hugging my coat around me. "Taxi, please."

Waving his hand, a taxi drove up to the curb. He opened the door for me and I stepped in. "Thank you," I said before he closed the door with a smile.

After I gave the driver the address of where I was headed, we were on our way. Elated, I looked out the window. Excitement tingled every nerve in my body. I couldn't wait to be inside the New York Fashion Show that I'd been dreaming of since…well…ever since I was born. Thankfully, the driver didn't ask many questions, so in order to pass the time, since the traffic was horrendous as expected—the reason why I'd left early—I observed the pedestrians on the sidewalk. Building after building, crowd after crowd of people going who knew where. Before I knew it, we had reached our destination.

"Thank you," I smiled, paying the driver, but I frowned at the cost. It had cost me thirty bucks, all because of the stupid traffic…oh well. "Keep the change."

Stepping outside, the wind swept me back several steps and I almost knocked someone over. "Sorry," I apologized. She looked at me like I was crazy. That was New York for you. She probably knew I was from out of town, especially since I didn't have a New York accent.

Looking for the entrance, I glanced around and noted how many people were there already. Weaving in and out of crowds hanging out, I pushed my way through the front entrance. Perhaps it was the fact that they were used to this kind of weather, but being from Los Angeles…well…that simply said it all. I needed to get inside the warmth. Taking out my small hand purse, I pulled out my ticket.

"Thank you," the lady said, pointing to her right. Then she handed me a pamphlet.

"Thank you," I said and headed to my seat.

"Jenna!" I heard my name from a distance. Twisting my head from left to right, I looked straight ahead when I heard my name again.

"Jake," I smiled happily, though surprised. I didn't know why I was. He was bound to be there with his team. He practically tackled me…that was surprising.

"You made it," he said, releasing me. "This is my team."

I waved to a group of guys, who waved back.

"Jenna, this is Megan," Jake introduced."

How could I forget? She took my job. "Yes, hello Megan," I smiled.

"Hello…what was your name again?" Her smile looked sort of fake.

"Jenna." To be polite I should've extended my hand to her, but from her tone and attitude it seemed like she wouldn't have taken it.

"Oh, yes. I remember now. You were interviewing for the position I got." She held a smirk I wanted to scrub off her face with a spiky sponge.

Way to sock it to me. And what was that for? But I wasn't going to let her put me down like that. "I did, but they needed my expertise in a different department."

Megan didn't say a word after that; instead she nodded, then pretended to smile and wave at someone from afar. If she was waving to a real person, I wouldn't have known. I wasn't going to look.

"Are we sitting together?" Jake inquired, looking at my ticket.

"Oh…I don't know." I glanced to his finger pointing to a number.

"You got the VIP seat?" He squealed. "How did that happened?" His eyes were beaming, looking excited for me.

Megan shot her eyes at me. I got her attention all right. "Are you sure, Jake?"

"Well, she isn't sitting with us, for sure. We're on the opposite side. But that makes sense. I'm with all the camera crew. But Megan—"

"We better get to our seat," Megan snapped, obviously heated over that fact that I was going to be in a VIP front row seat. Oh yeah!

♥♥

Sliding down the row of seats, I glanced at my ticket several times and finally stopped at the number that matched my ticket. Double-checking to make sure it was mine, I settled in. The temperature was neutral, but I still kept my coat on. Noting that many people were looking for their seats, I figured it must mean that it was close to show time.

Sitting there, glancing around, I recognized some movie stars. Thrilled beyond words to see them and to be there, I wanted to squeal from the top of my lungs. Trying to maintain my heartbeat, I flipped through the pamphlet.

I was so occupied with reading the list of names that I hadn't realized someone was sitting next to me. When a warm hand cuddled mine, I immediately knew it was Max. It had to be. No one else spread heat through my body that fast, and no one else smelled the way he did, awaking me.

"You made it before I did." He grinned in ways that made my heart flip.

It had been less than twenty-four hours since I'd seen him…how he could make my stomach flutter like that was unnerving. "I…I…yes," I muttered, looking at him and then quickly turning away.

"I assume you got my note?"

"Yes," I nodded, trying my best not to look at him.

"Did you eat lunch?"

"Yes."

"You didn't replace me with another lunch buddy, did you?"

That got my attention. I flashed my eyes to his. Trouble! "I…no." Not meaning to, I gave him the biggest, almost laughing smile.

Something happened at that moment. His lips curled up with warmth…with tenderness…staring…studying me.

With much effort, I turned away, slightly fanning the pamphlet I gripped tightly in my hand. Breathe…breathe…breathe.

"You got a pamphlet?" His tone went up a notch.

Like a dummy, no words escaped my mouth; instead, my eyes shifted to the pamphlet still in my hands.

I gasped and stiffened when his shoulder touched mine. Leaning in, his breath brushed against my ears when he spoke. "I guess they only give pamphlets to beautiful ladies."

Thankfully, the upbeat music blasted and a speaker came into view, breaking my nervousness. Max reached into his bag and handed me a packet and a pen. "Here you go," he whispered as I shifted my attention to him. "Your job is to pick several dresses for the cover of our next shoot, and I'll pick my favorites, then we'll compare."

No pressure there…the reason why I was asked to go, I guessed. I wasn't exactly sure of the reason for my trip. Not given much information before hand, I figured I would get more instruction…but I didn't know it would be from Max. "Sure, of course." It was all I could say.

I thought of two things as the models gracefully strutted down the long runway; how lucky I was to be there, and how Max's eyes occasionally shifted to me as I felt the weight of his stare. Model after model, dress after dress, brand names from Gucci, Dior, Dolce and Gabbana, Oscar de la Renta…I was in a heavenly show. And yes…there were hot male models, but I forgot to take pictures for Becky. Oh well…she'd have to imagine it when I told her about it.

Jotting down notes of several of the dresses I thought would look great on the front cover of the next issue of Knight Magazine, I stopped when I saw something crimson sway back and forth. My eyes glistened seeing the most gorgeous gown I had ever seen. In ways, it reminded me of the red dress Julia Roberts wore in an older movie called *Pretty Woman*, one of the movies my friends and I watched during our time together. But this dress was a hundred times prettier…no, a thousand times prettier…at least to me.

It was Gucci brand. Slightly off-the-shoulder, it snuggled her curves and flared out, with a long sexy slit up the front. Over the material underneath, sheer chiffon layered the dress.

"What do you think of that dress?" Max whispered.

Unable to peel my eyes off it, I spoke. "It's absolutely…can I say…I'm in love," I giggled. "I believe that's the winner. It's my number one pick," I gushed, still glued to the model. Her long, soft curled brunette hair swayed not just with the music, but with the rhythm of her sexy stride, making the dress even hotter. I wanted to be her…I wanted to be wearing that dress…shoot…I wanted to be the dress. And that thought made me giggle. I heard a soft chuckle beside me, and I could see Max's grin from the corner of my eyes.

When the show was over, everyone stood and applauded for what seemed like forever. Max turned to me. "There is a gathering you need to attend tonight. It wasn't in your agenda, but you need to be there."

I swallowed a lump down my throat. "I…I don't have…I didn't shop…I didn't bring…what time do I need to be there? Maybe I can go shopping for a dress." Oh God! I started panicking, but obviously Max saw the expression on my face.

When he placed his hands on my shoulders, I immediately calmed down. "Don't worry. Go back to the hotel now. I'll have several dresses brought to you. You can decide which one you like most."

My eyes thanked him, but I couldn't get the words out of my mouth. He was just…amazing that way.

"Oh…I'll send a limo for you, and don't forget to bring your cell phone." Then he turned me toward the exit, leaned down, and his breath brushed up against the side of my neck. "Go."

Quivering from his lips slightly touching my skin, my body gravitated off the ground as I headed out to find the exit door. "Limo?" I mumbled under my breath. Excitement brewed even more.

Chapter 15

As soon as I got to the hotel, I headed straight to my room. Waiting as patiently as I could, I thought about texting Max. There were no dresses there. Had I misheard him? Okay...no big deal. I had time to get ready. Digging into my suitcase, I pulled out my little black night purse that was just big enough for my cell phone and small items. Switching items into the small purse, I noted I had several text messages. Darn! Why did I keep forgetting to push the sound button back on?

They were from Becky and Luke. First, I clicked on Becky's text.

Hope you're having fun. Your room looks fantastic. I want to come. Lol!

I texted back. *Love it here so far. Tell you all about it when I get home.*

And I couldn't wait to tell her. She would flip to hear Max was there.

Clicking over to Luke, my face flushed. It was a combination of guilt and...I didn't even know if there was something else. It was just that...mostly guilt. I was having a blast, and even though I wouldn't admit it out loud, I was happy to be there...and...Max...I wasn't sure what I was feeling, or allowed myself to feel. Whatever this feeling was, it was winning, taking over my logic that I shouldn't be dating my boss's son. Perhaps when we were back home I could think straight.

A soft knock on the door pulled me back to the present. Peeking through the small peephole, I saw someone holding a long black garment bag. "Yes?"

"I have your dress, ma'am."

Cracking the door open, I smiled. "Thank you."

"May I come in and place this down for you?"

I stepped aside. "Oh...sure." Reaching into my purse, I fidgeted with my wallet as I watched him place the garment gently on my bed, along with a fancy box.

Eyeing me, he raised his right hand. "Ma'am, that is not necessary. I don't work for this hotel."

"Oh...umm...I thought there were several other dresses I could pick from." I tried not to sound snooty.

"I was told to bring this one and this box."

"Oh," I said, feeling like a dork. I hoped I didn't offend him. "Then...you came from...?"

"I work for Mr. Knight." He paced to the door, opened it, and turned to me. "Have a great time tonight, ma'am." Then he closed the door behind him.

Glancing at the clock, I saw that I had half an hour to get ready....plenty of time. Gingerly, I unzipped the bag and.... No, it couldn't be...could it? Taking it out of the bag...yup...it was. How? Surely it wasn't exactly the same dress the model had worn. She was taller than me...unless they had spares. Silly thoughts ran through my mind as I stared at the box. Spares? For what? Who knew about these things? I could ask.

Without any further hesitation, since the box was for me, I opened it. Holy sweet Jesus...they sparkle like...diamonds. Crystal clear, shiny...can't breathe...I'm holding a diamond necklace. Round-shaped diamonds were joined together to line up as one. I'd heard of tennis bracelets, but was there such thing as a tennis necklace? Was this real? I was sure it wasn't a gift. Perhaps borrowed? Actresses did that all the time. I was sure it was borrowed. And if by some chance it wasn't, I would return it to him. But...it was absolutely gorgeous, and it was going to look stunning with the dress.

♥♥

Though it was freezing outside, the temperature was perfect inside the huge rented building, so I checked my coat. It was a stand-alone building, the type of building companies rented to have a party to accommodate all their employees. White lights hung throughout the room, making the place magical. Soft instrumental music filled the air, and the smell of appetizers churned my stomach. With all the excitement, I had forgotten to eat dinner.

Striding toward the reception room, I was cautious not to stumble on my dress. Thank goodness it covered my black heels, but at the same time I wished it was little bit off the ground, mostly because I knew the dress was borrowed and I didn't want to dirty it.

Clutching my night purse tightly, I swayed across the room looking for Max or anyone from our company, but I found myself uncomfortably turning other people's heads instead. They must think the dress or the necklace is beautiful too. With all the eyes on me, I mostly kept mine rooted to the floor, but sometimes I peered up so I wouldn't run into anyone. That would be totally embarrassing. To be polite, I would return a quick smile when I accidentally gazed into a stranger's eyes, but must they make it so obvious they were staring?

There were many groups of people mingling, smiling, laughing, talking, and truly enjoying themselves, but I felt alone at that moment as I stood there by myself...until my phone vibrated inside my purse. Though I was standing smack in the middle of the room with several eyes on me, I almost wished I hadn't worn the dress. Opening my purse, I took out my cell phone. It was a text message from an unknown caller.

Hello, lady in red. You look breathtaking. I could just stare at you all night.

I blushed just as red as my dress. *Who are you?*

You don't know? Shame on you!

Sorry!

You should put your hair up like that more often.

Why?

It would be easier for me to nibble on your ear.

*Okay...you either know me well or...*Shoot! I'd accidently pressed send.

If you want to know, look to your left.

Putting my phone back in place, I did as the messenger suggested. As if on cue, Jake turned around. His eyes fell from my hair down to my shoes. There was an awkward pause, then he beamed a huge smile and came toward me. "Jenna. You look absolutely beautiful. I mean, not that you don't everyday, but...."

His compliment made me blush, but the flush deepened when he gave me a long tight squeeze and a kiss on the cheek. A part of me felt disappointed the text was from Jake. Who did I expect it to be from? The phone buzzed again, but I ignored it this time. "You look great too," I replied.

He kept eyeing the dress...or was it me? "Is that the Gucci dress from the runway?"

"To tell you the truth, I'm not quite sure." Before he could ask me tons of questions I couldn't answer, I changed the subject. "So...is your team here?"

"Yes. We just got here. They headed directly to the bar," he snorted. "And Megan is here somewhere." He looked around, as if searching for her.

Ignoring the phone buzzing again, I placed my hand on his shoulder. "It's okay...no need to find her. I'm sure I'll catch her later...soon." Soon would be too early. Ever since she was snooty to me, I wanted to avoid her much as I could.

"Jake, I'm so sorry. Can you excuse me? My phone keeps buzzing."

"Sure, but don't forget to save me a dance later."

"There's dancing?" I said under my breath as I reached in for my phone.

Not that left, the other left. And I hope you're not disappointed it wasn't Jake.

I scowled, knowing he was hiding there somewhere, toying with me. At least I could relax knowing the text wasn't from Jake...not that he wasn't attractive. And why was I even thinking this? Being far away from home, thoughts of Luke faded somewhat. But that wasn't fair to him. Speaking of which, I had forgotten to text him back. I placed a mental reminder in my head, turning to the other left. What other left? I guessed he meant his left. It was confusing, so I just turned the opposite way from where I'd turned last time. There were crowds holding their cocktail drinks, but nobody approached me to let me know who it was.

Where? Do I even know you? I texted back, feeling frustrated.

That's not a nice thing to say. Look up.

Too busy looking at the polished white floor, I hadn't realized it was a two story building. My eyes first followed the stairs and then up to my right, then…. Wow…he made me breathless, making time stand still by locking his eyes to mine with that smile he did so well. His expression said it all, calling out for me, and I was responding with my eyes. Wearing a black tuxedo and a crimson tie to match my dress, his body was leaning forward to rest his elbows on the banister, and he looked ever so debonair. I had simply died and gone to heaven.

Spellbound by him, my heart was shown no mercy as it thumped rapidly against my chest. Intensely setting his eyes on mine, his stride toward me was graceful, steady, yet powerful, and dangerous, like a predator setting on its prey. I was immobilized, and he was going to have me for dinner. Oh God! He was coming for me.

With every step he took toward me, my heart pounded harder, wanting and needing him. I could already feel his strong yet gentle hand on my cheek, his breath on my skin, and I was already quivering from his presence alone. Naughty thoughts began to dance in my head, filling me with blazing heat.

Suddenly, his gaze broke, and I saw something purple filter through my vision. With open arms, Megan was quickly approaching him. In fear of what I may see, I turned quickly as my heart dropped to the floor. She might as well have dug her heels through it. Snapping out of the spell, I headed to the bar. When I got there, I had no idea what I was ordering.

"Do you have something sweet with no alcohol?" Forget that. I needed a drink to cool me down from the heat and anger...anger toward him and Megan, and toward myself for being stupid. "Wait...something with a little alcohol...please?"

The bartender was trying to hold in a laugh, most likely knowing my low tolerance to alcohol since I'd said the words "a little." He reached for a wine glass, poured some liquid from several bottles, and handed it to me. "Here you go. Something sweet, and not too much alcohol."

"Thank you," I said. Turning my heels to walk away, I almost ran into Jake. Thank goodness he had retreated several steps, or I would have poured my drink on him. But then again, he would have deserved it for sneaking so close behind me like that.

"There you are. I've been looking for you."

At that moment I needed the distraction, and Jake was there. "Hey Jake." I lifted my drink to him. "I'm here. I went to get a drink."

"Me, too. And I also got a drink for you. It's red wine, nothing special."

"That was sweet of you. Thank you."

"Since you already have one, I'll hold onto this one."

It went quiet for an awkward second as I glanced around the room for Max. I told myself not to, but I couldn't help it. When he was nowhere in sight, I took a sip of my drink. Sweet, but I could taste the alcohol. Most people wouldn't, but being a lightweight, I did for sure. It had the usual effect when I drank a few sips. It felt warm in my chest and my cheeks.

A waitress holding a plate of shrimp in her hands, started to head our direction. She caught my gaze on her plate so she stopped.

"Here you go." She handed Jake and me napkins as we both reached in to grab some shrimp.

"Thank you," I said, already devouring the shrimp. Eating that shrimp reminded me that I hadn't eaten dinner, and how starved I was.

"They've done a great job in decorating this place," I said, breaking the silence. "I mean, even though it's just a bunch of lights and sofas here and there, it really looks...beautiful. Don't you think?"

"Yeah, I guess...I don't really care for the decoration. I like their appetizers and free drinks...and now your company."

I knew I should say something to respond, but I froze when I saw Max with another lady...one of the runway models. She was tall, blonde, and attractive like the other models. Not wanting to stare, I tried to look away as I wondered what they were talking about to make her giggle like that. But every woman giggled like that around Max. Oh God! Do I? Telling myself to turn around didn't help. At that point I probably looked like a stalker or a jealous girlfriend, but I was neither. Then something purple got in my way.

"Jenna. Where did you buy your dress?" Megan asked, without even a greeting or a smile.

Not wanting to tell her, I pondered what to say. I had been so excited to see it that I hadn't questioned it. All I knew was that Max had told me to wait for a few dresses, but only one came...the one I was marveling at, the one that I told him should be on the front cover. Hmmm....

"Jenna. Is that real?" Her eyes were deadlocked to my necklace.

"Borrowed," I stated, and looked away. From the corner of my eye, I could see the model's hand brushing against Max's arm. Pure jealousy raged through me. What is wrong with me? I was just about to turn away when Max caught my stare. He ignored the blonde and winked at me.

Oh please, not the wink! That wink that produced all sorts of crazy flips in my stomach. Without responding or acknowledging him, I turned and gulped down all of my drink. What had I done? Any minute now I'd be looking as red as a stoplight. I needed water. When I turned, Megan was still staring at me.

"So…you came with Mr. Knight? I mean, Max?" She started with her questions. "And, now you're wearing one of the runway dresses. Hmmm…you do know what this means, don't you?"

"Excuse me?" I was starting to get a little heated from the drill of questions she had no right to ask. It was none of her business.

Megan shifted her weight and took a sip of her wine. Her purple dress was beautiful, but not on her. "Well…there are rumors, and I don't know if you want to know, but—"

Jake gaped between Megan and me, then back to Megan. "I don't think she really cares, Megan."

She shot him an evil eye that made him back away. "Well…as I was saying. I'm just thinking of you. This really doesn't concern me. Rumor has it that Max likes to pick an apple, shine it up, eat it, and spit it back out when he's finished. So do be careful. You should stay away from him." Then she walked away, waving to someone from afar.

"Hey," Jake cheered, slightly rubbing my arm. "It's probably the alcohol talking. She really isn't that—"

Before Jake could finish his sentence, I took the wine glass out of his hand and gulped it down. Either I was really buzzed or the phone was really buzzing in my purse, but I ignored it. I was already feeling light-headed, but the alcohol was helping me forget…forget what Megan had said…forget Max…especially Max.

"Let's dance." I tugged Jake toward the band where people were swaying to the music.

As Jake and I danced—though I couldn't really dance since I was in the stupid dress that I now wanted to take off—Megan's words echoed in my mind, lingering a bit longer than I wanted them to. No way was I going to be that apple that shone for him, and no way was I going to be that apple he would spit out…oh…what else did she say? I couldn't remember any more.

Swaying to the music, strands of my hair that were pinned up fell onto my bare back. Though it was not a backless dress, it did reveal half of my back, but I didn't care. Twisting to the left, I saw Max. He had moved closer to the dance floor too, and he was still with that blonde chick and several others, but it looked like he was not paying attention to them. Whatever…I didn't care. But I knew I did care for only one reason…his eyes, staring at me, were too intense; he could've burned holes right through me. Or was he burning holes through Jake? Not only that, he twitched a little when Jake's hand went around my waist. After that, I looked away…somewhat intimidated by Max…somewhat afraid.

The music that pounded through the floor changed its pace to a calmer one, which was a relief because I couldn't move another muscle. Plus, the room was scorching hot, like a harsh, searing summer in Los Angeles when it was over one hundred degrees. Was I sweating, too? I wasn't dancing fast for that long. The room started to spin, and there was a humming sound in my head. Everything seemed to move at a slower pace. I could feel my arms draped around Jake's neck, but I didn't remember doing it. I couldn't even register when Jake's mouth opened to say something. Even through my haze, I realized that I was utterly high.

Wondering where Max was, I turned to look where he'd been before, though it felt like it took a great deal of effort to do so since my mind and body were not in sync. He was gone. Then I heard his sexy voice singing in my eardrum. It was not my imagination. Max was standing next to me, and I felt Jake's grip on my waist loosen.

Max's strong arms held me in place as he swayed to the music. I wasn't sure what I was doing…maybe just standing there. One thing for sure, somehow my arms were on his. "How many drinks have you had?" His tone was stern but gentle.

"I…I think…one…no, two?" I replied softly, unable to look him in the eye. Basically, I was talking to his chest. I was worried I had lost my job.

"You want to talk to my chest, or do you want to look at me?"

I was in trouble…a huge amount of trouble. Not only was I buzzed, I was sure I was red from head to toe, blending in with the dress. And clearly, this was totally unprofessional. Feeling ashamed, I let my emotions get the best of me. I let Max get the best of me. Maybe he couldn't tell? I hoped.

"Look at me," he ordered.

I peered up slowly, squinting my eyes. My head was throbbing, pulsating like my heart.

"Just as I thought," Max said in monotone.

"Sorry…I'm sorry. I'm so hot." I was sure I slurred my words, because they sounded unclear and strange to my ears.

"You're hot…in more ways than one," he said, gliding his arms to my back. When he touched me, I quivered, aware of his hands on me even in this condition. "Geez…Jenna!" His voice was loud. I heard it vibrate in my head, but I was pretty sure the loud music drowned out his voice. Max touched my cheeks and pulled me away, with his fingers tightly gripped on my arm. "You're burning." Now his arm was around my shoulders. "Come on. I'm taking you out of here."

Chapter 16

Blinking my eyes open, I couldn't recall how I got there…elevator, I thought. It was quiet, away from the crowd, away from the noise, but I was still roasting inside, as if my body were an oven, baking at the highest temperature. Feeling something cold underneath my bottom, I looked down to see myself sitting on a granite counter, and the slit on my dress parted open, exposing my legs from my upper thigh down. Lazily glancing around, I noted there were two sinks and three stalls. I was in the women's restroom. Someone walked out of the stall. No, I was in the men's room. What the heck?

"Are you okay?" Max's face was in my view. His hands were on the counter on either side of me, examining me with an amused grin on his face.

Thank God it was Max…what was I thinking? Not good at all. But better him than a stranger, I supposed. "Hot Max," I slurred.

"Yeah…you can call me that any time, babe." His lips curled up, brushing his hand against my cheek.

His hand felt so cool on my face, I welcomed it by letting out a soft moan. Did he just call me babe? That was the only thing that I understood.

"Yes…I understand," he continued. "You feel very hot. Are you okay? Do you need something? I should have gotten you some water, but I didn't want to leave you here by yourself, and I certainly didn't want to bring you down there."

Taking in his cool hand on my cheek, I grabbed it and placed it on the space between the necklace and my cleavage. That felt so good, but Max stiffened. I had never seen him stiffen like that before…or maybe I was wrong.

"Jenna…what are you doing? I wouldn't do that if I were you. Now you're making me feel hot," he sighed, pulling back, creating a wider space between us.

I managed to let go, only to refocus on his tie. "Pretty," I giggled. "I…like…ved." Then I yanked him closer to me and rubbed his tie on my face.

"I like red too," he chuckled. "But I like red on you. And you are way too buzzed."

"Soffft," I mumbled, ignoring what he had said.

"Jenna," he pulled me back again. "How many drinks did you have?"

"No dinner…so hungry…." I waved up three fingers and pointed to each one as I spoke. "Two…one…two."

Max chuckled out loud. "You're holding up three fingers." He closed one down. "There…two."

"Thanks…Max!" I said out loud, and pulled him in for a hug. "I…like…touch…you."

"Yeah…I'd like to touch you too, babe, but you need to agree to go out to dinner with me first."

My head had made its way to his shoulder, and it rested there. "Dinner…hungry…yes."

"Okay…you said it. So only two drinks, and this is how you are? Such a lightweight. And seeing how you look as if you were badly sunburned, you must be allergic to alcohol, too."

"Aller…ic," I sighed deeply.

"If you knew what would happen, and knowing you, with all that 'gotta be professional talk,' why did you drink?"

Only hearing some of what he said, I didn't answer.

"Jenna, answer me. I know you can hear me." His tone startled me so much that I twitched. "Sorry…I didn't mean to scare you."

It was mostly the alcohol talking and a part of me was screaming to hold back, to get a grip on myself. I didn't know if it was the quiet or that just the two of us were there alone in a small space, but I opened up. Though slurring my words, I opened up way too much.

"You...." I poked him on his chest. My finger bounced back from his hard abs. "Bad."

"What do you mean?"

"You...and...girl...ssss."

His eyes enlarged and his face lit up with an amused smile, seemingly liking what I was saying. "So...you were jealous?"

"No...yes...no...." I shook my head, desperately trying to compose myself, running my hand down my face. What was I jabbering about? Then Megan's words invaded my mind, making me upset. "You eat app....les...sh...ine...spiiit." Trying to make a spitting gesture, I bit my tongue and blew.

Max chuckled. "You make no sense."

Sliding the palm of my hand from my face, down to my neck, over my breast, I moaned as I tried to pull down the dress. "Hot."

Max's eyes got wider, then leaned closer. "Don't do that." He sighed against my ear. The puff of air from his mouth felt soothing and cool.

"More," I stuttered, running my hands on his face.

Max pulled back and started to blow softly...on my face...on my shoulders...and a little lower, shooting tingles through me. When he stopped, my bottom lips puckered to pout.

"Jenna, don't do that. You are just too adorable when you do that. Okay...I need to cool off." Max took sidesteps and splashed water on his face.

"Tired...hot," I groaned.

"I know, but I need to cool you down first." His eyes lit up with an idea. Reaching over, he pulled out several paper towels, folded them into squares, and ran them under the sink. After squeezing them somewhat, he placed them over my forehead, and a soft moan escaped my mouth.

"Don't make that sound, Jenna. You're turning me on," he squirmed.

"Hot."

"Yes...I know you're hot, but you're not as hot as I am right now, babe." He sounded agitated, and a deep growl parted his lips. Reaching over, he ran the paper towel under water again. Instead of placing it back on my forehead, he placed it on my cheek, gliding it slowly down my neck, my shoulder, to my collarbone, and what he did next awakened my sex drive. He squeezed the water, letting it pour down the middle of my cleavage, which sent all sorts of crazy shivers through every part of me.

"Ma...." I moaned, reaching for him, but he caught my arm.

"No, no, no. You can't touch me and I can't touch you. You don't know how badly I want to take you right here and now, but it would be wrong...wrong by you, and plus you have no idea of half of what I'm saying to you. There is also that sexual harassment policy, and we're here on business, not for pleasure...although the pleasure is mine to see you this way...opening up and all. Hell, I should have given you a drink the first time we met. Yes...the first time we met, 'cause I wanted my hands all over your body. I know you won't accuse me of anything, but anyhow...not this way...not here. After you go out with me...on a real date...then I can touch you anywhere you like."

Running my fingers through my hair, all I could do was stare while my head pounded, understanding most of what he said. I wanted to tell him I wanted him too, but no words escaped my mouth. I had already said too much, and I was fighting the urge to just seize him and kiss him madly, but there was that word again. He was my boss's son. And what the hell was I doing?

With a sigh, my head thumped on Max's chest. "Tired...hot."

Max's hand stroked my hair, making me relax, making me sleepy. "I know. Just hang in there. The redness looks better. Maybe in five minutes. Don't worry. I'm right here. I'll take good care of you."

"Sorrrry," I mumbled, wrapping my arms around him, snuggling up to him. In his arms I felt comfort...in his arms I felt safe...and in a strange way...this felt right.

Chapter 17

"Jenna," Max called softly, pulling me into his trance. The way he said my name sounded so sexy to my ears. Piercing his eyes at me with a wicked grin, his hands on the back of my dress were making their way down slowly...sensually. My dress had come undone, that I knew for sure from the sudden exposure of my breasts, that caused me to shudder from the cool air and lust. Somehow Max had unhooked my bra at the same time, but it didn't surprise me; he was good with his hands in more ways than one.

Excitedly, my nipples hardened, wanting and needing to be touched by him. "You're beautiful, Jenna. I'll never get enough of you," he said, caressing my breast with his face, teasing me with a flicker of his tongue on my left nipple.

"Oh...Max," I moaned as I ignited between my legs. Wanting and needing more of him, I gripped a handful of his hair. When he sucked my nipples harder and slightly bit one, I moaned louder, arching my back.

Releasing me, he gripped my hair, pulled my face into his, and sucked my lips. Sliding his body in between my legs while his lips were still on mine was easily done since I was on the restroom counter with my legs spread apart. Letting go of my hair, his hand glided down to my cheeks, to my shoulders, and then squeezed my breasts. With a pinch on both of my nipples, I bit hard on his bottom lip, which seemed to inflict both pleasure and pain. Sliding one hand lower, he found my G-string panties and rubbed his thumb right over the most sensitive part.

"Max…please," I begged through gritted teeth. Throbbing, burning, and aching for him, I wanted him inside me. As if he knew what I was thinking, with a strong quick yank, he tore my underwear, which left me even hotter and panting for him even more.

"You want me Jenna? I know you do. Show me," he demanded as he continued to touch my wetness.

Reaching for his belt loop, I pulled it to the right, and it unbuckled. Max released me, bent down, and stood up again, but somehow I couldn't see it. Why couldn't I see his hardness? But it didn't matter. He was already inside me, growling.

Oh God…he felt so good. With every thrust, my heart pounded with ecstasy, fulfilling my desire for him. Then with a yank, he cupped my behind sternly and pumped, grinded, and pressed deeper and faster, riding me like he couldn't get enough. I was…I was screaming. My body felt like it was going to explode as I felt myself climaxing. Then…it all stopped. What the heck?

Suddenly, Max disappeared and everything went dark, but the ache between my legs was still there, pulsating like a thumping heart. It was worse than it was from the start. Then I realized it was a just a dream…a very hot, wet, steamy, aching, needing-to-get-rid-of-this-throb dream. It felt wonderfully real, and a part of me wished it were. This wasn't the first time I'd dreamt about him like that.

Though I was still groggy, feeling like I had swallowed a handful of sand made me want to wake up—that and the need that was still inconveniently there—but I couldn't open my eyes. My eyelids were heavy and tightly shut, as if they were glued together. The need for a glass of water to quench the overwhelming burning sensation in my throat forced me to sit up, but when I did, a moaning sound escaped from my mouth from the throbbing headache. Not only that, the room was spinning, so I kept my eyes closed.

Knowing I could get to the kitchen in my apartment with my eyes closed, I headed out of my bedroom. Then bam! I ran into the wall. What the...? I shot my eyes open...at least, as much as I could. Then it dawned on me. I was in my hotel room, the expensive, beautiful room that I was probably never going to get to stay in again after today.

Oh, this headache...and...I need water...and why am I feeling this way? Trying to recall the previous night, I couldn't since I was extremely parched. I decided I would get relief first, then try to remember. Squinting my eyes as I looked at the clock, I saw that it was close to ten in the morning, but since the curtains were drawn, it felt as though it was still night. Seeing a bottle of water that had been opened, though I had no idea how it got there, I reached for it and froze. Next to the bottle was a note on a small peel of a sticky yellow notepad. It read: Drink me. It looked like Max's writing.

The past night's occurrences vividly rushed to the forefront of my mind, and both my eyes flew wide open. I went to the party and got wasted. *Oh no!* This was terrible...so unprofessional. I had never drank that much before. How much? I had two...I thought. Then Jake and I danced...then...Max. How did I get here?

While I was thinking, I started to gulp the water. It felt cool and refreshing slipping down my throat, so I gulped more down. Wanting to sit down for a bit, I turned, and there he was, sitting on the sofa, sprawled out, comfortably watching me. He looked too gorgeous in the morning light, with just a plain white T-shirt and cotton shorts on. Half of the water I had just gulped spit out of my mouth like a mini fountain, and the other half went down the wrong pipe.

As I coughed relentlessly, Max came to me. "Are you okay?" He massaged my back. "Here...take another sip. It should help. You did mention something about spitting last night, but I didn't really think you meant it," he chuckled. "And you must have had some wild dream, or you were in awful pain to moan like that."

Oh God! My face burned with heat, and I was too embarrassed to look at him; if I did, he would know I dreamt about us having sex in the restroom. I only hoped I hadn't said his name, or said the things I'd said in my dream out loud.

Taking the bottle out of his hand, I took a couple of sips, placed it down on the nightstand, and looked up at him. He was right. The horrendous coughing stopped, but left me with some lingering ones. "I don't remember. What happened? I mean…how did I get here? I mean…." How do you ask these questions to your boss's son? Not that he would squeal on me, but….

Before he could answer, I sat on the edge of the bed. I suddenly realized I was wearing a plain white T-shirt that looked just like his. And to top it off, I had nothing on underneath except for my G-string panties; and even worse, I wasn't wearing a bra. Not having a chance to look in the mirror, I was horrified. I could imagine my makeup all smeared, and my hair looking like a bird's nest. Pulling the blanket, I covered my breasts and tucked the blanket under my arms.

Instead of sitting next to me, Max stood in place. "Everything is alright, Jenna," Max started to say. "Don't worry about this…okay?" His tone was so tender that I believed him, but I needed answers.

"How did I get here?"

"I brought you here. No one knows about this. You were red…really red; or, as you said it…you were 'ved'." He gave a devilish grin.

"I did not," I stammered. Did I?

"Oh yes, you did. You also said a bunch of other stuff." Max sat on the bed, creating massive flutters in my stomach by his proximity.

I gulped and closed my eyes, then opened them to ask him a question I was dreading to ask. "Did we…umm…did you and me…did you spend the night?"

He looked at me with a sideways glance. "Don't bite your finger, Jenna." He pulled it out of my mouth. I was totally unaware I was doing that. Looking baffled, he answered my question. "Depends on what you mean by 'spend the night.'"

Unsure of why anger was brewing inside me, besides the fact that he wasn't giving me a clear-cut answer, I tried to calm myself down, but it wasn't working. "Who changed me? And why am I wearing your T-shirt?" My tone came out a little bit angrier and louder than I wanted it to.

Then there it was...that hurt and anger in his eyes that made me want to take back what I had said and how I had said it. Under those thick eyelashes, his eyes daggered at me for long seconds without a word, but I could tell he was mad from the way he wrung the comforter. Finally, he bolted up like he had sat on fire, and ran his hand through his sexy short hair.

"You...you think I took advantage of this situation? You think I could be that low?" Now he was pacing back and forth. "First of all...I took care of you so you wouldn't make a fool of yourself. For someone who can't tolerate alcohol, you sure didn't care last night. That was very unprofessional of you. You represent the company when you're at a function, not yourself."

My headache was throbbing again, and this time it was from guilt and shame. I should have been more careful with my words, and I should not have assumed things like that, but what was I supposed to think? Water pooled in my eyes, but there was no way I was going to shed a tear.

Max continued, but his tone was softer this time. "You were burning up last night. I was worried for you. I've never had an experience with anyone who couldn't tolerate alcohol, so I didn't know what to do, and I sure as hell wasn't going to leave you by yourself. I didn't want to fumble through your drawers, so I gave you my T-shirt. I swear I didn't look, which is the reason why it is on backwards. You changed yourself. When I tucked you into bed, I managed to make you take a couple of sips of water....you were very stubborn by the way...then you were knocked out. Just in case you needed me...." He pointed. "I slept on the sofa. Now you know what happened." Then he stormed out of my room.

The whole time he was speaking, my head was down in shame. I felt so awful. He took care of me, and this was how I thanked him. The tears that threatened to fall were making their way down my cheeks, and when Max left, I couldn't fathom the reasons why, but my heart ached...really ached...for two reasons; I felt bad, and he'd just walked off, like we had broken up. A part of me told me to stay put, but the other half told me to run to him and apologize. The second half won.

"Max," I muttered under my breath, and walked out of the bedroom into the living area. I had forgotten I was half-naked, but I didn't care. I needed to apologize, and by the time I put my clothes on, it would have been too late. Either he didn't hear me or he'd chosen to ignore me, because he kept on walking through a door that wasn't the front door. All this time, I hadn't realized there was an adjoining door; but then again, I had never noticed because the place was too damn big.

Max was out of sight, so I started jogging to reach him. I had only turned my head for a split second to observe I was in a bedroom, and not another living room like the one I had, when I slammed into something hard. Instinctively, not wanting to fall flat on my butt, I reached for something stable. My arms were suddenly wrapped tightly around the nape of Max's neck, and I felt something warm around my back. My...oh my...my flesh...my bare butt, my G-string butt. I tried to pull away...I think...or maybe I didn't, but Max's grip on me was too strong.

One of Max's hands was holding me steady on my bottom, causing me to be on my tippy toes. Our bodies were pressed so tightly I could feel my nipples perk, feeling his heart thumping hard, making my body move in the rhythm of his. Heat combusted like a wild flaming fire throughout my body, and I completely dissolved in his embrace.

Quivering from the warmth of him, I stared at his manly, sexy Adam's apple as neither one of us moved a muscle. Knowing one of us had to move, I slowly peered upward. I felt his neck muscles stretch as he peered down. We were eye to eye, nose to nose, lips to lips, and heated tingling sensations shot between my legs. "I'm...I'm so sorry," I managed to breathe out, worried that if I spoke any louder he would hear how hard I was panting.

He didn't respond to my apology. Instead, his angered eyes softened with tenderness, and perhaps even…desire…wanting. Every puff of his heated breath on my lips was tantalizing me to the point I was unraveling. With a sharp intake of my breath, I felt the tiniest, idly circular motion on my bottom, causing an aching need between my legs. It got worse when his eyes shifted to my lips while he bit down on his bottom one.

While I concentrated on his lip that I wanted to devour so badly, I hadn't realized my hands had slid down to the sides of his neck. With every angle, every curve, my hand glided downward to his ripped muscular chest that was perfect in every way. He was beautiful and he knew it.

When his clenched hand loosened on the back of the T-shirt I was wearing, I knew he was finally letting me go. Reaching for my face, he blotted the wetness with his thumb. "You were crying?" He sounded shocked. His relaxed body stiffened, more alert. "Shit…I'm sorry to blow up on you like that. It's just that…." He raked his hair back and parted his lips, seemingly wanting to say something. Instead, he pressed his forehead against mine. "I'm sorry too. Don't cry. I don't like to see you cry. Go take a shower; I need one too…an icy cold one."

When Max twitched his brows playfully, I knew everything was back to normal…except for the aching need between my legs that still lingered. I needed a cold shower too. With a huge smile that was returned from Max, I pulled the back of his T-shirt down as I started to walk out of his room. Though it looked like a dress on me, I needed the security of knowing he couldn't see my behind.

"Nice ass," I heard him say faintly. Whether or not it was said for me to hear, it produced a huge, giddy smile on my face. In some twisted way, his words were hot, and I blushed all the way to the shower.

M. Clarke

Chapter 18

A cold shower was what I really needed, but a hot shower was even better. Feeling the beaded drops of water on my body helped me relax the tension in my muscles. Though the headache was better, it was still there, but knowing food would take care of that, I dismissed it. Standing under the soothing running water and seeing the steam fog up the glass door put me in a trance, and my mind started to wander with thoughts of Max.

Why was my room so much bigger than his? For goodness sake, he was the boss's son. Hell...he practically owned the company. Then it occurred to me. The front desk lady took a bit longer than usual to check me in. Not only that, Max knew where my room was before I did. Oh my God! He did. He switched rooms with me so I could have the bigger room. Now I felt really horrible, and guilty, and everything else I could think of. He was just...and something warm glowed in my heart.

A part of me wondered why I was chosen to accompany Max on this trip. The team was just the two of us. That didn't seem right. Did Max arrange it that way? He knew how much I wanted to go from our lunch conversation. I didn't know if I should be angry or happy about it, but I didn't want to ask him after he had taken care of me, and after the sweet things he had already done. I decided to do what Mrs. Ward had told me at our meeting—don't ask questions and enjoy.

After washing my hair, I opened the bottle of gel soap that smelled of lavender and poured it on the round white puff wash sponge that was provided. How I was going to miss this bathroom that was bigger than the size of my bedroom...make that twice the size of my bedroom. Gliding the soap down my neck, over my shoulders, down my arm, and over my breast, I stopped. Feeling my nipple pressed on Max's chest had done all sorts of crazy things to me, and I was feeling that same feeling again. The ache, the desire, the want was back. Wanting that feeling to go away, I turned the cold nob, but I had pushed too far. Ahhhh! Cold...so cold. I jumped.

Slipping into a long, white bathrobe, I tied it loosely and twisted my hair into their long white towel. Practically everything was white, except for the walls and the floors that were made from marble—the color of caramel to be exact. After I washed my face, brushed my teeth, and felt refreshed—and a whole lot better—I stepped out of the bathroom.

From afar, I saw Max holding a laptop. His eyes were on the screen as he headed toward me. Though I was completely covered, I panicked, and I couldn't move. Neither one of us had closed the door. I guessed it was fine...after all, we were on opposite ends of the room.

"Jenna," he called excitedly, peered up, and halted. His brows arched and gave me a flirty sideways glance. His lips curled in a crooked sly smile, but he didn't say a word. He didn't have to. I could only assume what he was thinking in his dirty mind, because mine was there for a second until I snapped out of it.

"Max," I said, tightening the robe to secure.

"You okay there?" He approached closer...a lot closer. He brushed my cheek with the palm of his hand. "Your cheeks are red."

Placing my hand where he'd just touched, I spoke. "I took a really hot shower."

"Oh...well let me show you something on my computer." He sat on the edge of the bed and gestured for me to sit next to him. "Look at our front cover for our next issue. The lady in red. It's only a lay out, and we need to have the model or an actress actually do a shooting, but I think it looks great. What do you think?"

It was the same red dress I had worn last night, and the same dress I told him should be on the front cover. He'd actually listened to my opinion; and not only that, he took my advice and put it into action. "That looks fantastic," I cheered. My body was filled with genuine excitement. "It's...absolutely gorgeous...though I think her hair should be slightly up, like with loose curls. Then she would look stunning."

"You mean the way you had it?" His eyes blazed into mine. "She wouldn't look half as beautiful as you did last night," Max said sincerely, softly, melting me into the mattress.

Speechless, I sat there, feeling dazed, as I stared back at him...until he looked away first.

"Anyway...I'll show you the finished product."

"Max," I said softly.

"Jenna?" He gave me his full attention.

My hand had a mind of its own. It went straight to Max's forearm and it stayed there. "Before I forget, I would like to thank you for taking care of me. I've never been like that before, and it was very unprofessional of me." I didn't want to say the word buzzed or wasted. It sounded so adolescent. "Umm...it was my first time."

"First time...really?" His brows arched with amusement.

"Yes," I replied shyly.

"Are other things firsts with me?" He smirked.

"Be quiet," I giggled lightly, pushing him away with my hand, but his hand caught mine and then he let go. Heat...dangerous heat...spread from my hand, up my arm, to my cheeks. "Anyway, also, thank you for allowing me to wear the same dress. That was so sweet of you. And the necklace...I don't know what to say. And speaking of the dress and the necklace, I don't know where they are," I sighed worriedly.

"I took the necklace off you, and before you get any funny thoughts, I didn't look. I helped you with the zipper on the dress, but that is all. After you got into bed, I took them to my room. They were picked up this morning when you were in the shower."

"Oh...and I was wondering how you knew my size. The length and fit were perfect."

"They carry more than one size, and being in this industry long enough, I know. All I need to do is just examine your body with my eyes, which I have been doing a lot lately," he winked.

Oh...blush...blush...blush. I looked down, not knowing how to respond to that.

"I'm hungry," Max said, brushing the tip of my nose with his finger. "You must be famished, since you didn't eat dinner last night. Why don't you get ready?"

"How do you know I didn't eat dinner last night?" I fidgeted with the bathrobe belt. The thing was so long.

Max took it from my hands and placed it on the bed. "This robe is too long on you. Be careful. You may accidentally trip on it." He stood up. "Oh...to answer your question. You told me lots of stuff last night, babe."

Did he just call me babe? Taken back by his words and wondering what the heck I'd said to him, I stood up. "Did I say many crazy things?" I gulped nervously.

"What you said to me is a secret, so I can't share," he chuckled.

"What?" I smiled, glaring playfully at him.

"Well...we better get ready. We can have brunch, then head out to the airport."

"Sure," I said, moving to my right while Max moved to his left. Bumping hard against each other, the momentum pushed me back. Max, being the gentleman he was, reached for me, but when he did, he stepped on my robe. Somehow, the robe slipped down to my waist, and Max fell on top of me on the bed.

The sound of his laptop hitting the floor was what I heard first. Thank goodness it didn't sound like it had been broken, but Max didn't seem to care enough to look. His eyes pierced mine, heated and shocked, just as much as mine. Topless, breasts exposed, my nipples flared through the thin layer of his T-shirt when I felt his chest, and the yearning between my legs exploded. Feeling my chest rise and fall rapidly, I struggled to control my urges and my breathing. *Boss's son*, I kept telling myself, but it wasn't working.

"I'm so sorry," Max chuckled. "You know, you don't have to get almost naked to get my attention. You already have that, and a lot more." His muscles were now flexed, supporting his weight on his elbows. "I promise I didn't see anything. I mean...I'm sure there is much to see, but I didn't see what you thought I saw, or might have seen." He sounded really nervous. "Okay...so what I will do is...um...." He glanced around the room, seemingly looking for something.

"Max...can you just pick me up? Or maybe you can close your eyes." The truth was, my muscles felt so weak from his close proximity that I had lost control of my body.

"Well, if you're giving me a choice...." He didn't finish. He helped me up with my body still pressed against his. The towel on my head loosened, and my wet hair tickled down my back, producing a different kind of shivers. "Then I'll do it this way."

What was the matter with me? I could've pulled up the robe myself, but I couldn't move. I was enjoying his hands on my naked back, and the delicious seductive heat that blistered through every inch of me. Max didn't seem to want to move either. He stood there, holding me, when he could've let go. Instead, his feather light touch smoothly glided down my spine and created more dangerous tingles. He kept on going and took hold of my robe that stopped at my waist.

"You drive me crazy. What am I going to do with you?" he whispered, hardly audible, but I heard. I also heard a low groan that sounded way too sexy to my ears.

Feeling that soft cotton rubbing against my skin, I could tell he was fidgeting with it, most likely contemplating whether to drop it or pull it up for me. As much as I wanted him to let go of it and let it pool around my feet, I was glad he didn't, because my self-control was completely gone at that point. Gingerly, the robe went over my shoulders, and he even fastened it for me.

Still standing there body to body, he spoke without looking at me. "So...like I said." He cleared his throat. "You may step on your robe and trip. We'd better get ready. I'll move first."

When he turned to reach for his computer, a cold empty space took his place. Standing there, breathless, I was immobile for I don't know how long, until Max brought me out of it.

"Jenna...."

I turned. He was outside of my room, so I followed his voice...across from where I stood, still in my bedroom, him in his. He was topless, with a bath towel around his bottom half. Oh dear Lord! I had imagined what his chest would look like underneath his sweater or T-shirt on many occasions, and he did not disappoint. With ripped muscles along the curve of his arms and six-pack abs that sizzled, he made my dreams come alive.

"Just to let you know, you agreed to go on a date with me."

"What? I don't remember. Was it when I was not myself? 'Cause that doesn't count."

"Everything counts, babe." That was the third time he'd called me that. My heart did a pleasant flip, and I wasn't sure if I liked that feeling. "We'll talk about it later."

"There's nothing to discuss."

Then I heard the water running from his side of the room. "What are you doing?"

"I'm going to take a shower."

"I thought you already took one."

"Babe, after what just happened, I need another one, and a lot colder this time."

Chapter 19

Stretching and yawning, I woke up in my own bed. It felt good to be back home and see the sun again, except...I was back to reality, something that was both good and bad. Arriving late last night, Becky had already gone to bed. A part of me felt guilty for not replying to all her texts, but I knew she would understand. Then there was Luke. Not that Max and I were an item, but what I had experienced with him in New York was something I'd never felt with Luke.

Knowing this was one decision I couldn't just decide in bed, I thought perhaps when I saw Luke again, my feelings may be stronger, since I hadn't seen him for at least ten days. A part of me also felt guilty for texting him back only twice. Hearing footsteps sound, I knew Becky was awake. Jolting out of bed, I could not wait to see her.

Tiptoeing to the kitchen as quietly as I could, I observed her fidgeting with the coffeemaker before I could find the right time to make my move. Silently waiting...silent giggling inwardly...wait for it...wait...now.

"Becky!" I said out loud, draping my arms around her from behind.

She jerked back and panted. "Shit, Jenna. You nearly gave me a heat attack." She squeezed me tightly, then let go and placed her hand over her heart. "I knew you came home last night, but for sure I thought you would still be sound asleep. What the...? Don't ever do that again."

"Sorry," I pouted.

"Don't pout. You look too darn cute. It makes me actually forgive you," she smiled then frowned. "So…how was New York? Was it everything you hoped it would be?" Placing her mug under the coffeemaker, she opened the refrigerator and took out a container of eggs.

Leaning against the counter, I thought about how I would tell her everything that happened in New York, and I mean…EVERYTHING. "So, the show was fantastic."

Becky poured the oil in the small frying pan. "That's great." She looked up at me. "I'm listening, okay." She smiled. "I'm just starving. Want some eggs?"

"Sure."

"So…go on." She cracked the eggs. "Scrambled?"

"Sure…so…I got to sit at the VIP front row seat."

Becky started to stir the eggs with the spatula. "You did? That is so cool. I wish I had been there with you."

I crossed my arms and braced for what I was about to hear. "So…Max was there, too."

Silence…she stopped moving…then there was the scream. "Are you serious?"

"Becky…stir. You're going to burn the eggs." I took the spatula from her hand and took over.

"What the hell, Jenna? Why didn't you text me? Oh my God! You're terrible."

With Becky freaking out like that, I had to intervene. Opening the cabinet, I took out two small plates. "I wanted to tell you when we got home so we could talk about it."

"Hell yeah, we're going to talk about it…you're going to tell me every detail of every second, every thought…everything else," she rambled, still staring at me with her jaws dropped.

"You want to pour me a glass of juice while I take the plates to the table?" I asked. "And don't forget your coffee." Becky looked like she was somewhere else, so I reminded her of what she needed to do.

While we ate our eggs, I told her everything. I provided her every detail, every emotion that I had felt there...about the fashion show...the dress...the hotel...about Megan...and definitely about the accidents. While I spoke, her eyes were sparkling, and she was giggling like a schoolgirl. Most of all, she wanted me to thank her for cleaning out my underwear drawer.

Becky took a sip of her coffee. "So, what are you going to do?"

"I'm not sure." My fingers glided idly around the rim of the glass. "Max said I had agreed to go on a date with him, but he hasn't really asked. I mean...we don't have a date set yet. And I need to see Luke so I can be sure."

"I think you know the answer. But I understand. You need closure with Luke."

I swallowed the last gulp of my juice. "You're so sure of what I'm going to do?"

"Honey...your eyes are sparkling more than the diamond necklace you've described. Now that speaks volumes."

I inhaled a deep breath. "I don't want to hurt...him."

"Well...too bad." Becky's tone went up a notch. "He should've made you sing hallelujah. If you snooze you lose, and that's what's going to happen to you with Max if you pull that string too long. Anyway...don't forget we're doing ladies' night out this coming Saturday."

"I won't forget." I was really looking forward to seeing Nicole and Kate.

Becky was right. I'd always taken her advice seriously since she had more experience with relationships than I did. After we cleared the table, we agreed to go shopping at the local mall. She suggested that I buy some new attractive clothes. I had to agree...she was right.

♥♥

Monday morning was just that. It was dreadful to get out of bed, but once at work it didn't seem like Monday anymore, especially when I got a warm welcoming smile from Lisa and the rest of my team. They asked me questions about the fashion show, but of course I left out many details.

Checking my emails and responding to the customers took up most of my morning, but I couldn't help thinking about Max and wondering what he was doing. Reaching over to grab a pen, I noted I had a couple of text messages. Clicking, I saw the return text from Luke confirming our dinner that Friday. And then there was one from Max. My face burned.

Good Morning. I'm busy this morning, but I'll see you soon...very soon.

Rubbing the back of my neck, I smiled giddily and pushed the phone aside.

After a quick bite to eat, I got right back to work. The office was filled with the sound of computer keys clicking away and phone conversations to customers. When the phone shook on the table, knowing the possibility it was Max, I checked it right away.

What are you wearing? T-shirt or bathrobe?

What?

Come to my office.

No!

I guess I have to try harder...please!

No!

Letting out a quiet giggle, which I totally didn't mean to do, I peered up to see if anyone had heard. Thank goodness they were too busy to notice. Then my phone rang. The screen read Maxwell Knight. My heart did a backward flip. Should I answer?

Since I let the phone ring too long, my group all looked at me. "It's a wrong number," I smiled.

The ringing stopped. Relaxing my shoulders, I looked at my computer screen. There was an email from Max. Should I click? With my hand over the mouse, I glided the arrow to open.

Please come, or I'll come and get you myself!

Startled and worried that he would come and make a scene, I stood up.

"Jenna," Lisa said, holding the phone receiver. "Mr. Knight asked me to tell you that you have a meeting in his office right now."

He called her, too. This must be a real meeting and not a flirting meeting. Crap! I need to get my butt down there and apologize to him. How was I to explain why I said no? I didn't even know what the meeting was for, and I certainly wasn't prepared for anything...whatever we were supposed to talk about. And where the heck was his office?

After Lisa informed me where his office was located—it was the last one on the right—I speedily headed down the hall. The only sound I heard, besides the thumping of my heart beating close to my ears, was the clicking, irritating sound from my heels.

Brushing my hair with my fingers, straightening my black pencil skirt, and making sure my white blouse was buttoned, I knocked softly at the door that was slightly ajar.

"Come in. I've been expecting you."

Grrr! I hated how his voice alone could stir up arousing emotions in me.

Pushing the door open, I walked in and closed the door behind me. The first thing I noted was Max's eyes twinkling, seemingly enjoying what he was seeing, and that beautiful grin on his face.

"I'm so sorry," I blushed. "I didn't mean to...I didn't know...." How was I going to explain? I didn't even know what I was saying. I stole a quick glance at his big office, which was nicely furnished. A mahogany desk was placed in front of the large window, a few chairs sat in front of his desk, and a sofa was settled in front of a large bookcase filled with picture frames and books. To the right of his desk was a coffeemaker and coffee amenities.

"Jenna, relax and take a seat."

It wasn't a long distance to the chair in front of his desk where I was headed, but having Max stare at me like that made me nervous, and that darn clicking sound from the heels made it worse. Not only that, he looked so good in his suit and tie, with his arms behind his neck for support, I thought I was going to faint. Finally, I sat stiffly, and gave him a small smile. "Yes?"

With his arms folded on his desk, he leaned forward. "For someone so sweet, you can be very stubborn. But it's okay...it turns me on," he winked.

Yikes! He just did not say that. My eyes went straight to the desk.

"Anyway...after several texts, after an email, after calling you, then Lisa, you finally came. What are you going to make me do next time to get you to come to my office?" he chuckled.

I shrugged my shoulders sheepishly. "I'm...sorry...."

"I didn't ask you to come so you can keep apologizing to me. Come take a look at what we have so far. I was at the shooting this morning. I think your idea was fabulous. I'm going to give you credit for this."

I was pretty sure my eyes grew ten times their size as I stared at him in disbelief. "Really? I don't know what to say!"

"Don't just sit there, come take a look." He gestured with his hand. "It's on my computer."

Feeling exhilarated, I stood up and started to pace around his desk. Unexpectedly, I tripped over a small wastebasket I did not see since my eyes were glued to the computer screen. Max stood up to catch me, but the weight of my body caused us both to crash on his chair.

With his arms wrapped tightly around me, my skirt had slipped up and I was straddling him. "Oh my God...I'm so sorry," I said, my lips next to his ear.

"We gotta stop meeting like this, or I won't be able to control myself," he murmured as his chest rose and fell quickly.

Shakily gripping the arms of his chair, I pulled up somewhat, but I couldn't get myself to stand. Max wouldn't let go. Twisting my head to the left, I was now face to face with him. He was too beautiful. With perfect skin, a nice defined nose, and warm brown eyes that could totally melt you with one glance, and those lips...those kissable lips. I had to stop staring. My trance broke when Max spoke.

"I wanted to take you out this Friday, but I'll be in New York. I'm leaving tomorrow, so I won't be able to take you out to lunch on Wednesday either, lunch buddy. And waiting till next Friday is too long, so I would like to take you out on Sunday. We'll have brunch. We can sleep in late together, then have brunch if you like."

Trying to register what he had just said, I blinked. My mind told me to say no, but my heart told me to say yes, and so did my body. Becky was right. If I waited too long, I would lose him. And I didn't like the idea of Max being with anyone else. Being jealous seeing him with that blonde model confirmed that I didn't, and those hot, wet dreams that kept invading my mind and body...well...that just said it all. Before I could change my mind, I lit up a shy smile. "Brunch sounds great, without the sleeping in late together."

"You said yes," he squealed happily, then arched his brows. "Get your mind out of the gutter, Ms. Mefferd. Sleeping together doesn't necessarily mean having sex, unless you can't handle yourself around me. We can cuddle, just like this. And we don't have to be just lunch buddies, we can be cuddle buddies."

I smirked. "Is that a challenge, Mr. Knight? We can try one day." I couldn't believe those words escaped my mouth, but with Max, it was so easy.

His lips curled into a huge grin as he arched his brows in astonishment, most likely thinking he couldn't believe I said it either. "I like challenges. You're on."

I gulped my nerves down. "Can I get up now?"

"You need my hand service. Let me help you," he said with a cool, steady tone.

Oh no!

Purposely, his hands on my back gingerly, carefully, caressed down my spine, making me quiver in all the right places. Then his hands slid to my sides, over the material that had gathered up, then to my exposed thighs. I sucked in air hard, and I knew Max heard it because of a satisfied grin on his face. Feeling his touch, his hands felt so smooth, so sensual across my legs as he lifted me up, but I wasn't standing.

Losing my mind and control, I was still utterly dazed, and sucked in more air when his face was inches away from my chest. My breathing was heavy and fast, and so was Max's. I felt the warm air he exhaled way down south. Panting and worried that someone may walk in, I turned my head to the door.

Max's arms around my upper legs were now dangling by his side. "Don't worry, Ms. Mefferd. It's locked. I made sure of it."

"I'm…I mean…I'm not worried." I struggled to get up, but just before I did, Max twirled his chair and I ended up in his lap with my back toward him, facing the computer, locked between the table and him. How the hell did he do that so fast?

"Don't bite your finger, Ms. Mefferd." He guided my finger out of my mouth and kissed it. "Next time, it's going in my mouth."

My body stiffened from the small short kiss and the thought of it going inside his mouth.

"Now that we can concentrate better, here is the front cover."

And there it was, just as beautiful and stunning as I remembered it to be. The model did it justice, and so had Max with the layout.

Chapter 20

It was going to be our last date, so why did I worry so much? Perhaps it was the fact that I was going to break Luke's heart, or the guilty feeling washing over me...guilt for not telling Luke about Max before, and guilt for going out with Luke and not telling Max. But Max was in New York, and I needed to break up with Luke in person and not over the phone.

Luke picked me up, but this time it was awkward, perhaps from knowing that it would be our last dinner together...well, at least I knew. Instead of dressing up, I wore jeans and a sweater. I guessed it was a way for me to express that this wasn't a date. However, Luke was dressed a little bit more than casual since he had just gotten off work.

"How was your trip?" he asked, cutting his steak with a knife.

Thinking about Max and what happened, my face felt warm. "It was great. I enjoyed it," I replied, twirling the linguini with my fork.

"I can tell...I mean...since you didn't reply back much, I figured you were very busy."

I gulped guilt down my throat. "Yes...very busy." Feeling the vibration from my purse, I checked. It was from Max. Max had called and texted me everyday. We flirted a lot on the phone and by text, which made me miss him even more. Though we hadn't even kissed yet, the powerful, raw emotion he stirred inside me felt like we had, and a lot more.

"Excuse me," I said, and read his text.

What are you doing?
Thinking of you.
Good. You know what I'm thinking of?
What?
You wearing my T-shirt or the robe.
Keep thinking that.
Not quite sure what that means. I have a surprise for you.
You don't need to give me another surprise. I love the roses you sent again.
There are a lot of fun things you can do with the rose petals on your naked body.
I'm sure there are...lol! Gotta go.

Feeling hot from his words, my finger went up to my lips then stopped. Giggling inwardly, I thought about how many times Max had to take my finger out of my mouth. Oddly, I never had the urge to put my finger in my mouth with Luke. Placing my phone back, I peered up to see Luke chewing on his steak, staring at me with an irritated expression. "Sorry about that."

"That's okay," he said sharply.

I felt a sting of anger so I took a sip of my water. While playing with my food, my heart pounded from nervousness as I built up the courage to tell Luke it was over.

"Max."

Oh shoot!

His eyes shot daggers at me and then looked away.

That was just great. I didn't need that evil eye thrown at me. Flushing redder than his wine, I built up the courage again and continued as if nothing happened. "Luke...there is something we need to talk about."

"I need to talk to you too," he said with a full mouth. He didn't even let me continue, nor did he even look at me. "Listen, I don't think this is going to work. Don't get me wrong. I think you're attractive, but obviously we don't have much in common."

Is he kidding me? I wanted to break up with him. He's breaking up with me? And all this time I was worried about his feelings, and obviously he didn't care about mine. What the hell?

Had I known he was going to do this, I would have told him to meet me here instead, or just done it over the phone. Wait...he should have asked me to meet him here. Why would he pick me up unless this wasn't planned? He didn't take me out to break up...he must have sensed it from my lack of attention to him, and by me telling him we needed to talk...and especially since I called him another name.

"We can still be friends," he continued, cutting his steak a little bit harder than before.

The rest of the dinner was awkward. Still be friends, my butt. I didn't even want to see him after that. Wanting to be cool about it, and especially since he was my ride home, I just gave him a fake smile. "Sure."

Awkward silence filled the air on the way home, so I glanced out the window to pass the time. Only a few stars graced us tonight, but it very dim and sad looking, like me. It wasn't the fact that our short-term relationship was broken, it was the feeling of how strange it would be to run into him again after tonight, if that ever happened. And if we did, would we ignore one another and pretend we never knew each other? That was the saddest part of breaking up.

Sure, we could be friends, but come on. The chances of that happening were slim to none. I'd seen it happen many times with my friends' relationships. It was almost impossible to be friends afterwards. And here I was, sitting in his car, thinking this was the last time we'd ever see each other, and that was very depressing because in a way, he was my friend.

Luke wasn't like Max, but he didn't treat me badly. He wasn't a perfect gentleman, but at least...nah. I didn't want to think of reasons to make him look better than he was. Turning off the ignition, Luke didn't say a word. The headlights behind us blinded me for a second from a flash of their high beams. Seriously, was that even necessary? We know you are parked behind us.

Stepping out of the car because I knew Luke wasn't going to open my door, I swung around to see him in front of me.

"Jenna, look. What I said back at the restaurant...I didn't really mean it."

"What?" I was confused. Did I hear him right? "Luke...don't—"

"Please...I was upset. You didn't want to come with me to San Francisco, and you hardly returned my texts or my calls in New York. Then you called me Max. Who the hell is Max?"

"Luke, please. This is over, and you need to go."

"Just think about it...okay?" Luke's eyes were pleading. "I'm sorry that I didn't call you enough or take you out enough. It's just that...I wanted someone who was more driven, career orientated, someone bolder, with more self-confidence. Now I see that you are...but in your own special way. Just give me one more chance."

I couldn't look at him. It was too late. His words alone confirmed that I didn't ever want to see him again. He didn't even see the real me while we were dating, but Max did from the very beginning. When I didn't respond, he continued.

"I'll call you later. Maybe we both need to sleep on this." Without warning, Luke looped his arms around me so tightly I couldn't break away.

"Luke...I can't breathe."

"Sorry. Just think about it."

Exhaling deeply, because this was how I had imagined this might play out, I focused my eyes on the tree across the street and thought about how I should respond.

"Jenna," Luke said, breaking me out of my thoughts. "Maybe you'll change your mind after this."

When I peered up, Luke's lips crashed into mine. I was taken aback, and it took me a few seconds to push him away, but his body weight on mine made it difficult. As I struggled to break away, he finally let go. Without a word he got into his car and took off, and I stood there feeling staggered as to how that had happened. I didn't even enjoy it.

What happened next spun my world upside down...and then some. Max stood frozen, with his body halfway out of the car, his eyes searing with hurt and anger. I opened my mouth to speak, but nothing came out; and to make it worse, my legs were planted to the ground and I couldn't run to him. All I could think at that moment was how much he had seen.

"Max? I thought you were in New York." I managed to mutter, and started toward him.

"Stop! Don't take another step. You were sure thinking of me."

Before I could say another word, he got in the car and sped away. My heart dropped within seconds of his absence. He might as well have run over it. Feeling the sting in my eyes, I let them fall. And seeing a dozen red roses on the ground where he'd thrown them, I welcomed the pouring tears even more.

M. Clarke

Chapter 21

"Are you going to lie in bed all day?" Becky asked, lying next to me. "He'll come around. After you explain, he'll know what a fool he's been…that arrogant bastard."

With a Kleenex tissue in one hand, I wiped my tears. "I should have tried harder to push Luke away. I should have bit him, or kneed him, but it didn't come to mind when it happened so fast."

"I know. It's not your fault. Men are so stupid. Sure…just run away."

"The funny thing is, Max and I hadn't even kissed. We didn't even go on a date, but I feel such a strong connection to him it's kind of frightening. I mean…look at me. I'm a mess, as if we broke up after a long relationship." I let out a short laugh. Sitting up, I blew my nose.

Becky paced to the door and held onto the frame of it. "Nicole and Kate are coming soon. I'm going to prepare a chicken dish. You lay here and mope all you like, but when they come, hell…whatever. Let's have a moping fest. I have some moping to do myself."

"Thanks, Becky. Next time I'll cook. I don't know what I would do without you. You know that, don't you?"

Becky ran to me and wrapped her arms around me. "I know. And just so you know, even though you think I'm here more for you than you are for me, you're totally wrong. You were there for me in college way more than I could ever make up for. You took care of me when I was wasted, you helped me through bad breakups...and don't forget how you helped me with the classes I almost failed...okay? I'm just glad that we have wonderful friends we can count on. You know what I mean."

Still holding on to Becky, I nodded. I knew exactly what she meant.

♥♥

"Nicole, Kate," I squealed, embracing them in my arms.

"Missed you too," Nicole said, returning the hug, then let go.

Kate, the more affectionate one, kissed me on the cheek and handed me a bottle of wine. "So...tell us all about New York."

After packing our plates with food and a glass of wine, and water for Kate, who was still breastfeeding, we sat at the table in our usual spots. With all eyes on me, I told them everything that happened in and out of New York.

"Sounds like Max was really hurt by seeing you with Luke," Nicole said, sticking a fork into the chicken. "I don't blame him though. If I had been there when that happened, I would've thought the same thing. I mean...I'm not siding with him, but he's been after you for some time, and when he finally gets you...well...you know what I mean. It's sort of like giving your heart away to have it handled with care and caution, but instead, it gets stepped on, flattened on the ground, squashed, mutilated, ripped apart—"

"Okay. I think she got the point," Becky intervened, seeing the crushed look on my face. "You're making it worse, Nicole," she scolded.

"Sorry. I didn't mean...I was thinking about the time when I was...I'm so sorry." Nicole apologized and placed her hand over mine.

"After you have a chance to talk, he'll come around," Kate mumbled with a mouth full of fruit salad.

"That's what I keep telling her, but Max doesn't answer her texts or phone calls. That's the problem," Becky explained, pouring a second round of wine in her glass and doing the same for Nicole.

"What did you say in the text?" Kate asked.

Taking a sip and holding lazily onto the wine glass, I stared at the space where the vase of roses was. My mind reverted for a bit as I recalled the red roses Max had tossed on the street. I was in shock and hadn't had the energy to pick them up. I wondered if I should go back out and do so, but I couldn't get my legs to move. They were probably gone by now anyway. Knowing Max, he would have gotten the expensive kind, like the last two times he had gotten them for me. Surely someone would have picked them up. Those flowers were not meant for me...anymore.

"Jenna," Kate called, bringing me back to our conversation.

"Ummm...I texted that we need to talk, and that it wasn't what he thought it looked like. I can't text everything I need to tell him."

"True."

Becky poured more wine into my glass. I hadn't realized I had emptied it...well...half of it anyway, but I knew I was buzzed. It was confirmed when I began feeling like I had been out in the sun way too long.

"I know you can't drink, but you're home, and we're here. Drown out your sorrows, hun. We'll take care of you."

Looking from my half-eaten plate to Becky's eyes, I gave her the most thankful smile I could give. "Thanks. After this drink, I won't be able to think or...feel." And that was fine with me. I didn't want to feel...anything.

"Dang, Jenna. I've seen you turn red before, but you look like a lobster," Nicole snorted. "I see why Max was so worried about you. I'm worried for you right now. Are you okay?"

"Don't worry," I sighed, feeling my heart thumping faster. Not only that, my head started to throb, my body was burning, and every movement seemed slowed. Pausing for a second, trying to process my thoughts, I changed the subject. "Soooo...Kate. Are you...still...breastfeeding?"

Kate held an amused smile. "Someone is buzzed," she giggled, touching my cheeks. Her hand felt so cool to touch. Enjoying the sensation, I closed my eyes and opened them when she spoke again. "I'm weaning her off so I still can't drink, but once I'm done…well, no need to ask no further, girl friend." She accentuated the word girl friend with a funny accent.

With the palm of my hand on my cheek and my elbow on the table to support my head, I shifted my eyes to Nicole. The whole dinner conversation was about me, and I didn't want it to be about me anymore. Plus, I was certain my friends had things to share. "How…about…you, Nicole?" I wasn't sure what I had asked. Every word in my ears seemed like an echo and slowed.

Her whole face was beaming while her body shuddered slightly. She looked like she was about to explode. "I can't hide it any longer." She stood up, pulled something out of her pocket, and sat back down. Doing something with her left hand underneath the table, she smiled mischievously.

"Hurry up," Kate shook her hands.

I yawned and put my head down on the comfort of my crossed arms on the table.

"Be patient. I hope this is the last one I'll ever have," Nicole said excitedly. "I dare you not to get excited."

"Ahhh!" I heard the screams from all three of my friends. Popping my head up, I saw Nicole's hand up in the air and something very shiny on her finger. "Nicole?" I stood up and pulled her finger closer to me. It took a great amount of effort to peel my eyes open. From what I could tell, it was bigger than a karat…a round, gorgeous ring. "You're en…raged?" I shook my head. "En..gaged?"

Nicole giggled. "Yes…I'm engaged."

I   embraced   her   with   all   of   me. "I…sooo…hapeee…for…me…you," I slurred, running my hand down my face, trying to focus.

"When did this happen? Didn't you guys break up?" Becky asked, looking confused.

"Yeah…well…we did a lot of talking the past week. We spilled our guts and got everything out in the open. At the end, he said he couldn't live without me. We got back together…which I didn't tell you about. And then he proposed last night."

"Details…we want details," Kate blurted.

"It's coming…hold on, impatient one," Nicole giggled. "I need to ask you guys a question." Draping her hand over my shoulder, she looked at each of us with a heartfelt smile while water pooled in her eyes. "When I need a helping hand, you're always there for me. When I'm down and I need someone to lift me up, you're always there for me. I'm so blessed to have you in my life. My life wouldn't be fulfilling and the same without all of you. Will you all be my bridesmaids?"

Next thing I knew, I heard sniffles from all three of my friends and lots of arms wrapped around Nicole and I. Pure joy filled my heart and soul. Though I was hot as hell from the alcohol, I welcomed this special warmth. How I loved my friends.

M. Clarke

Chapter 22

Sunday was the slowest day of my life. Whatever I was doing, my eyes were glued to my phone in hopes that Max would call or text back, but he didn't. Luke called me several times, but I ignored him. A part of me blamed him for what had happened, but I didn't want to think of him, so I brushed the thought of him out of my mind. But every time I thought about that awful, unwanted kiss and the "what if's", I saw Max's expression and it killed me.

Becky left a note, letting me know she would be back before dinner. She had gone out to run some errands since she would be going to San Francisco for a literature convention. Having alone time, I sat on the sofa with the cell phone on my lap, just staring. That felt pathetic. I looked pathetic. Being that tomorrow was Monday and I needed to be at work, I had to snap out of it. Needing to hear a comforting voice besides my friends, I called my mom on her cell phone.

"Jenna?"

"Hi, Mom." I tried to sound cheerful, but instead my lips quivered. I had to hold it together or I'd start sobbing on the phone. Mom would worry, then I would have to talk about my love life, which I wasn't comfortable doing.

"How are you, sweetie? It's good to hear your voice."

Pausing, I took a deep breath. "It's good to hear your voice too." I've been better, I wanted to tell her, but that would sound suspicious, so I lied. "I'm great, just busy with my new job. How's Dad and…anything new?"

"Just the same old thing. Will you have a chance to visit?"

"Christmas for sure, Mom. I'll be there."

"Fantastic. I'll tell Dad. I can't wait."

"Me, too." I paused for a second, pondering if I should ask her this question, but I needed to know. "Hey, Mom?" My voice sounded like I was a child again.

"What is it, hun? Is everything okay?"

"Everything is fine...I was just wondering. Did you love Dad when you first met him? I mean...how did you know he was the one?"

"I can't explain it. I just knew. I knew that I couldn't live without him. So when that time comes, make sure to pick the one you can't live without. The one that makes you levitate off the floor and never lets you touch the ground. The one that loves you so much, he'll put you first, above anything else. The one that will love you on the sunny days, but he'll love you most of all through the heavy, thunderous storms. Let him pamper you, shelter you, and romance you till he's given his all. And in return, love hard and give back everything you've got. You deserve all the happiness, Jenna. Don't settle for anything less."

"Okay." I nodded, though she couldn't see me. As a tear escaped down my cheek, I quickly wiped it away. I thought about how her words were enduring and took them to heart, glad that I'd asked her. It made me re-evaluate the men in my life.

"Oh...before I forget, I want to let you know that Dad and I will be on a cruise for the first two weeks of December. We're doing the fourteen day European cruise."

"That's great. That's like in three weeks. It sounds fun," I said cheerfully.

"I hope we don't get seasick."

"You'll be fine, Mom. Have a great time. I'll talk to you again before the trip. Well...I better go. I'll call you soon."

"Okay sweetie. I'll talk to you soon."

"And Mom...thank you," I said sincerely, needing to hear all her words of comfort, though she had no idea what was going on.

"Anytime. That's what mothers are for."

After the phone conversation, I felt somewhat better, so I did my laundry, cleaned the house, and took care of bills. Somehow I had to find strength, because one way or another, I had to go to work, and I would run into Max, unless he found a way to avoid me.

♥♥

Dragging myself out of bed, I didn't know how I got to work. Everything about the place seemed too big and too cold. Trying to act like there was nothing wrong, I smiled as often as I could. This only confirmed that I had been right all along...never get into relationships with people you work with, especially your boss's son.

I checked my emails—it seemed like every minute—but there were still no emails, texts, or phone calls from Max. Curiosity got the best of me, so I tiptoed down the hall to his office. It seemed very obsessive of me, but I needed to at least explain to him what had happened, because the thought of him hating me produced acid in my stomach. Even if he didn't want to work things out, I would be okay with it, as long as he knew the truth.

Seeing his secretary, I walked up to her. "Hi...umm...I was wondering if Mr. Knight was in his office?"

"Ms. Mefferd, he's not in today."

I knew I should stop asking questions, but I couldn't help it. I didn't know if I felt disappointed or relieved that I didn't have to face him. For some reason, the dagger in my heart cut in deeper. "Do you know if he'll be in today or tomorrow?"

"I'm not sure. He's usually in the office by now, but I know he has several meetings out of the office this morning. Would you like for me to leave a message for you?"

"No," I said quickly, then I thought, Why not? "I mean...sure. Can you please tell him I need to talk to him, and that it's urgent?"

"Sure." She started to scribble words on her pad.

"Thanks." I turned on my heel to walk away. My body felt heavy, and the clicking sound from my heels got louder as I headed back to my office.

♥♥

From my office window, I could see the thick, heavy clouds. Their bellies were so full that they were ready to burst. As more dark clouds gathered, it got darker and colder. Then lightning flashed deadly, yet beautifully, across the sky, followed by a loud boom of angry thunder that shook the window. Rain pounded on the ground, washing away the dirt, washing away the smog. I wished it could wash away my pain, but of course I knew it was impossible.

After work, I went straight home. Becky had left for San Francisco that morning, so I was home alone. Luke had called me every day—sure...*now* he called me everyday—but I never picked up. And as for Max...well...he never replied at all. I chuckled out loud at the irony of this. The three of us were somehow connected and doing similar things. I was avoiding Luke, and Max was avoiding me. Luke wanted to get in touch with me, and I wanted to do the same with Max.

After eating last night's leftovers, I took a shower and went to bed early. I didn't know if the thoughts of Max were wearing me down or if I was coming down with something, but my body began to feel heavy and cold...very cold.

The next day, I went to work, looking and acting like a zombie. After some persuasion from Lisa, begging me to go home, I did. I had caught some kind of bug, and it was terrible. Without any dinner, I snuggled into the comfort of my bed as I thought of Max and went to sleep.

Shivering...sweating...my whole body burned. Kicking off my blankets, I reached for them when I suddenly got cold again. I wished my body would make up its mind, but it didn't. Tossing and turning, I had a restless, uncomfortable night.

When I woke up, I didn't feel any better, so I called in sick. Though I wasn't hungry, I knew I needed something to eat, since I hadn't eaten anything the previous night. Wanting to head to the kitchen, my feet dragged across the floor like they weighed a ton. After drinking a glass of water, I tried eating something, even a slice of bread, but I couldn't take a bite of anything.

Looking into the medicine cabinet, I found some Advil, so I took it. Though I knew I should feel better, I didn't. I felt myself burning up again, and it wasn't from alcohol this time. All I wanted to do was sleep and close my eyes, because right now, even Max wasn't on my mind...my burning throat and the feeling that a bus had hit me was. Forget Luke, forget Max...forget...I couldn't think or feel anything anymore, except for the need for sleep, and my heart, which hammered against my ribs so fast I thought it would burst right through.

♥♥

Something besides my head pounded as I drifted in and out of sleep. It sounded like it came from the kitchen, but I didn't care. Nor did I have the energy or strength to get up and see where the sound had come from; either that, or I was clearly delusional from my current condition.

Feeling something cool touching me, I welcomed whatever was on my cheek. I let out a soft moan and shifted my head from side to side.

"Jenna." I heard a male voice calling my name. "Are you okay? Shit...she's really hot."

This must be a dream. I missed Max so much I was dreaming about him, but I didn't mind. Hearing his voice somehow soothed the ache in my body. At least it gave me a temporary escape.

The cold hands left my face. "Nooo," I moaned. Max was fading...come back.

"Should we call the ambulance?" another voice said. I didn't want to hear him. Who was he?

"She'll be fine. I had the same thing. I'll take care of her. Thank you for letting me in," Max replied.

Max wanted to take care of me. This was too good to be true; it was just a dream, but I would take it. Then the voices faded in and out.

"I'm not suppose to be doing this, but since her mail box was full...she didn't pick up the phone, and since she works for you and she hasn't returned your phone calls, it was something to be alarmed about. I'm glad I could help. She does look really sick," the other voice said.

"Here's my business card," Max said.

"Wow! Are you *the* Mr. Knight from Knight Magazine?"

"Yes, but my father is the founder," he said flatly.

"Why didn't you tell me in the first place? Well, I'd better go now. I'm sure she's in good hands."

Then I heard the sound of retreating footsteps and cold hands on my face again. And my dream ended.

Chapter 23

Blinking my eyes open to the sun gave me the warmth that I needed to let me know I was going to be okay. Though there was a little lingering ache in my body, it was definitely much better. But one thing was for sure...I had lost several pounds. As I lay there trying to recall the dream I'd had about Max and some stranger, I couldn't. It was gone, and the knot in my heart that was temporarily pushed aside came back fast and heavy.

Suddenly it dawned on me that I had no idea what day or time it was. I racked my brain trying to figure out how long I had been passed out. My cell phone would tell me the information I needed. I only had to reach over to my nightstand, but I needed to get up and use the restroom. Getting out of bed wasn't as bad as I thought it would have been, but my legs were shaky, and my muscles were weak all over.

I had only taken a few steps when I heard a loud, female, screeching scream, and I immediately knew Becky was home. Wondering what that was all about, I opened the door and ran out of my room. Becky was standing by the front door. She looked shocked, like she had seen a ghost. I followed her line of vision and.... Oh my God! Max was standing there, holding up both of his hands, seemingly gesturing he was not a thief.

Max wearing jeans and a black sweater made me think it was the weekend, but I knew Becky was returning on Thursday, so it had to be Thursday. What was Max doing there? I couldn't recall any of it. I wondered when and how he had gotten in. Even in casual clothing he still looked hot…so good, it made my heart skip a beat. Looking a little bit younger and a little bit less serious, he looked like he hadn't slept in days, nor shaved. They both stood there looking astonished until I broke their stare.

I cleared my throat. "Max…what are you doing here?" My voice was hoarse, but I said it as gently as I could. The hurt and anger in his eyes was still there. I wasn't sure if he wanted to talk to me. God…I needed to talk to him, and fast. Seeing him like this was making me ache even worse.

Max's gaze lowered to my T-shirt. I was wearing his white T-shirt and only a panty underneath, but I knew he could see my nipples protruding out, so I crossed my arms. Since he didn't ask for it back, I'd kept it. I didn't know why, but needing to feel things would work out, I'd worn it to bed. I only hoped he didn't think it belonged to Luke.

Since he was still staring and didn't answer, Becky held a giant smile, walked toward him, and extended her hand. "Hello, Max. I'm so sorry about that. I'm Jenna's roommate. I thought you were…gosh, I'm so sorry."

He snapped out of whatever was on his mind, shook her hand, and then let go. "Becky, it's nice to meet you. It's okay. I would've screamed too if I saw a stranger in my apartment…but not like a woman, of course." His tone was sweet and charming as usual.

Becky let out a giggle, and things got awkward after that. Max wouldn't look at me. He didn't even answer my question.

"Well…." His eyes went straight to the front door. "Now that you're here and she's in good hands, I'll be on my way home. It looks like you just got back from somewhere…a business trip, perhaps?"

"Yes," Becky replied, placing her bag down.

"You're not leaving again, are you?"

"No, not for another month."

Max nodded. "I didn't pick the lock, if you're wondering. Your landlord let me in. Jenna had called in sick for two days and her assistant, Lisa, needed to ask her an important question, and she never returned the phone call. I…we were worried. Several of us that got back from the New York trip called in sick too, including myself. I guess we caught the same nasty bug."

I had been knocked out for two days? Max had been sick too, but he was here to take care of me?

Max continued. "Knowing she didn't have her family nearby, it's our policy to take care of our employees...just in case...you know what I mean. Anyway, I should go."

"Thanks for taking care of her." Becky looked grateful and awed.

Max nodded with a small grin. "I've left a bottle of antibiotics the doctor left for her. Oh...I had my doctor friend come check on her. I hope that was okay?"

Becky's eyes grew wide and she nodded with admiration. "Sure...of course. Thank you."

"I had to crush the pills so she could sip it, but I think she's okay to swallow pills now. Please make sure she finishes the remaining three. Since the dosage is high, she needs to make sure she takes it on a full stomach."

Why was he taking to Becky as if I wasn't there? Did he hate me that much? He'd crushed my pills? Now this was too much. I hated myself for hurting him. Anxiety was taking over my body as I fidgeted. I needed to explain to him right now.

Max still hadn't looked my way after he turned from me. After Becky thanked him again, he headed straight for the door. I froze...I completely froze. My heart pounded in my chest and burned from the possible rejection. He said I was stubborn...he was worse than me. Shaking on my legs that were too weak to move, Becky looked at me with a "what the hell are you still standing there for" look. She was right.

"Max," I breathed his name, but it came out too soft, and maybe it hurt too much to say it; I didn't know which one it was. But I was sure he heard my stomping steps, which was the reason he turned around. Just as I almost reached him, my weak legs gave out. I almost stumbled onto the floor, but Max caught my fall with one arm, as if holding me with two arms would be terrible.

"Why are you running in your condition?" he scolded.

I didn't answer. My body in his arms, tightly against the side of his chest, overwhelmed me and made that tingling feeling come alive again. Staring at his chest, I couldn't look up, especially when his hand wrung my T-shirt tightly. Either he was mad or he was fighting something. I couldn't tell, but I wished I knew. "Max...please. I need to talk to you. It's not what you think."

My eyes became watery. No, I won't cry in front of him. It will make me look pathetic. This wasn't working. When he didn't answer me, I slowly craned my neck upward, passing his sexy Adam's apple and his stubble along his jaws that I wanted to touch so badly.

His eyes gazed on mine without even blinking.

"Please...I tried to call and text, but you wouldn't answer." That sounded like I was begging, but at this point I didn't care. He was going to leave with that look in his eyes, and I couldn't handle it.

"I know," he whispered. Releasing a deep sigh, his eyes gazed lower.

Was that all he had to say to me after he had wanted to be with me? There was that dagger in my heart again, twisting. One tear found its way down my cheek.

He closed his eyes as soon as he spotted it and inhaled a deep breath.

"You can hate me all you want, but let me explain. At least give me that." My lips quivered.

He flashed his eyes open as if my words surprised him. With his free hand, he wiped my tears. "Don't cry. You know I can't stand to see you cry."

Don't let me, and do something about it, I wanted to yell at him.

"Not here. Not now. I don't want to talk to you here with your roommate, and I don't want to talk to you in a restaurant. I'll text you my address. I'll let you know what time. Don't go to work tomorrow...I've already called in sick for you. You should be a lot better by Sunday. We'll talk then."

I nodded as he shifted me to steady my stand. "You okay to stand?" His eyes went straight to my breasts.

If I had covered them with my arms at that minute, he would know I knew he was looking...awkward...but I couldn't help the thought of his hands on them. Trying to make this as smooth as possible, I ran my hand through my hair and crossed my arms. He shuddered slightly, and I didn't know what to think of that.

Max blinked. "I better go. Don't forget to take your medicine, and eat something before you do, or your stomach will let you know you forgot."

I reached over and opened the door. "Max...thank you for being here. I'll pay for the doctor's bill and the medicine, and whatever that—"

He didn't let me finish. "See you on Sunday," he said wearily, then walked out the door.

Trying not to make it obvious, though it may have seem a bit stalkish, I stuck out my head just enough to see him walk down the hallway and enter the elevator.

M. Clarke

Chapter 24

Sunday couldn't come fast enough. The past night had been another rough night's sleep compared to the other rough nights' sleep the days before. Max had been there on Thursday, so I had to wait three days before I got to tell him my side of the story. I was feeling a whole lot better, and I had to thank Max for that.

My mind was blown away by the fact that he cared enough to come to my rescue. Though he had mentioned that it was his company policy, I wasn't too stupid to realize that he was worried about me, and this gave me hope that things could work out. I hadn't known Lisa was trying to reach me, but then again, I didn't recall the phone ringing, and my cell phone was on silent mode…it had also ran out of battery power.

Becky had a lunch date. She told me we would exchange stories that night, and she would give me more details about the possible new man in her life. I couldn't wait to hear all about him. As I stared for God knows how long, I glanced at my closet full of clothes and saw nothing worth wearing. How was that possible? Becky and I had gone shopping recently. Needing to get to Max's house, I decided to wear a pair of jeans and a red button-up sweater.

After slipping on my coat and a pair of boots, I was on my way. Max didn't live far from work. I had expected to be looking for a house, but instead I found myself standing in front of a tall building. He lived in a pent house. Nervously, I headed up the elevator as my finger found its way to my mouth. I didn't realize how hard I was biting until I pulled it out from the pain. It was a very bad habit I needed to break.

Standing in front of Max's door, I inhaled deeply and rang the white circular button on my left. After a long few seconds, the door cracked open and anxiety flooded through me. Exhaling and inhaling quick breaths, I wanted to pass out. Most of the anxiety went away when I saw that gorgeous smile on his face. At least it was genuine this time, like he was happy to see me.

"Hi, Jenna. You look…." He paused. "You look better. Come in."

Max was wearing cotton shorts and a plain white T-shirt, just like the one I'd borrowed… kept…and he was barefoot. He still hadn't shaved, which made him look even sexier. I had to find a way to stop staring. Trying not to glance around was almost impossible. After Max took my coat, I took in the breathtaking view from his window, which took up the entire back wall.

The city lights dazzled against the black sky. A multitude of colors shined like Christmas lights, holding their vibrant hues. As my boots clicked away on the dark wood floor, I followed him to the living room. The furnishings were simple but elegant, and I approved of his taste. His place was big, spacious, open, and wide. You could even see the kitchen from the living room.

"Sit anywhere you like," he said.

Already standing next to the sofa, I just plopped myself down to the nice, expensive, leather spot.

"Would you like anything to drink?" he asked, pouring himself some liquor into a wine glass. "Some water or juice perhaps?"

He had only given me two options since he already knew my lack of alcohol tolerance. "No, thank you," I replied. I didn't want to be there longer than I needed to be. The longer I stayed, the stronger the likelihood of me not wanting to leave.

"So…." He cleared his throat after taking a sip of his drink. "What did you need to talk to me about? You made it clear before that we shouldn't date, and you made it clear by being with him that night. From the way I've been behaving, I have to say you were right. We shouldn't be dating."

His words pierced through my heart with a sharp sting. Looking down, I nodded. I needed to be brave. This was more difficult than I had thought it would be. It would have been easier to express myself when it had happened, but to say all that I felt a week later, not to mention being really sick, and to hear him say we shouldn't be dating, was extremely difficult. Then I knew I had lost my chance.

Placing my purse down next to me, I rubbed the palms of my hands on my jeans and focused on my hands. It was easier to talk to my hands than to look into his eyes. "I needed to tell you...that night... what you saw wasn't what you thought you saw." I paused. "He...I called him so that I could end things with him. We went out to dinner so I could tell him, then he brought me back home. I told him goodbye and that's...that's when he kissed me. I was completely shocked, and was not expecting that at all. I tried to push him away, but he was too strong."

Max's body tensed and his hands balled up tightly. "Did he hurt you?"

"No...yes...I mean...he hurt me in the sense that I didn't give him my permission, and he wouldn't let go. I didn't have an option. He was holding on so...tight. I was trying so hard to push him away...but...."

Max's shoulders relaxed, and something had changed in the way he looked at me. I wasn't sure if it was for the better or worse. Standing up, he headed for the window. "If what you are telling me is true, then I was the fool not to let you explain it to me. But you have to understand...I'd wanted to take you out since the first time I saw you at the restaurant. I remember seeing you there with Becky. After all the no's and the reasons why we couldn't go out, you'd finally said yes, and made me the happiest man in the universe.

"I was suppose to be in New York that weekend, but now I wished I hadn't cancelled just to surprise you. I didn't want to wait another week to see you, so I rescheduled for this week...which I rescheduled again because I found out you were sick. And when you didn't call Lisa back, she let me know. I was very worried. I didn't mean to step over the line, but I just needed to know you were okay, especially more so when you weren't answering your phone. I didn't want to leave you a text message. I needed to see for myself.

"Going back to that night, the only thing I saw was…that…Puke…." He had the most disgusted look on his face. I wanted to laugh so hard, but I didn't want to correct him. Knowing he knew Luke's name and called him "Puke" was hilarious and cute. Max continued. "…Kissing you like there was no tomorrow, and the fact that I told you I was going to be out of town…." He stopped pacing and surprisingly sat on the floor in front of me. Taking my hand, he gently caressed the back of it, seemingly apologizing through his gesture. "But…I'm so sorry. I didn't let you explain, and I don't mean to go all possessive on you like that…it's just that…I've never felt like this with anyone before."

When Max's hand cupped my left cheek, I let out a soft sigh and shuddered, and I tried so hard not to lean into his hand. "I was really hurt," Max continued, placing his hand back to mine. "We haven't even gone out, and how you could make me feel this way…I don't understand. You have this hold on me that's exciting and terrifying at the same time. But if I held onto my fears, then I would never have taken the leap, but I did. I wanted to dive right into your heart and permanently stay there. I fell for you the first time I looked into your eyes. That's all it took. Then I knew I'd found the one I've been waiting for all my life."

I wanted to say that I felt the same, but the words wouldn't come out. My lips were sealed shut as I listened, because for the last eight days I'd felt like I was in hell because of him, and like he said, we hadn't even dated. Was this wrong? I only went there to explain so he wouldn't hate me…that's it. But hearing his words confused me. After that night, I was thinking of trying to find another job.

When my free hand went straight to my mouth, Max pulled it away. "Don't do that, Jenna. You have no idea what that does to me." Then Max pushed his way between my legs, reaching closer…oh please don't! His hands cupped my face. "I'm sorry for being…a jerk. Let's start over again. Hello…I'm Max, and I really want to get to know you and take you out." His brows twitched playfully, looking so adorable.

My eyes grew wide, trying to hide my smile, but it curled up enough for Max to see it. I hadn't expected that at all. He already "had me at hello," but I had to talk some sense for the both of us. We weren't thinking clearly about all of this at all. "Max…after what we've both been through, I think we…ummm…." He felt what I was going to say, so he placed his hand straight down with that funny look in his eyes. "Like you said before, we work together, and if things don't work out, then…it would be really difficult…and I think...like you had indicated, it wouldn't be good for—"

"It's too late, Jenna," he said softly, placing his hands on my arms. "I only said that not knowing what you would be saying to me. I know you feel something. I can see it in your eyes…the way you respond when I'm close to you. And because I know this, there is nothing that I wouldn't do to convince you now. I'm not letting you slip through my fingers again."

Somehow I was standing. How did he get me to stand without me even knowing? Darn his eyes, that made me get lost in them. "Look what we've been through, and we haven't even gone out," I said.

"I don't know, Jenna. I've only told you what I've been through." His eyes widened and glowed, and those lips of his curled up wickedly. "Tell me…did you feel the same way as me when I didn't text or call back? Did you miss me as much as I missed you?"

"I…I…." He was standing so close. I couldn't speak. I couldn't breathe. This was not how I had played it out in my mind. He wasn't suppose to ask me about these feelings.

His stance over me, demanding an answer, was hot and frightening at the same time. "Jenna…tell me? Did you miss me?"

His tone was so commanding that it made me twitch. And since I knew he wouldn't back down until I told him the answer, I lied.

"No!" I said sternly into his face, and ran to the front door. The word stung me more than it might have him, and I felt my eyes pool with tears. I hated that I had so many emotions with him. No, I take it back…I liked it. I liked all the emotions I felt with him, that I never felt before with anyone else. The emotions that made me come alive, the emotions that made me want to be naked in bed with him…to touch him…to feel him inside me…oh…I needed to stop thinking.

"You're lying," Max said from behind me. He had almost reached me. "You're just afraid I would give you something great. You're afraid to fall in love with me."

"I'm not afraid to love you," I snapped, and I couldn't believe the words came out, or what I was about to say. "I'm…I'm more afraid of losing you."

Max pulled me in so tightly that I could feel his hard muscles against me. His piercing eyes looked me squarely in my eyes with so much conviction it was terrifying. "You haven't really given us a chance to even know what losing means. You think you're the only one afraid here? Does life just revolve around Jenna Mefferd? My heart isn't made out of stone. I feel pain, I feel anger, and I feel every emotion that you feel. You don't think I'm afraid of losing you? Yes, someone like me, who's got it all, is afraid of losing what I want the most. I've wanted you since the day you captured my heart. It was the first day you looked at me with the same look I'm giving you right now, the look of want and need and searching for something great. Yes…you are my great. Can you see what I want you to see in my eyes? My body aches when you're not around. I see the image of you in my mind, and I see so much in our future, but we can't get there if you're too afraid. I'm fighting for you. I'm fighting for us. So what are you waiting for?"

From his beautiful words, from his body touching mine, I was panting like a wild animal, and the erotic heat blistered through me so that I had to look away to cool down. I wanted him. I wanted us. All my life I'd played it safe, no risk and no adventures. Changing jobs was the first step to something better, and having Max in my life could be something great. I'd rather know what having something great was, than not knowing what it was at all.

At that moment, I realized I hadn't lived to my full potential. Life was about taking good risks, to learn and grow from them. What good was it if I was too afraid to try? I would never know the meaning of true love or happiness. If I got hurt in the process...so be it. There was no self-control at this point. As I blinked, my eyes found his again and gave him the permission he needed. "I don't want to wait anymore, Max," I said softly.

M. Clarke

Chapter 25

There were no words after that. My back contacted the wall when Max claimed me with his lips, those lips that I'd been wanting to taste for so long. And he did not disappoint as the urge between my legs awakened. Feeling his tongue pressed deeply, wanting me, took me to another level. My tingling hands shot up to his hair and gripped it tightly, letting him know I wanted more than just a kiss. He let me know too, as his body, already pressed against mine, got harder.

Feeling his hardness drove me wild as his hand slid down my back and cupped my behind with a firm grip that made me suck in air. "Mine," he said with conviction as he continued to kiss me. "You taste so sweet. I can't get enough."

His possessive words had me spinning out of control. My hands on his hair slid down his rough manly stubbles, down his Adam's apple, over the curve of his firm chest, and stopped by his waistband. Hearing Max groan, he pulled back to breathe and took both of my hands and pinned them against the wall. With a naughty grin, taking me in with his eyes, he reached in and tenderly kissed my neck, slowing things down.

Making his way downward, he released my arm and placed his hands on my waist. When his tongue played with the base of my breast, I yelped while I arched my back, and the ache between my legs intensified a hundred fold.

"Do you want more, Jenna?" he teased. "Tell me you want more or I'll stop."

His hot breath on my skin just added to what I was feeling. "More," I cried out with my eyes closed as his tongue slipped inside my sweater. With a slight twist from his head, I felt it on the side of my breast. When he dug in deeper, his stubbles brushed my nipple, and I quivered from the pain and how they made me feel….so good. I thought my knees would buckle.

When I felt a sudden coolness, I stiffened. Max was using his teeth to unbutton my sweater, already half way down. "My lady in red…you…are… beautiful," he said, asking my permission to continue with his eyes.

I locked my eyes on him and unbuttoned the remaining three buttons. Helping me slip out of my sweater, he held me tenderly as he unhooked my bra. Taking in my breasts with his eyes, he pulled off his T-shirt and crushed my lips into his. My nipples, that had been yearning for his touch, perked up. With one of his hands caressing one of my breasts, his tongue was soothing the other. Flicking, nipping, and sucking, then sucking really hard, sent me over the edge. I could not control the burning, wanting sensation anymore.

Running my hands down the curve of his biceps, they found their way to his shorts again, and I accidently brushed his enlarged hardness. With a deep groan, he sucked my nipples harder, then looked up at me, out of breath. "Don't do that, Jenna. You'll have me begging. I didn't plan this. We can stop. I wanted to take you out. You're not a one-night stand. You're more than that. I didn't mean to do this. I want something great with you. We don't have to—"

But I wanted to. "I know, Max," I said, panting and taking him in with a mad passionate kiss as my hand went straight down to his hardness. He shuddered and groaned loudly, and I was more than happy I could make this beautiful man become completely weak. "Just so you know," I said between kisses. "I don't do this, ever, not until I at least—"

"How many?" he asked, kissing me back. His hand gripped my legs and pulled me up. My legs were wrapped around his waist as he headed toward the stairs.

"Just one."

He smiled hugely. "Just one?" Burying my face into the space between his neck and shoulder as he climbed higher, he asked another. "When was the last time?"

Feeling too embarrassed to tell him I wasn't that experienced, I muttered into his shoulder. "Three years ago."

"Shit! It's been three years?" He sounded completely surprised.

I nodded.

"Then it's like I'm your first." He let out that sly grin. "Let me make you waiting for three years worth the wait. I'm going to brand every inch of your body with my hands, my lips, and tongue, so that your body will know only me. You'll be begging me to stop, because I'm going to give you pleasure like you've never known before."

That shot another tingle right to my core, sending fireworks to every nerve, every vein, every fiber of my being, and I wanted to rip his clothes off him.

Kicking the door with his feet, we were now standing in front of his bedroom. Not only was it spacious, and had a breathtaking view of the city, it was made for a king. He had the biggest bed I had ever seen. Wondering how many women he had brought there, I pushed that thought aside. For tonight, he was mine and mine alone. He wanted me as much as I wanted him, if not more, and that thought alone did all kinds of craziness to me.

Lowering me to the mattress, he pulled the satin blue cover away. Cupping my face, he kissed me softly, then headed toward my neck. "I'm going to make your first in three years the most memorable one," he whispered in my ear. "I'm going to make you come...all night. Don't worry about going to work tomorrow...I'm going to tell them you have a meeting with me."

It took me a second to register what he had said. He had already lowered me down to the bed, taking in my breast. Trying to keep it together was hard enough. If I had been in the right state of mind, I would have said no, but I wanted him more than work.

Max unzipped my boots, then my pants, and managed to take both off with one single slide, except my G-string panty. I blushed. "I like…red."

He arched his brows, taking of his shorts. Knowing what he was doing made me nervous…a whole lot nervous. After all had been stripped down…there it was, long, hard, and beautiful as him, and he had no problem showing it. Smiling, he hovered over me, using his elbow to anchor his weight, and laced his hand through my hair. "So beautiful. Are you ready?"

Withering underneath him, I nodded. Feeling the anticipation of him being inside me, the ache between my legs fired up. He was teasing me, taking his time, kissing where his lips could touch down south. When his lips found my panties, he used his tongue to move them aside and teased my clitoris with his tongue. "Max," I exploded. I had died and had gone to sex heaven. The ache became stronger…stronger as he licked inside. Squirming from ecstasy, I pulled my legs up. I couldn't take it any more.

He was enjoying me totally coming undone, and I loved the things he was doing to me as he took his time, giving me pleasure I never knew could be possible. I had imagined and dreamt how it could be with him, but never in my wildest dreams did I envision this. "Do you want me?" Max asked, teasing me with his erection on the tip of my vagina.

"Oh, God…yes," I panted.

"We don't have to. We can just taste each other," he said, placing his hand where his penis was. "You're so wet, baby."

"Max, I want you inside me," I said quickly, breathlessly. My fingernails dug into his shoulders, pulling him closer. "I've dreamt about this."

Max's eyes sparkled, reacting to my words. "I couldn't stop now…but you didn't dream nearly as much as I dreamt about you." He reached inside a nightstand drawer and pulled out a condom. As I watched him do it with ease and precision, I wondered again how many girls had been there. I had to stop thinking about that.

Max started to insert. "So tight, babe." Gripping my legs, he pulled them up, and my legs spread even more. With several penetrations, he punctured through, and I moaned with pleasure and pain. "Are you okay?" he asked sweetly.

"Yes," I shivered, taking him in, but I didn't get a chance to say anything after that. Max was devouring me with his lips as his hips moved in and out slowly, then gradually moving faster. His hand moved down to the curve of my breast, and with a pinch from his fingers, I moaned louder. I never knew I could moan that loud.

"You like that, babe? Tell me what you want. I'm all yours."

I couldn't. Not being that experienced, I didn't know what to ask for. "Max," I cried. His eyes never left mine as he pumped faster...faster. Closing my eyes from this overdrive, my head was spinning, filling with pleasurable sensations that drove me to the edge. My arms fell on the mattress and my fingers clawed into the sheets. Gripping and pulling onto it, my back arched. "Max," I cried again out loud as I felt myself...erupting...exploding...climaxing...then there it was. I couldn't take it anymore. It was too much of fulfillment, too much of him, needing him to stop, but wanting more. And hallelujah rang in my head. God, I didn't know it could be this good.

"Jenna," Max cried out. Loud groaning, pleasurable sounds escaped his mouth as he threw his head back. Then his eyes came back to mine with intensity and need. Embracing me in his arms, he gave me more of him. I didn't know how long it lasted, but I'm pretty sure I reached another level of nirvana. Max brought his eyes to mine as he slowed things down. Sweat trickled down his forehead and he looked so delicious and sexy that I couldn't help myself, and ran my hand down his face.

"You feel so amazing, Jenna. I want to see your beautiful face when I come." His tone was deep and blazing hot.

Before I could reply, he bit his bottom lip and thrust harder and faster than before. I had utterly lost control of my thoughts, muscles, and myself. Trying to keep my eyes on him, my eyes fluttered as my back arched with intense pleasure, and I couldn't believe the sounds that escaped from my mouth. When Max pulled out, our eyes radiated with fulfillment and my sex continued to pulsate. I was too weak to move and I believed Max was too.

After pulling off the condom, he dropped it on the floor, plopped down next to my side, and snuggled me into him. Hot air puffed out of his mouth as his chest rose and fell rapidly with mine. "I didn't think it could be better, but it was. And it was all because of you," he managed to say with a hot, breathy whisper. Pulling me closer to his chest, he placed his right leg over mine and held me tenderly. "I'm glad we made up. No more misunderstandings…okay?"

"Okay." I nodded, still catching my breath. "That was…I never…umm…felt like that before," I muffled through his chest, feeling completely exhausted as I lay there, unable to move.

Max let out a chuckle, and my body moved with his. "My sweet, innocent Jenna. It's one of the things I like about you. You're different. You're not like the other women I've dated."

Hmmm…what did he mean by that? "Is that a good thing?"

Max's finger lifted my chin so my eyes matched his. "It's the innocence I saw in you that drew me to you, besides your sexy body and beautiful face." He winked. "I can tell you're beautiful on the inside and outside. You're a diamond in the rough. My once in a lifetime chance, and I'm not letting you go."

His words tugged at my heart. My eyes twinkled in the dim lighting, I was sure of it, just as bright as the lights below his window. Not only did he call me sexy and beautiful, but his words were sweet, and it sounded like he really meant them. Was this real? I couldn't believe someone like him would want someone like me.

Chapter 26

Still tucked in his arms, he kissed my forehead. "Do you have family here?"

"My parents live in San Francisco. My father is a dentist, semi retired. My mom never worked." I trembled from the cold.

"Are you cold?" Max didn't wait for me to answer. He reached over and pulled the sheet over us. It was silky soft against my body. I quivered and melted into it. "It feels so good," I gushed.

Max's eyes shone with amusement, and that playful look crossed his face. "I can give you something to make you feel better." His hand teased my nipples.

I jerked a little as my clitoris pulsated from his touch. I giggled and shyly looked away.

He continued with his questions. I wasn't sure if he really wanted to get to know me, or if the guilt of not taking me out before we ended up in bed was eating at him. "Do you have any brothers or sisters?"

"No. I'm an only child."

"Really? You don't act like an only child. I mean…I've dated an only child, and she wasn't anything like you." Max's tone went up a notch as he ran his thumb across my cheek. "So soft. I could touch you all day." He paused for a second, then continued with his questions. "What kind of food do you like to eat?"

"I'm not picky. I eat all sorts of food."

"That's perfect." He caressed my hair, making me sleepy.

Since he asked me tons of questions, I wanted to get to know him better too. "I know you have parents. I read an article about them before. You have a younger brother, but I don't know much about him."

"Ms. Mefferd, you did your homework. My brother is younger than me. He is somewhat irresponsible, but I guess I can't blame him. He was the younger one, and he was spoiled since he was born. I guess we both don't need to work, but I enjoy what I do, though I have been working a lot less lately. Soon enough, you'll meet my family."

Meet his family? So soon? "Max."

"Yes…." His finger trailed up my back.

"What time is it?"

"Why, you going somewhere?"

"I have work tomorrow, and so do you. I'm sure it's close to ten."

"You don't remember what I told you?"

"Yes, but—"

"No buts, Jenna. You're spending the night with me. I want you to stay…please." With that pouting look that could make your heart melt, I didn't have the strength to turn him down.

"Okay…but I need to work a little in the morning, and I'll call Lisa. I've been out so long, being sick and all."

"Sure. And Jenna?"

"Yes."

"I'm glad you said yes." He sounded sincere, and so happy.

"I can't say no to you when you pout like that." I poked him on his chest.

"That was the plan." He arched his brows.

"You…." I tickled him a little. "But seriously, what time is it? I need to text Becky that I'm not coming home. She'll worry about me."

"Babe, it's past midnight."

"What?" I got to Max's at eight. "We've being doing it…I mean…that long…I didn't…."

Max let out a full-blown chuckle, obviously finding this amusing. When he chuckled, his Adam's apple moved. Without thinking, my hand went straight for it. Max was still, seemingly enjoying my touch. Then I moved my fingers along his strong jawline, feeling every inch of it, trailing upward to his hairline, curving along his thick dark eyebrows, and down his perfect nose to his lips. I wasn't sure what I was doing, but it made him moan. When I felt his hardness against me, I sucked in air and unknowingly stuck my finger in my mouth, looking right at him.

Max moaned again. "Jenna…." My name rolled off his tongue in a smooth, deep, yet scolding tone. I never knew my name could sound so sexy. "Does your finger taste good? I bet it does. I told you not to do that." He pulled it out of my mouth. Without warning, he stuck it in his and started to suck.

I tried to pull it out, but his suction was stronger, and when that pleasurable feeling shot down between my legs, I wanted more. Letting go of my index finger, he shifted his mouth to mine, and his penis slowly rubbed against me. I was wet….and getting wetter with each stroke. I couldn't take it anymore. Having just climaxed I didn't know if it was possible to do it again. I guessed I'd find out.

"I told you the next time you did that it was going straight to my mouth," he said in between kisses. "Do you want more, Jenna, or have you had enough?"

How did he expect me to tell him to stop when his hand was playing on my breast and warmth spread where his penis was touching me? "More…Max," I panted, whispering in his ear. I had never asked my ex for more before, and in a way I was really shy about it, but Max's touch put me over the edge.

With his knee he spread my legs apart and hovered over me, placed a condom, and put his fingers between my legs. "You're so wet. I love how I make you wet, babe." With his body slightly pressed on mine he moved up and down, but not inside, while cupping my face. "You want this, babe?" he asked, drilling his eyes to mine with fire in them.

The ache between my legs was already erupting, throbbing, and I needed him to release it so badly. "Yes, Max...please," I begged.

With one thrust, Max was inside me, causing me to suck in a lump of air. Rolling to the side while inside me, he rode me faster and deeper, and I followed his rhythm with my hands on his hips. Having done it once took me out of my shyness, and the second time was even better. When his mouth covered my nipple, sucking as hard as he had with my finger, I exploded even more. Throwing my head back as my back curved, I pressed my breast into him even more.

"Are you exploding, Jenna?" Max asked, groaning.

"Yes," I whispered, gripping his hair so tightly, I was surprised he didn't tell me to stop. I got my answer...it was possible to climax again. Loud sounds escaped my mouth as I bit my bottom lip, and tears dampened the side of my face. Why was I crying? But they were blissful, fulfilling, can't take any more, tears.

"Louder, baby. No one can hear you. Scream for me. Cry for me," Max's breath was heavy as he pumped even faster...faster...never ending faster. I screamed louder, and I would have sworn the whole world heard me. He was that good.

"I'm coming, babe." Within several seconds, he dropped next to me, and hot puffs of air blew out of his mouth. I was doing the same thing as my body pulsated, making me weak all over. Without a doubt my need had been fulfilled, if not more.

After a short while, Max stood up. "Take a shower with me, then we can go to bed or not." He twitched his brows seductively. "I have extra tooth brushes and a bunch of toiletries under the sink."

"Okay," I said shyly, then wondered how many girls had spent the night. Oh...I had to stop thinking those thoughts. But I couldn't believe I was doing this. I didn't want to be those girls on his list. This was something I would never do, especially when I hardly knew him, but in a way I felt like I did.

Max broke my thoughts when he reached out his hand to me. When I was just about to take it, he scooped his arms around me and lifted me up into his hold. We were buck-naked together. That thought was thrilling, exciting, but my face flushed with warmth all of a sudden. Though he had seen all of me, standing there in the shower for full exposure was not my cup of tea.

"Don't be shy. I've seen everything. You're beautiful, Jenna. And I can't take my eyes off you."

I blushed even more. Max's words were so sweet, making me feel comfortable, sexy, alive, and at home.

M. Clarke

Chapter 27

Silk bathed my naked body, soothing, calming. Where was I? Perhaps I was dreaming. When I managed to peel my eyes open, I realized I was in Max's room in his extra large king size bed. Twisting my head, he was nowhere to be found. He must have gotten up. What day was it? Oh yeah...Monday. What time was it? I couldn't tell since the curtains were drawn, but it was still dark inside.

Sitting up, I reached for my cell phone as I blinked my sleepy eyes to clear. There were several texts, one from Lisa and from Becky. Instead of calling Lisa to let her know I would be staying home for one more day, I decided to text her, being afraid that she could hear my lie over the phone. Yup...I was that paranoid. Her return text read that she was out sick, and for me to rest up at home. This terrible flu must be going around.

Clicking off the text messages, I noted it was close to noon. Oh my God! He let me sleep in that late? But then again, we were at it all night. Those naughty thoughts not only shot tingles in my stomach, but hunger pangs as well. I hadn't eaten well the past week, and now that I was feeling better, my stomach was aching for food.

Wondering where Max was, I got up to find my clothes, but they were nowhere to be found. Finding only Max's white T-shirt, I slipped it on and headed for the double doors. Hearing Max's voice, I found him just outside the door talking on the phone. Upon opening one of them, Max turned around and stared at me with a sparkle in his beautiful eyes, and smiling like I'd never seen him smile before.

His gaze kept me standing still, making me turn hot in all the right places, making my lips curl to give him the warmest smile I could give him. "Sure," he said to the person on the other line. "Maybe next weekend. Yeah…I'm loving the view right in front of me too." Max winked at me, and knowing his view was me made me blush even more. "Listen," he continued. "I gotta go. I'll talk to you after I ask her, okay? Bye."

Ask her? Who is her? Then my heart tugged a little, and not in a good way.

"Good morning," he said, his eyes never leaving mine as he came for me and gave me a tender kiss on my forehead. It warmed my heart.

"Good morning." My voice sounded hoarse. "You let me sleep in so late."

His fingers were playing with mine, tingling and tickling at the same time. "You needed that sleep. And you also must be starving."

"I am," I smiled. "And I can't find my clothes."

"I want you in my T-shirt all day, or maybe naked. You can decide, but I'm not giving your clothes back until you're ready to go home. I prefer to keep you here forever." He held me tightly, slightly rocking me back and forth in his hold, then let go.

What could I say after that? I peered up. "I like your T-shirt. It's so soft on my skin."

"You can have it." He bit his bottom lip, seemingly wondering if I would take it.

"But I already stole one from you," I said shyly, and stuck my finger in my mouth. When I saw that funny look in his eyes, I gasped and pulled it out as fast as my reflexes allowed.

"No, no, no," he shook his head, grinning playfully. Then he paused, seemingly thinking. "You stole one?"

"I kept the one you gave me when we were in New York."

"Uh…I see…thus the T-shirt when I was in your apartment. But I already knew that."

"How?" My tone demanded an answer.

"I had a feeling, and I also looked at the tag…which there was none. It also has my initial on it, MK. I had it especially made that way." Max must have seen a questioning look in my eyes. Before I could ask, he spoke. "Don't worry, I'm not a pervert. I didn't look anywhere else, except…your beautiful face that looked like an angel when you were sleeping. And I did want to climb into bed with you, but I didn't think you would approve."

I smiled warmly, not knowing what to say as I stood there feeling grateful for his care.

"Let's go feed that stomach of yours before you eat your finger." Next thing I knew, my hand was in his as he led me down to the dining table.

Pulling out a chair, he gestured for me to sit down. Plates of bagels, bacon, muffins, and all sorts of fruits were in my line of vision. As Max poured me some juice, there was another glass filled with water in front of me. As parched as I was, I waited until Max sat down. Instead of sitting across the table, he sat beside me. "Hi," he said, grinning like a schoolboy. Then he placed a napkin over my lap and a plate in front of me.

I giggled. "Hello."

"What would you like to eat?" he asked.

"Everything." But I didn't mean it.

"Everything it is." He started to fill my plate with food, and no matter how many times I told him to stop he wouldn't listen. "You need to eat. You lost so much weight when you were sick."

"Okay," I said, and gulped half the water down my throat. Oh…that felt so good. Then I picked up the fork and went straight for the blueberries. "Did you sleep well last night?" I asked, trying not to be shy about this whole situation. This wasn't something I'd done before.

Max swallowed a bite of his bagel as he nodded. "How about you?" he grinned.

"Good, thank you. Your bed is so comfortable."

Max leaned over, creating that heat again. "You know you can sleep in it every night if you'd like. We can be sleeping buddies and breakfast buddies, too."

I smiled and looked away, not knowing how to answer his question or if I was meant to answer it, because I wasn't sure if he meant it or if he was just flirting. "What's wrong?" he asked, looking concerned.

He must have seen me stiffen. "I…it's just that…I've never slept with…I mean…we didn't even date…." I was turning red. I felt so hot that I wanted to take his shirt off.

"Jenna, it's okay." Max's hand rested over mine and idly rubbed my knuckles. "I know you're not the type of woman that has one night stands, or the type of woman that sleeps on first dates. I know you take your relationships seriously. I can tell by the way you act and by your words. So…don't worry. And I'm not so bad that I would take advantage of you like that."

I must have produced the biggest smile of my life. Max knew me…unlike Luke. And I believed that he wouldn't take advantage of me. Feeling less embarrassed, I happily took a bite of my bagel with cream cheese on it. Max was sweet enough to spread it on for me before I could reach over for the container.

"Do you have plans next Saturday?" Max asked, placing his glass down from taking a sip of his orange juice. "That was my brother on the phone. I would love for you to meet him."

"Umm…." My eyes flickered to think, and was happy that when Max said, "I'll ask her," he'd meant me. "I think I'm free."

"Good," he said excitedly. "I'll pick you up before we go to my parents' home."

"What did you say?"

He gave me a sideways glance. "My parents," he repeated slowly. Then he blinked his eyes, seeming to be thinking. "I'm sorry. Is it too soon?"

It was a little too soon for me, but seeing the sparkle leave his eyes, I couldn't say no. "No…I think I'll be okay. Just as long as they know I'm coming and they are fine with it."

"Of course they will. But I don't want to have to wait a week before I see you again. Let me check my schedule so I can take you out on a real date."

"Okay." My smile was big. "So…is this for a special occasion, or is your brother in town?"

"Just because," he said, and took a bite of his bagel.

"I was just wondering if I needed to wear something special, or how I should dress in front of your parents."

Max chuckled. "This is why I think you're so hot. You care. Jenna, you can wear jeans and a sweater if you like. My parents are humans, not gods. Don't worry too much. They will love you. But if you're asking me what you should wear…." Max arched his brows playfully.

"Never mind," I smiled giddily, blushing. Max had just told me I was hot. "Eat before your food gets cold."

Max leaned over, smacked a good kiss on my lips, and pulled my bottom lip with his teeth. And the glass of cold water wasn't cold enough to cool me down.

M. Clarke

Chapter 28

"You're meeting his parents?" Becky didn't let me answer. She had changed into her sweat outfit that we had bought together when we went shopping. Hers was purple and mine was black. "*The* Mr. and Mrs. Knight?" She accentuated the word "the". "Already? Really? Wow! He's really head over heels all over you, isn't he?"

Pondering her words, I carefully settled myself down on the sofa with a mug of hot green tea in my hands. "He made it sound like it was no big deal."

"No...you're trying to make it sound like it's no big deal." Becky sat next to me and took a sip of her hot tea.

"I don't know. He's moving too fast, maybe 'cause I gave him permission by sleeping with him." I groaned, burying my head in the palm of my hand, then looked up. "I've never done that before."

"I know." Becky nodded, taking another sip. "Nope...never since I've known you. So I was completely surprised when you texted me that you were spending the night. Anyway, it's nothing bad. You know my history...I've had a couple of those in our college days. Two consenting adults fulfilling their needs...I think it's perfectly fine. But I understand...cause...." She took another sip and let out a sigh. "I know you."

Taking the warmth from my mug, I sank in deeper as I thought of Max. "I'm okay with it 'cause he makes it okay for me. I mean...he says the sweetest things. He knows I'm not like that. At least he says he knows…I hope." I blew into the mug and took a sip.

"Just be careful, okay? I'm not saying that he's going to hurt you. But I've been with enough men to know that you don't take any girl to your parents' house unless you're serious about her."

"He said he wanted me to meet his brother. It's just that…I'm now officially dating my boss's son, which I was trying to avoid." The realization of that didn't hit me when I was in Max's penthouse. It had just hit me. And I would be officially meeting the couple I'd looked up to since I first wanted to be in the fashion industry. Though excited, a part of me was extremely uneasy about this whole situation.

"Who cares, Jenna? Don't worry too much. Just take it one day at a time. He actually may turn out to be something great. Anyway…it's nine. I need to get some work done, and you need to go to work tomorrow since you took Monday off."

"I know." And there, those words were spoken again…something great. I wanted him to be my something great.

Becky was already up and walking toward her bedroom door. "Oh…don't forget. We're going out to lunch this Sunday to celebrate with Nicole."

"I won't. Good night, Becky." I headed to my room.

"Good morning, Lisa, Rachel," I cheered, walking in. Then I turned to my right. "Good morning, Dan, Eric." After they greeted me with a smile, I went straight to my desk.

"You feeling better, Jenna?" Lisa asked. "You must have been really sick. It seemed like everyone who went to New York got the bug."

"Yes," I agreed, blushing, wondering if they could see right through me that yesterday I was out because of Max. Not liking the attention on me, I changed the subject. "Are you feeling better, too?"

"Yes…thank you. I had a twenty-four hour bug. I guess that's what you would call it."

After I told them about my trip to New York, we got right back to work. Things were crazy since I hadn't been there for several days. I thanked Lisa for taking care of what needed to get done while I was out. Though I knew I didn't need to, I made a mental note to get her something extra special for Christmas.

Typing a reply on my email, I jerked slightly when my phone started to make that buzzing, vibrating sound. Looking at my cell phone, my face turned warm and I wondered if they could tell.

What are you doing?

Haha...what do you think?

I hope you're naked.

No...lol!

Do you have any plans for lunch?

No, but I really need to work. You know...cause of yesterday.

Would you like me to repeat yesterday?

Hmmm...yes...maybe...no! We are at work.

I'm coming!

I didn't understand what he meant by that, but that kind of sounded hot. I didn't need to wait to see what he meant. After few minutes, sounds of footsteps increased. Max walked through the door.

"Mr. Knight," Lisa said quickly. "How may we help you?"

"Hello, Lisa, Rachel, Dan, Eric." He grinned nicely to them as he said their names. I loved how he was professional and friendly to his employees, unlike some bosses I'd worked with before. Then Max turned to me, trying to hold in a smile. "I'm actually here to see Jenna."

"Sure." Lisa sat back down and turned her head to the computer screen, but I could see her peering from the corner of her eyes.

I swallowed nervousness down my throat and tried to be professional. "Mr. Knight. Won't you please take a seat?"

Max settled into the chair and scooted himself forward...way forward, till his chair was right at my desk, sitting on the opposite side of me. I wondered what I had done wrong. When he gave me his biggest grin, my shoulders relaxed. "Lunch," he whispered.

I didn't say a word as I wondered if they had heard him. Not wanting to speak, I shook my head. Max stood up, pulled his cell phone out of his pocket, sat back down, and started texting. In a way I was glad his attention was not on me, hoping he would be called for a meeting or something... anything. I was starting to feel really embarrassed. Nobody knew I was dating Max. Then my phone vibrated. Wondering who it could be, I looked. Since Max was busy I didn't think there was any harm in it.

Come to lunch with me!

He was sitting in front of me, texting me. My lips perked up, trying hard not to laugh. I texted back.

I can't. I already told you

If you don't come with me, I'm going to carry you out of here. You decide.

He's asking me to decide when there really isn't a choice, since I don't want him to pick me up in front of everyone. Shoot! He wouldn't...would he? I peered up to see him nodding and the serious look in his eyes. Though I didn't know Max that well, from what I'd experienced in the short amount of time being with him, there was no stopping him whatsoever. When he wanted something, he would find a way to get it.

Where are we going?

I have lunch ready in my office.

Oh...why didn't you say so in the first place?

What would be the fun in that? And by the way, I'd rather have you for lunch. The dress frames your body nicely. Not to mention easy access.

I started blushing, giggling...really giggling, then realized I was in Max's world and not in reality. Turning to my left and right, their eyes were curious, most likely wondering why we were texting and not speaking, if they even knew we were doing that.

"Ms. Mefferd. I'll see you in five minutes." Max winked and stood up.

"See you in five, Mr. Knight," I said softly, trying my best not to look up to reveal my red face to my coworkers. After a few minutes, I inhaled a deep breath and stood up. "Are you going to lunch?" I asked, trying to pretend nothing happened.

"Do you want to come with us?" Lisa asked.

I had already headed for the door. "I believe it's a lunch meeting," I fibbed, sort of. Pulling the door toward me that was already ajar, I turned to Lisa again. "Thanks though. Have a good one."

"Okay," Lisa said in a funny tone. "Have a good one." That tone was even stranger...too friendly. They knew. He had made it obvious.

"Mr. Knight." I knocked even though the door was slightly ajar.

"Come in." Max was on the phone, gesturing with his hand for me to come in.

Walking in, I closed the door. Instead of heading to the chair in front of his desk, I went to the bookcase that took up one side of the wall. With a quick glance over my shoulder, I checked to see if Max would disapprove. Since he didn't, I tuned out his phone conversation and proceeded forward.

Running my hands over his picture frames, I spotted his parents first. Max looked more like his father with his mother's eyes, and Max's younger brother, Matthew, looked like his mother with his father's eyes. Regardless, they were both handsome. I didn't know how old his parents were, but I was sure they looked young for their age, especially his mom. She was blonde, which explained Matthew's lighter colored hair. But Max had his father's hair—full, thick, and dark.

Thumbing through the books that lined one side of the bookcase, I ran across more picture frames of him and his brother and with a group of friends. Happily, I didn't see any pictures of any women that may have been the loves of his life. But then again, they would have broken up, so why would he still have them up?

I gasped when I felt Max's chest on my back. His warmth spread blissfully down to my toes. "I missed you all day," he said, turning me to face him. His loving eyes met mine, cupped my face with his hands, and gave me a nice, juicy, tender kiss.

"I missed you, too," I said shyly, already heating up from his kiss.

"Let's go eat." He took my hand and led us to the table next to his desk that I had not seen coming in. Arranged on the table was a bowl of seafood salad, a plate of grilled salmon, and a plate of asparagus.

"Max. This is so nice. Thank you. Do you eat lunch like this all the time?"

"No. I'm usually eating lunch with a client or something I bring from home. It depends."

Knowing that he had done this for me, I felt grateful. I peered up to him again. "Thank you," I said as sweetly as I could.

"Are you hungry?" he asked, running his hand down my black silk blouse. "Your blouse feels almost as soft as your body, which I'm pretending to feel right now." His eyes were glistening, wanting, calling out for me. How could I be hungry when all I could think of was him inside me?

"I can eat, but I'm not starving...if that's what you're asking," I managed to say, feeling his thumb brushing against the side of my breast. Then a little higher...oh goodness...then purposely crossing over my front. The ache between my legs was throbbing. Knowing how good it felt to have him inside me, I wanted more...now. But we couldn't, we were at work. He had to stop, or I would have no control over what I would never do at work.

There was no point thinking about that now. Max had taken me in with his lips with mad, hungry, passionate kisses. His tongue touched every part of my mouth as if it were his hands caressing every inch of me. Pulling out, heavily breathing, his kisses trailed lower...lower...lower as his hand slid down with him.

I had no recollection of him unbuttoning my blouse, but it was undone for sure, and somehow my bra was unhooked. Moaning from his tongue bathing my breast, I squeezed his forearm tightly, and when he sucked hard on my nipple I quivered, utterly out of control.

"Max," I pulled away, dazed and confused. "We're at work." My breathing was so heavy, I didn't know if he'd heard what I said.

"The door is locked. Everyone is out to lunch. This room is sound proof, but we don't have to—"

I didn't let him finish. Grabbing a fistful of his hair with both hands, I tugged him closer and slammed my lips on his.

"Oh...Jenna." His voice muffled in my mouth, but there was an excitement in his tone. Needing more of him, I took charge this time and slipped my tongue into his mouth and sucked his tongue the way he sucked my breast. He responded by sliding his hand down my back, then stopped on my behind. His massaging it drove me wild.

Breaking out of the kiss, he sat on his chair and pulled me to him, my front to his. His hand easily slid up my legs since I had a skirt on, and when his finger found my front, I achingly shuddered. G-string panties sure came in handy. With each flicker, with each stroke to my clitoris, I moaned, wanting him inside me now.

"Max," I cried, pulling his tie, silently telling him what I needed.

"You ready for me?" he asked, standing up. "This isn't going to be slow and sweet. I'm going to fill your need." He whipped me around as my chest lightly mounted on his desk. With a zip, he pulled down and stood up. I don't know where he got it, but I heard the plastic tearing sound. Then unexpectedly, I felt his tongue on my vagina. "Max," I moaned loudly. That felt so...unbelievably good.

He moved my G-string to the side with one finger, then he was in. Holding both of his hands on my waist, he rocked, then faster...faster, so fast I thought my heart would leap out of my chest. Grabbing my hands on the edge of the table, he was taking me somewhere I'd never gone before. The ache between my legs was gone, and for sure I had reached beyond exploding. Ecstasy filled my head, making me breathless, making me weak, and making me dizzy.

Just when I couldn't take it any more, Max slapped my behind, not hard, but enough to climax even more if that was possible. I had never been slapped playfully before. In a twisted way, I liked it and wanted more. Just as I climaxed, Max pulled out and held me from behind. We were both out of breath as the heavy puffs of air escaped our mouths. "That was incredible, babe," he heaved. "That was the best lunch I ever had in my office."

Blissful giggles sang out of my mouth. I had completely unraveled this beautiful man, and how I enjoyed doing it. After he helped me, and then fixed himself to look presentable, he served me a plate full of food, then forced me into his lap and showed me the front cover page he was so proud of again.

"Aren't you going to eat?" I asked, still in his lap.

"I'll eat later." He sounded relaxed, content.

Feeding myself didn't go well with me, so I stabbed my fork into the seafood salad and fed it to him. With a look of surprise and a huge grin, he graciously took it. Surely, one of the ladies he had gone out with had fed him the way I did, but I didn't know. I didn't want to think of someone else feeding my Max. Oh God! I called him my Max. At least for now he was. But I had to agree with him. This was the best lunch I'd ever had.

Chapter 29

The rest of the week went perfectly, and that was the only lunch date we had that week. Friday night Max wanted to take me out to dinner. Since he was across town for a meeting, I told him I would meet him at the restaurant. He didn't like the idea that he wasn't picking me up and taking me there directly, but I told him it was ridiculous to drive all the way back to work and then back to the restaurant. Not only was it a waste of gas, it was a waste of time, though Max wouldn't have driven...he would've had his driver do it. Following the address he gave me on my GPS, I got there in plenty of time. The Japanese restaurant was cozy, small, but elegant. The dim lighting gave it a romantic feel, and I had to admit, I was overflowing with happiness.

"We have a reservation under Mr. Maxwell Knight," I said to the hostess.

She studied me for a second, then gave me a big smile.

What was that for?

The hostess told me I could wait at the bar for Max, so that was where I headed. Sitting at the bar, there were several seats taken; probably people who were waiting for their tables as well. With a quick smile to the strangers, I sat with my back to the door and admired the clock on the wall.

Just as the long hand touched the number twelve, a warm body cuddled behind me, and I knew it was Max—just in time. The scent of his expensive cologne was intoxicating. He nibbled on my ear and whispered sweet nothings to me. "Hey, beautiful. Everyone has an addiction. Mine happens to be you. You're my only addiction, and I don't ever want to find a cure."

"Max," I gushed, giggling, recalling him saying something like that to me before.

Then Max twitched from the sound of his cell phone. "Sorry…let me check," he uttered. A frown crossed his face.

"Who is it?" I asked. I was concerned, seeing his unpleasant facial expression. Though I knew it was none of my business, and I shouldn't have asked, I couldn't help myself. That facial expression worried me deeply.

"Nothing, babe." Shifting his eyes away from his phone and shoving it back into the holder on his side belt loop, he peered down at me with a smile and held my hand. "Let's go to our table."

Getting out of the bar area and into the dining area, I thought he was headed to our table, but instead he took me to a private room, set just for two, with a candle flickering on the center table. Helping me take my coat off, he pulled out my chair, waited for me to sit, and sat across from me. Always a gentleman.

"Do you own this restaurant?" I asked, placing my small purse behind me. The hostess hadn't escorted us in, and I thought it was unusual to walk into a private room without her knowing.

"My parents do, so I'm not sure how to answer that question," he chuckled lightly. "I knew they were not coming here for dinner, so…here we are." He grinned. "How was your day without me?"

Before I could answer, the waitress walked in with two glasses of water and a glass of wine for Max. "Good evening," she smiled warmly.

I smiled, but Max greeted her. "Hello, Ana. How have you been?"

"Good, thank you, Max."

A strange, knotted feeling twisted inside me, and I couldn't help but wonder if they'd had something before. I guessed that it would be natural for them to know each other, but the fact that she was pretty with a gorgeous body, she had called him by his first name, and the way he smiled at her…I had to stop thinking like that. What is the matter with me? Trust…I need to trust him. He hadn't done anything wrong. Whatever it was, it was in the past…if there was anything there in the first place.

After placing the drinks on the table, she gave us each a menu. "I'll be back to take your orders." When she turned, I expected Max to turn to check her out, like most men would have, but he didn't. He turned to me with an even bigger grin. In a silly way, that put a smile on my face.

"So, as I was asking…how was your day?" Max continued, opening my menu for me. "Pick whatever your heart desires…or I should say your stomach."

"The same old," I said, referring back to his question. "But…yes, I have to admit, I did miss you…a little."

As if I had thrown a dagger into his heart, he placed his hand there with a pretend hurtful expression. "Just a little?" he frowned. "That's okay. I'm not afraid to say I've missed you more."

His words tugged at my heart. Since I wasn't sure what to order, Max ordered lots of sushi, sashimi, and things I'd never tried before. This concerned me a little…I was never the adventurous type to try new things. I had always stuck to the same old, usual, safe stuff. But I had to admit, I was glad Max made me try them, because they were delicious.

As we sat there and ate, Max wrapped his long legs around mine underneath the table as if his legs were arms, wrapping me inside his hold and keeping me there. It was the sweetest thing, like he couldn't get enough of me, or a part of him had to touch me. I was falling…falling too fast and too hard. Max raised his glass. "Sorry…no wine for you."

Blushing with embarrassment, I recalled the night when I got really buzzed. "Don't you want to take advantage of me?" I teased.

"Babe, I don't need to get you buzzed. You're high with my presence right now. And if I could close that door and put up a 'Do not disturb' sign, I would have you on this table, stripped naked, and eat sushi off your body."

He was right. Heat exploded, and his words made my clit explode like fireworks.

"You're turning red as my wine," he teased, and changed the subject. "Let's toast." He held up his glass again and I did the same. "To being lunch, cuddle, sleeping, breakfast, and finally dinner buddies, and to our first date...and more to come."

With a clink, I gulped practically the whole glass of water. Not only was I thirsty, I was still hot from his flirting.

"So which one did you enjoy the most, or do you have a favorite?" Max asked, taking a bite of the tuna.

"I like the ikura one." I held it up and carefully placed it in my mouth to look ladylike.

"Why? Do you like the taste or the texture? Each fish has its own unique taste and texture."

"I like the taste...and...it's kind of silly...but I like how they squirt in your mouth." That did not come out well. Max had the most amused grin on his face. I sank into my chair.

"Do you now?" His eyes were glistening, reflected by the candlelight. "Would you like for me to squirt in your mouth sometime?"

I wanted to hide under the tablecloth. "Max," I whispered, feeling too hot.

Max only chuckled. He knew how I would react, and he enjoyed seeing me all tense and yearning. "Sorry...it just slipped. I didn't mean to make you blush and get hot and...it's so sweet how you look so innocent like that."

I took another sip of my cold water and shoved another salmon piece into my mouth so I couldn't talk anymore. I wished he would do the same.

"Oh, by the way, referring back to your question about taking advantage of you. Yes, I do. Not here though," he winked.

I almost choked...not because I thought his words were inappropriate, but because of how he made me feel.

During the rest of the dinner, we talked about our families. Max told me that he practically grew up with a nanny, and that his parents were always busy traveling. Getting deeper into the conversation, he told me he didn't really have a choice of profession. His dad wanted him and his brother to take over his pride and joy, his company. Seeing no choice and not wanting to disappoint, he had followed in his father's footsteps. Matthew, on the other hand, did so only for a short period of time, then stopped.

Though at times he'd wished he had a choice, he said that finding me was the best part of his experience with the company. He partially blamed Matthew's irresponsibility on his mother. Since she was hardly around, and since Matthew was the youngest, he was spoiled and got everything he wanted, when he wanted. Max, on the other hand, wanted more in life, and didn't want to be like his brother.

As for my family, I told him we were just an ordinary family. My dad worked all his life as a dentist, working six days a week, and Mom was always a stay at home mom. Max said he envied me in the sense that my mom was around instead of a nanny, and I felt for him. This only proved that love and being there for someone was more important than having all the riches in the world. Though I had friends, being the only child got lonely at times, I told him, so he understood from our conversation how much Becky, Nicole, and Kate meant to me. They were my family.

After dinner, we had dessert…green tea ice cream. While we ate, the phone buzzed several times, but after he checked to see who it was, he ignored it. Though I shouldn't read into it, I couldn't help wondering who it was. He had that same disturbed look he had produced earlier. Since he'd turned back to me with a smile, I didn't pursue the questions I wanted ask.

After dessert, Max took me home. He wanted me to spend the night with him, but I told him perhaps another night. I had done it once, but I wanted to wait, and the fact that I was going to see him the next day made it easier to say no. The plan was for him to come pick me up by ten in the morning to head to his parents' house for lunch.

♥♥

Thumbing through the hangers in my closet, I decided I had nothing to wear. How was it possible I couldn't find one decent sweater that was presentable to wear in front of Max's parents? Of course I had plenty, but everything looked so plain. Then all sorts of thoughts circulated in my mind. Would they know we'd slept together? Did they even know I was one of their employees?

The sound of something broke me out of my thoughts. It sounded like our doorbell, but was very faint, so I wasn't sure. Becky was blasting the music in the living room, and with the sound of the heater running, it was hard to tell. Ignoring the sound, I continued to rummage through my closet as I shook my behind to the beat of the music and sang along. When I heard my name, I froze. Mortified that Max had seen me shake my behind, I dared not turn.

Inhaling a deep breath, I buried my face in the palms of my hands as I tried to build courage to face him. Covering my front with my arms crossed, since I was only wearing a bra and a pair of skinny jeans, I turned slightly to my left, but not all the way. "Max. You're early. Like…one hour early." I tried to sound casual, but I was burning hot with embarrassment.

Max closed the door and headed toward me as he spoke. "Jenna. Don't stop on my account," he smirked. "The music and dancing becomes you, not to mention you almost being topless." With both of his hands on my waist, he turned me around and gave me a kiss. "Hello," he said, looking at me with such tenderness while his hand had a mind of its own, being dirty. His finger started from my collarbone, slowly making its way down my breast, making me shiver like crazy.

"I…I…was looking for something…," I stuttered, but paused when he tugged my bra and his tongue started to caress my right nipple. "To…wear."

"I can…help you…with that…department," he said in between sucking my nipples.

"Max," I gripped his dark gray sweater that formed to his chest in a delicious way. I was glad he'd worn jeans, too.

Max pulled up and turned me around again to face my clothes. Panting and blistering inside my panties, I stood there feeling dazed and unable to concentrate. Max reached over me, slid some hangers to the left, and pulled out my pink sweater with ruffles down the buttons. "You look pretty in pink."

After I put my sleeves through, he buttoned from the bottom, but when he reached toward the top, he purposely brushed his knuckles on the side of my breast, making me ache for more.

"There you go," he said, closing my closet door. "You're all set."

I smiled shyly as he took my hand, leading me out of my bedroom door.

M. Clarke

Chapter 30

After Max kissed his mom on the cheek, he turned. "Mom, this is Jenna Mefferd, the one I told you about."

"Hello, Mrs. Knight." I smiled warmly, walking further into the house on the hard wood floor. The aroma of whatever was cooking in the kitchen churned my stomach, especially since I had eaten a very light breakfast. "Oh…I bought you these flowers, and dessert." I turned to Max, who was holding a bouquet of various flowers and a box of cheesecake.

"I'll hold them for you," Max said.

"Welcome, Jenna. And thank you so much. It wasn't necessary, but it was very sweet of you," Max's mom greeted as she hugged me. She was a couple of inches taller than me. "Call me Ellen. And come in." Ellen took the flowers from Max's hand. "I'll put these in a vase." Then she took the box from Max. "I can take this too. Take Jenna into the family room." She smiled.

Ellen was even more beautiful in person than in the picture. Her beautiful blonde hair, just above shoulder length, was silky and shiny. I wondered how often she went to the beauty salon. With the amount of money she had, I wouldn't be surprised if she went everyday. And it looked like, compared to the pictures, she had a lost a few pounds. But then again, I'd heard that a camera added unwanted extra pounds on photos.

Looping his arms around my shoulders, Max guided me into their foyer and dropped his arms, allowing me to take in the grandeur of the room. With a high ceiling and a staircase on either side of the wall, it was just as big as I thought it would be. The crystal chandelier caught my eyes after that, sparkling like a star…no brighter than the stars, twinkling from the sunlight reflecting through the window above the front double doors.

"Is Matt here yet?" Max asked.

"He's in the kitchen, helping Carlos cook."

They have a cook? A male cook?

"This way." Max placed his hand behind my back as he guided me further in.

"Max!" Matthew said out loud. Matthew practically ran Max over and tackled him into a hug. Matthew was just as tall as Max, with lighter hair. He was handsome too, but not as gorgeous as my Max.

"Nice to see you too, little bro," Max chuckled, then let go. "Matt, meet Jenna."

Matthew raked his eyes over me from head to toe. His gaze made me uncomfortable, like he was undressing me with his eyes. "Where have you been all my life?"

Max slapped his arm. "Snap out of it. She's mine."

"Hello, Jenna." Matthew gently wrapped his arms around me, as if worried he would crush me, then let go. "Max and I share everything," he teased. "Don't we, Max?"

"Shut up." Max pushed him out of the way, held my hand, and led me into the family room. It was like walking into a home magazine. With the finest of furnishings, the area had definitely been decorated by a professional, unless Ellen had an eye for it— probably not. It was all color coordinated, down to the pictures of the family mounted on the wall, to the crown molding I loved so much. It gave a feeling of warmth and home.

"Dad, this is Jenna," Max said.

As soon as I heard the word "Dad," I froze, stopped glancing around, and turned. "Mr. Knight, it's a pleasure to meet you." I extended my hand. A tall, handsome guy, with salt and pepper-colored hair, stood in front of me. It was amazing to see how much Max resembled his father.

"The pleasure is all mine," Mr. Knight said. "Call me Rob." He shook my hand. "Please…have a seat. I'll be right back." Then he went to the kitchen.

"My dad likes to cook, too. At least he tries," Max said, sitting right next to me. He obviously wasn't shy about displaying emotions in front of his parents. "In our house, men do the cooking."

"Really?" My eyes grew wide. How sexy was that? "Whatever they are cooking in there smells delicious. And who's Carlos?"

"He comes when my mom calls. She wanted everything to be perfect, so that meant she wouldn't be cooking," Max chuckled lightly.

Matthew headed our way with open beer bottles in his hands. Max took one. "No thank you," I said as politely as I could when Matthew offered me one.

"Then two for me," Matthew said, and sat across from us. Leaning back into a comfortable position, he crossed his right leg over his left.

"Babe, would you like anything to drink?" Max asked after a taking a sip.

"No, thank you." I didn't want Max to leave my sight. Being under the microscope with Matthew was nerve wracking enough.

"So, how long are you in town, Matthew?" I asked, breaking the ice a little.

"Actually, I'll be in town for awhile." Matthew looked at Max when he replied.

"Really?" Max seemed surprise, raising his tone a bit. "Do Mom and Dad know?"

"They know. I've been doing a lot of soul searching on my trips. I know I need to settle down and help my family, especially since Dad wants to retire," he said, running his thumb over his bottle. "I'll be back to work soon."

"Good," Max said. "It's about damn time."

How lucky he was to have the luxury to travel and not have to worry about anything.

"So...." Matthew's brows arched with a crooked smile. "How long have you two been...?" He paused, waiting for an answer.

My chest burned and I stiffened. Was he going to ask how long we'd been dating, or something else? Surely not the latter, but just from the little I knew of him, he would be the kind to be very blunt. Max felt my sudden movement and looked at his brother. "None of your business," he chuckled. "And get your mind out of the gutter."

"What?" Matthew laughed out loud. "My mind wasn't there, but now I know."

Being as red as I was, I might as well have drunk the beer Matthew had offered. To ease this awkward conversation, I broke in with a question. "So, Matthew...." I cleared my throat. "Max told me you've been backpacking through Europe. Did you go by yourself?"

Matthew scooted forward, sitting at the edge of the sofa with his legs spread apart. "I went with a friend. You should go sometime. It's an amazing experience." He twirled the almost empty bottle.

"I've always wanted to. I've known a couple of friends that have gone, and they say the same thing, but I think I would prefer to stay at a hotel instead of other people's houses," I smiled.

"We can go some day soon, babe," Max said.

"If Max doesn't take you, I will." Matthew winked.

"Hey...mine, I said. Stake your claim on someone else," Max joked.

Never having a sibling, it was refreshing to see two brothers at each other like that. And though Matthew was flirting out loud, Max took it as a joke. It was the ease and comfort they had with each other that I enjoyed observing. It was exactly like that with my circle of friends.

Max peered up when his mom walked in. "Time for lunch," she said happily.

Max followed his mom with one hand behind my back, and Matthew followed behind us. Knowing Matthew was staring from behind, walking straight was almost impossible. It felt like he was studying me. Had Max not brought anyone to his home before? Perhaps Matthew was being protective of Max. But that sounded strange even thinking about it, since Max had told me Matthew was the irresponsible one who would never settle down and hold a job. So to hear him say that he would, Max must have been overjoyed.

Max sat next to me as we settled into our seats. Grilled halibut, assorted vegetables, baby racks of lamb, pasta salad, and the dessert I brought were all presented beautifully on the table. The flowers I brought had been placed in a vase and presented as a centerpiece in the middle of the table. Mr. Knight untied the apron he was wearing, took it off, and sat across from Max. "Carlos, this is Jenna," Mr. Knight introduced as Carlos paced around to fill the glasses with water.

"Hello, Jenna," he said with an Italian accent.

"It's nice to meet you," I said, watching him pour my glass. "Thank you."

With a nod, he left for the kitchen.

"Eat away," Mrs. Knight said, sitting across from me.

Max helped me filled my plate and everyone else followed after. As we ate, Max's parents asked me questions about where I went to school, about my parents, and where I lived. From the corner of my eyes, I could see Max giving his parents funny looks. Though I was comfortable answering them, I knew Max didn't like it. If I were in his shoes, I would've have done the same thing.

During dessert, Mr. Knight spoke about how he'd started the company, and what his vision was for the future. His story was long, but I was all ears. Everyone else seemed to be bored. I figured he must have told them the story a million times, but for me, it was fascinating.

As I continued to listen in awe, I jerked a little as if a bee had stung me. I was caught totally off guard. Max placed his hand on my thigh, and his pinky was rubbing me there. Hot...it was too hot. Trying not to make it obvious, I slipped my hand under the table as I listened and nodded to what Matthew was talking about without looking at Max. But Matthew knew. I could tell when he chuckled and raised his brows at Max. As I continued to smile, I tried to move Max's hand away, but he wouldn't let me. His grip was too strong...at least that dirty little pinky of his stopped moving.

Luckily I was wearing jeans and the material was thick, but it didn't matter. Max obviously didn't like the fact that I was giving his brother lots of attention and ignoring him. In fact, my attention was all on his family. They were fascinating. They lived a life style most families dreamt about. Having the best and the finest things in life, going anywhere on vacation and not having to worry about money...who wouldn't dream about that?

Besides spending lots of money, they were involved with charities, which made me love them even more. Max's parents were almost like my parents: good, down to Earth, except they were financially well off and then some. Having money didn't matter to me, but the fact that they were nice and knew that I was one of their employees dating their eldest son, and they still treated me as if I was part of their family, touched me deeply...way too deeply.

After lunch, Carlos and another lady cleared the table. Max's parents excused themselves to attend a function, and Max and I spent the afternoon with Matthew. As Max and Matthew gave me the tour of the grand house and their amazing backyard, they told me short stories of what they did when they were growing up, what types of sports they'd played, the mischievous pranks they'd played on their nannies, and all kinds of stories to make me laugh.

Matthew had plans for dinner with his friends, so Max and I had dinner at his house. I thought he would try to seduce me, but he was being really good. After that darn pinky rubbing against me, I thought for sure he would've tried, but that was not the case. He stole a few kisses here and there, but impressively, I was happy to know that sex was not always on his mind, and he was taking this relationship as seriously as he claimed to be.

Max walked me to my apartment. I didn't know if I was suppose to invite him in, but luckily he spoke first. "You made me really happy today," he gushed as his fingers played with mine.

"Just today?" I giggled. It was that look of warmth and want he gave me that made me all shy and bubbly.

"You know what I mean. I was afraid you would back out on me." His hand trailed up my arm, over my shoulder, caressing the side of my neck with his fingers.

Max was afraid? "Why would you think that? I told you I would go."

"I know," he said. His eyes became softer, sparkling against the light, looking dreamy. It was hard to resist the thought of devouring him. "It's just that…I don't want to scare you or push you away. I've never moved this fast before, so just tell me if I am…okay?"

I nodded.

Max continued. His eyes were deeply rooted into mine. "I'm a lucky man to have found you. I've never fallen so deep and so fast before. You've cast a spell on me. I'm going to be good, to be the man you want me to be, to be the man you deserve, the man you want to have a future with. I know your heart is big and delicate. You have to trust that I'll take good care of it when you decide to gift it to me. It will be my amazing treasure, and I will hold it as my keepsake, inside my heart."

"Okay," I managed to say when his finger slid down further as he stared at my lips. All his words were beautiful. It made my heart full, but his touch left me starving between my legs.

Seemingly taking his time, he slowly inched his lips toward mine. He knew exactly what to do to drive me crazy. Shuddering from his touch, his hands shifted to my sides, and now they were gingerly kneading my breasts. I lost control, as his lips were now in front of mine. As the anticipation of him kissing me grew, my heart hammered rapidly, and the heat flushed through my body really fast…too fast.

"Sleep tight, Jenna. And dream of me all night, making love to you anywhere you like, 'cause I definitely will be," he whispered. Every puff of air to my lips shot a shooting star between my legs.

Feeling my chest inflate in and out, I thought I was going to faint. Then Max pressed his body to mine and held me tightly. His

M. Clarke

kiss was tender and sweet, and leisurely. We were making out like teenagers. Then he pulled back slowly. His eyes were in a dream like state, and he blinked to gather himself. "You better go inside before I kidnap you."

Waking up from my own daze, I shoved the key that was already in my hands through the keyhole and opened the door. Max ran his fingers through his hair and released a sigh. "Go inside so I know you're safe, then I'll leave."

"Okay." I gave him a fast peck on the cheek.

"See you on Monday," he said, giving me a little shove inside the door as he closed the door in front of him.

Trying to cool down, I placed my back against the door, but I knew Max hadn't left yet. There were no footstep sounds. Wanting to see what he was doing, I looked through the peephole. Both of his hands were on the door and his head was down. This was too adorable...too sweet... straight out of romantic movies. When I heard the sound of his footsteps, I knew he was leaving, and that made me feel empty.

What do I do? My heart had taken over my mind. I opened the door to see Max walking funny. I guessed he had what Becky had mentioned to me before, something called blueballs—when the man got really hard and was unable to release the pressure. Giggling softly, I watched him near the elevator as I tried to make up my mind.

"Max."

Max whipped around. "Get back inside, Jenna. I need to know you're safe."

My heart was pounding. I had never asked a man to spend the night with me in my own bed before. The feeling was exhilarating yet frightening, because wanting to ask him was an indication that I had already gifted him with my heart. "Spend the night with me?" I asked shyly.

Max's lips slowly curled into a huge smile. He didn't walk toward me...he ran.

Chapter 31

Waking up and having Max beside me was thrilling. He was sound asleep, which gave me the opportunity to study his handsome face. Soaking in the fact that he was actually in my bed and the fact that I had asked him to spend the night...well...that was a first for me. Not wanting to wake him, I slid off the bed.

Max's phone vibrated, and though I knew I shouldn't, I took a peek. It was a text. *Call me!* The person's name was Crystal. Hmmm...it could have been a client, but it had me frozen for a second, draining my blood, sending me back to my college years. Since trust was one of the components of having a successful relationship, I had to trust Max. Just because my ex cheated on me didn't mean Max would. I had to give him the benefit of the doubt.

Brushing it off, I went to the restroom and closed the door. I figured I could freshen up and get back in bed with Max. After I took care of what I needed to do, I stepped out to hear Becky's loud scream. My bedroom door was open and Max was out of bed.

"Max? Becky?" I ran out.

Becky's hand was over her heart. Her body was shaking from her labored breathing.

"Sorry." Max's apology was very sincere. "I didn't mean to scare you...again."

"That's okay. We always have half-naked men...shirtless...jeans...did I mention shirtless?"

I knew Becky was trying hard not to stare, but how could anyone resist? Becky finally noticed me. Max turned to me with a smile and headed toward me. With a brush of his hand on my cheek, he went to the bathroom.

"Jenna?" Becky looked so surprised.

Thank goodness Becky was decently dressed. "Becky. I'm so sorry. You weren't home last night and I didn't know—"

"It's okay," Becky interrupted. "I'm just a little shocked…that's okay. Umm…I don't know if you got my text, but Nicole had to switch it for lunch. And umm…." She still looked distraught, seemingly thinking as her eyes shifted to my room, then to me. Her lips trembled and her eyes sparkled. I knew she was trying to hold in something, maybe a laugh. "In all the years we've been living together, you've never let a guy into your bedroom, even your ex-boyfriend. This must be really serious."

I didn't answer right away. Twisting my head to my room to make sure Max wasn't by the door, I inhaled a deep sigh, then turned to Becky. "I hope so."

Becky finally let out what she was holding, a huge, smug smile. "I hope so too."

♥♥

Max left shortly after, and Becky and I left to meet with Nicole and Kate. "So…." Becky started to say, keeping her eyes straight on the road in front of her. "Do you and Max talk about…you know…his past?"

"I know enough," I said, wondering where this conversation was headed.

Becky inhaled deeply, seemingly uncomfortable. "I'm just going to say it. This question is none of my business, but do you know his sex life…like how many he slept with, or how many girl friends he's had? You know, things that you talk about with the new man in your life."

"Don't worry, Becky. I know enough. I don't want to know more. He's mentioned he had some one-night stands, and dated many models. He had one serious girlfriend before, but he didn't want to talk about it much."

Becky signaled, then turned the steering wheel to the left. "Okay," she nodded, seemingly satisfied with the answer. "Does he know about yours?"

"Yes, he does. But you already know I don't have much to tell. Basically, I told him that I don't mess around. I don't like messing with people's hearts, and I certainly don't lead them on. I told him one-night stands are fine when mature adults agree, but I wasn't that type. Also, I told him that I did go on many dates, but the little spark that got me interested died quickly."

"Does he know about your ex?"

I chuckled a little. "My one ex? Yes, he knows. He knows he cheated on me. He knows I have trust issues; but then again, we're all three years more mature now." Knowing the other questions Becky would ask, I just answered. "Yes, he knows I haven't in three years." I lightened the mood a little. "And yes, he knows if he ever hurt me, you, Nicole, and Kate would hunt him down."

Becky turned to me for a second and flashed back to the road. A light chuckle escaped her mouth unexpectedly. She hadn't expected that to come out of my mouth. "You bet his ass we will."

And they would, especially Becky. Though we were the same age, she was the older sister I'd never had. Living together for the past fours years had brought our friendship to a family level. Knowing we had each other made new adventures not so scary, even a possible heartache.

♥♥

"Your ring is beautiful," the waitress said to Nicole, setting down glasses filled with orange juice and champagne on our table.

"Thank you," she said, glancing at her ring with a big smile.

Since it was a buffet brunch, we headed our separate ways. There were so many different types of cuisine to choose from, I didn't know which way to go—Italian, Mexican, Japanese, Chinese, Korean, and many others. Being that it was my first time, I placed a little bit of everything on my plate.

Nicole and Kate were already seated, eating, and Becky followed behind me. Soon as I sat, I dug right in.

"Have you picked a date yet?" Becky asked.

M. Clarke

"It's going to be a spring wedding...maybe in April or May, but after Easter for sure. Keith and I have already started planning." Nicole sounded so excited, I couldn't help be excited for her too. "I'll let you know as soon as I pick out the color and style for the bridesmaid dresses. I was hoping you all could come with me."

"Sure," we all said in accord.

Kate took a sip of her drink and swallowed her food. "It'll come really fast. It's already the beginning of November. That only leaves you with five months. You'd better get going," Kate advised, having been through it.

"I know," Nicole said with a full mouth. "I'll let you know soon."

"So...how's Max?" Kate asked, changing our lunch topic.

"Good," I said, turning red. That came out a little bit too chirpy and gushy.

Kate's eyes burned through me. "Oh...my...God. You did...you really did. He must be some kind of wonderful, 'cause we've tried to set you up with guys that we thought were highly qualified for our mighty queen, and nothing, but...when did this happen?"

I blushed even more since now they knew. Did I make it that obvious? "Recently," I mumbled, gulping down my orange juice. I wasn't good at talking about this topic, mostly because I wasn't that experienced. Was something wrong with me? They could talk about it so freely, like it was no big deal. Maybe I needed to get with the program. They were like my sisters, and I knew I could trust them with anything, so what was my problem?

"So...ummm...did he make you sing hallelujah?" Nicole giggled, slipping a slice of beef into her mouth.

I closed my eyes for a second, then opened them, knowing I shouldn't be embarrassed about this subject. There was a big smile on my face, and I was sure my eyes glistened like Nicole's engagement ring thinking about the times in his bedroom, dining room, family room, bathroom, on the stairs, my room, and—I couldn't believe—in his office. If only my friends knew, they

208

would probably have a heart attack. With a shy grin plastered on my face, I said. "And then some."

My three friends screamed...almost silently, smiling, and giggling. Nicole threw up her hands half way into the air. "Then...he's a keeper. When do we get to meet Mr. Wonderful?"

♥♥

Being at work on Mondays was no longer a drag. It meant that I got to see Max. That was, when he could get away. On occasion I was still his lunch buddy, and others times I would eat lunch in my office to catch up with work, or have lunch with Lisa and Rachel. Jake had stopped calling me at the office about two weeks earlier, when word had gotten out about Max and me.

"Hey, Jenna," a familiar man's voice greeted.

I peered up to see Matthew speed walking toward me with a big grin. "Matthew?" Getting out of my chair, I headed toward him. Lisa and Rachel's eyes practically popped out.

Matthew squeezed me tightly in his arms. "How've you been?"

After he released me, I looked up, smiling. "Good, and you?"

"Good." His eyes wandered, glancing around the room to Lisa and Rachel with a smile, and nodding to Dan and Eric. "I'm a floor above you. I settled in last week. Max told me to find you and take you to lunch. I mean...we three are going to lunch together."

"I'll be back," I told Lisa. Matthew had already grabbed my purse and my jacket. With one of his hands gently on my back, he guided me toward the door. He was just like Max, such a gentleman. Looking over my shoulder, I spotted Lisa.

"He's hot," she mouthed.

I giggled inwardly as I stepped out of the office.

M. Clarke

Chapter 32

Matthew was a sweetheart in the car, and so was his Porsche. I didn't know what kind it was, but who cared? I should be used to it, since Max had one, too. I knew Max was turning twenty-seven, and I found out that Matthew was my age, twenty-three. He didn't ask many personal questions…he mostly spoke about his trips and Max, letting me know what a great brother Max was and how he looked up to him. It was nice to hear Matthew talk about Max that way. It only confirmed what I already new. Max had a good heart…no…an amazing heart.

"We're almost there." Matthew paused, looked in his rear view mirror, looked to his right, then changed lanes. "How's work treating you? And, what do you do…exactly? I mean…I know your job description, but I want to hear it from you."

"Our team makes sure the magazines are delivered on time, answers any questions, and fixes problems. We're the customer relations…the go to people. We especially take good care of companies that get mad." I let out a short laugh.

"You have such a sweet voice. I don't think anyone could get mad at you," he said lightly, then turned left.

I blushed a little. "Thanks. But unfortunately people do. I haven't had any problems at this company so far. Everyone seems very professional and respectful."

"Good. If you have any problems, make sure you tell Max, and if Max isn't around, let me know. I'll take care of it. Max speaks highly of you, and he cares for you like I've never seen him care for anyone before. You are nothing like his ex-girlfriend. I'm so glad he moved on. Crystal was such a bit…." He stopped himself and became quiet, then his eyes cringed a little, as if he didn't mean to burst that out. "Sorry…Max told me not to cuss around you."

At that moment, the only word I heard was Crystal. Recalling Max's text, my mind began to wonder. I never wanted to know the names of any of the women he dated, but I knew one now. Not only did he date her, she was his one serious girl friend. She wanted him to call her…but why? Did she want to get back together? Was he dating her behind my back? Was he having lunch or dinner dates when he wasn't with me? I had to stop thinking or I would drive myself crazy.

"Thanks, Matthew." That was all I could say as he drove into valet parking. There were several cars in front of us so we had to wait our turn. "Enough about me. How do you like your job, and what do you do?"

"I do absolutely nothing." He paused. "Just kidding. Before I took off on my little adventure, my team and I were in charge of page layouts, which order or what model to schedule in. It sounds easy, but there is a lot of work, especially since our magazine goes out on a monthly basis."

"I can only imagine, but it seems like fun."

Matthew's eyes lit up and so did his tone. "Jenna, why don't you join my team for a couple of days and see if you'd like what we do? There are so many departments in our company; you should check it all out to see what your interests are. I know you are great with customer service…." He paused and squirmed a little, like he had done something he shouldn't have. "I looked at your resume. Sorry. Just wanted to get to know you better without asking you so many questions. After all, this is our company, and I wanted to know what you could offer. Max told me you went to New York with him."

There was no reason to believe Max had told him about what happened between us, so why did I blush. "Oh…what did he say?" I swallowed.

"He said you helped him with the front cover, and that you had a great eye for that. He also suggested what I just offered to you, and I thought it was a great idea."

"Really?" I sat up taller.

"Anyway, I know you're great at what you do, since that was what you did at your previous job, but here, you have unlimited possibilities. Just keep that in mind…and it does help that you are dating my brother, who happens to think the world of you."

"Okay," I nodded. When my side of the door was opened for me, my high heel contacted the ground first, and I was just about to put my hand on the side of the door to get out when I saw his hand.

"Max," I said blissfully, peering up, twisting my lips upward. The strong wind brushed up against my legs, feeling icy, cold.

"Hey, babe." With one strong pull from my hand, my body pressed into his. Burying his face to the side of my face, he held me tightly. "Missed you, babe."

I was warm again from his hold blocking the wind and the warmth traveling to my heart from just the sight of him. As I breathed in his scent, I repeated in my mind, please don't cheat on me.

♥♥

"Hello," the waitress said too cheerfully as her eyes shifted from Max, then to Matthew, but not to me. "My name is Amy. I'll be your waitress. What would you like to drink?"

"Hello there…Amy." Matthew's tone was friendly and inviting. Leaning back in a cool, relaxed manner, his eyes traced the curve of her body from head to toe.

The waitress flushed, and she looked like she was lost for words. I didn't blame her. Matthew was good-looking and he could make any woman blush, just as much as Max could. Him checking her out confirmed what I hadn't asked before, that he was single…I hoped so for Becky's sake, thinking they would make a cute couple.

"Water all around please," Max said quickly, then moved his eyes back to the menu.

"Sure. I'll be right back." She flashed a flirtatious smile to Matthew and left.

Matthew ordered their gourmet hamburger, Max ordered sea bass, and I ordered black peppered salmon. With a small, fresh green salad on the side, our lunch was served. Matthew was hilarious during lunch. I couldn't stop laughing at his stories regarding his European trip. He also told stories about how Max had looked after him when they were young. Max had gotten in trouble in sixth grade because he punched a bully who picked on his brother. Those were the younger days, Matthew said. Now he claimed, in the present time, Max needed him more. I wondered what he meant by that.

Matthew and Max switched cars so Max could drive me back to work. Matthew left right after lunch for a meeting, but Max and I decided to stay for a cup of coffee.

"Excuse me," Max said, looking at his phone. His forehead crinkled, looking disturbed. Shaking his head with a frown, he closed the phone.

"Is everything alright?" I asked, feeling concerned. What kind of message would make his face look distraught like that? And why did he keep getting those messages?

"It's nothing, babe," he replied, peering back at me. But I could tell something was on his mind. "Drink your coffee before it gets too cold." His tone was stern, but kind.

Reaching inside his workbag, he placed a little box in front of me.

"What's this?" I asked, placing my cup down. A spark of excitement shivered through me. I felt like a child looking at a Christmas or birthday present.

"I just want you to know that you're my something great." Max beamed a huge smile. "Open it."

Trying my best not to get too excited, I opened the box. Inside was a key, attached to an engraved key chain that read "Something Great."

Before I could say anything, Max jumped in. "I know it's too soon. If I could have it my way, you would be living with me…like, yesterday…but I don't want to push you too fast. This is the key to my place. You are welcome to be there anytime you like…preferably when I'm around. You can spend the night if you'd like." He twitched his brows. "Come and go as you please. My place is yours. You can also walk around naked. I don't mind at all."

"Max," I blushed as I shot my eyes back to the key, but the thought made me hot. Reaching over, I picked it up and ran my fingers over the engraved words. It was so sweet and touching. Feeling overwhelmed, I felt a pool of tears. No guy had made me feel the way Max did. The insecure part of me wondered if he was cheating on me and how long it would last, but I had to stop thinking such negative thoughts, because I knew it would get in the way of me enjoying the present. "I don't know what to say…thank you."

Max's shoulders relaxed, looked less nervous as he radiated a smile. Perhaps he'd thought I wouldn't accept it. I wasn't sure what he was thinking, but he let out a sigh of relief. "Believe me…it's my pleasure. Don't forget to use it." He winked.

After we finished our drinks, I placed the key inside the box and placed the box inside my workbag. Before I had a chance to grab my bag, Max picked it up from the floor and carried it for me. Such a gentleman! It was hard to get used to sometimes, but I had to admit , I loved that kind of attention from him.

Before we parted ways at the office, Max reminded me he would pick me up for Thanksgiving dinner. Though I hadn't forgotten, I was feeling a little bit nervous. Thanksgiving dinner was meant for family to spend time together, and I wasn't sure if his parents wanted me there. Though Max had told me they had invited me, I was almost certain he told them he was bringing me.

M. Clarke

Chapter 33

"Becky...you sure you don't want me to take you to the airport tomorrow?" I asked, watching her place items inside her suitcase.

"No, I'll take the taxi. It's not a big deal." Becky paced to the closet again. "I can't believe I have nothing to wear."

I started to giggle. "Yup...sometimes I feel the same way."

Becky turned to me. "Didn't we just go shopping recently? How is that possible?" She huffed and pulled a black sweater off the hanger. After folding it, she placed it inside her suitcase.

Sitting on her bed, next to her suitcase, I straightened some of her clothing items inside it. "You're only going to see your parents, right?"

Becky slowly turned. "Yes...but one of my parents' friends will be there with their son, whom I've had a crush on since high school. His name is Ryan. He was in college when I met him so he didn't pay attention to me. Since the age difference doesn't matter anymore...just maybe...." Becky paused. "Oh gosh...what if he has a girlfriend? Whatever...I'm just wearing whatever," she giggled.

After she zipped her suitcase, she placed it by the front door. Then she plopped back onto the bed next to me. "Dinner with the Knight family, huh?"

I arched my brows. "Yeah," I replied. My tone was half-excited and half-nervous.

M. Clarke

"I'm glad you have Max while I'm off to see my parents. I'm sure he'll take real good care of you." The last sentence came off too playfully. "We should communicate more often. You're here during Thanksgiving and I'm not. How did that happen?"

"I'm not sure. I think we didn't think about it...you know what I mean." I draped my arms around her.

"Don't miss me too much while I'm gone, okay?" Becky hugged me back. "You know you have the whole apartment to yourself, so you can do whatever you like." Her tone was playful, dragging out the word "whatever."

Giggling, I told her to take her mind out of where mine was.

"You have changed, my dear. Max is bringing out the wild side in you. Little miss angel is turning into little miss devil."

With wide eyes and stunned by her words, though I knew she was joking, I playfully pushed her off the bed.

♥♥

Becky had taken Wednesday off and left early that morning, the day before Thanksgiving, and Max picked me up Thursday evening. Upon entering his home, his parents and Matthew greeted me with open arms. A few of his uncles, aunts, and cousins had also come to dinner. Max hadn't told me there would be other relatives, but then again, it was Thanksgiving, so I guessed I should have assumed. But being an only child, and having cousins who were already married and had children of their own, our extended relatives didn't get together for Thanksgiving.

Since the dining table could not accommodate the number of people in the household, long rectangular tables were set outside with outdoor heating lamps. Though it was dark, the pretty white lights that were hung in the surrounding area, like the ones you would hang on a Christmas tree, gave it a lovely ambiance, especially against the dark sky.

A table adjacent to where we sat was filled with plates full of Thanksgiving food—the biggest turkey I'd ever seen, ham, mashed potatoes, green beans, corn, Caesar salad, cranberry sauce, gravy, and others I couldn't remember from a quick glance. Being the eldest, Max was in charge of carving the turkey. Instead of being social, I stood around the corner where he couldn't see me.

My eyes were set on his biceps. The way they flexed as he stretched his arm and pulled back, slicing through the turkey with the knife, while he bit down on his bottom lip as if he was concentrating, was too hot. I never thought carving a turkey could look this hot, but who was I kidding? Max could make just standing there look hot. Being hungry, I should be drooling over the turkey, but I was drooling over Max instead.

"Hey, Jenna. Are you going to fill your plate, or are you going to stare at my brother all night?" Matthew teased.

Startled by having Matthew next to me, my heart leapt out of my chest and embarrassed warmth shot to my face.

Max, hearing Matthew's words, peered up and caught my eyes. Flashing a satisfied grin, he slightly blushed and winked at me. "I'll be right there, Jenna. Go fill your plate," Max ordered.

Returning a shy smile, I took the plate Matthew offered and followed behind him.

Before we ate, we all stood around the table as Matthew said a prayer. "Thank you for our family and friends, and for this wonderful meal we are about to receive. Let us not forget how precious life is, and how every day should be lived to the fullest. And as families around the world gather around their tables to celebrate the meaning of this special day, let us not forgot the ones we loved that passed away; Grandma and Grandpa Knight, and others that meant...." He paused and got choked up.

Max looped his arm around his brother, and I wondered what that was about as he finished the prayer. Afterward, we all sat and started to eat. I had thought it may have been awkward for Matthew after that, but he played it cool as if nothing had happened and got back to being himself.

As dinner progressed, I thought Max's relatives would ask me bunch of questions, but they mostly kept to themselves. With a smile here and there, they were friendly, but not overbearing, which I appreciated. We sat at a long table, perhaps the reason the conversations were limited.

"Do you have any plans for Christmas?" Matthew asked me after wiping his lips with a napkin.

"My parents live in San Francisco, so I'll be visiting them for Christmas." Max and I hadn't spoken about what our Christmas schedule was like, so this was the first time he was notified that I would be gone.

"You'll be gone for Christmas?" Max sounded surprised and disappointed.

My body stiffened when Max placed his hand on my right thigh, creating warmth as it spread when he slowly moved upward. Thank goodness the tablecloth was long enough to hide what he was doing. Even Matthew, who was very observant, couldn't tell.

Placing my hand underneath the table on top of his, trying not to make it obvious, I tried to push it off me, but of course, as always, he was too strong. And if I budged a little bit more, I knew Matthew would know for sure that something was going on underneath the table. That would make me blush even more.

Sheepishly I shrugged my shoulders. "Sorry, I know we didn't talk about this. Maybe...you can come with me?" I wasn't sure what he would say or if he would even consider it, but I thought I'd ask anyway. After all, this would be a great opportunity to have Max meet my parents, since I didn't know when I would see them afterward.

"Let's talk about this later," Max said as his eyes lit up brighter than the surrounding candlelight. His hand already on my thigh started to gingerly caress the area between my legs. I guessed he was really happy I'd asked him. The material of the sweater dress I was wearing wasn't thick enough to protect me from Max's pinky. It purposely stroked the sensitive area that flared the urge and heat. I had to make him stop. I was having a difficult time answering Matthew's questions. Standing up abruptly, I excused myself to the restroom.

Hearing footsteps behind me, I didn't think much of it, but when they followed me to the bathroom, I turned. With my back against the door, I peered up to see Max. His arms were flexed on both side of the doorframe as he pierced his eyes on me in hunger and want. I didn't know why, but every time I was in the bubble of his arms like that, I withered from the strength of him, the dominant male side of him.

"I believe this is my stop," he said softly, weakening me from just the sound of his voice that slid off his tongue like ice. Thankfully, the restroom was down the hallway, away from everyone else.

Quivering from recalling the words he had said to me before, I remembered how he had made me feel, and was making me feel at that moment. Back then I couldn't do anything about it, but today was a different story.

"I think you should go in there with me," I said playfully, gliding my hands up his dark grey sweater, feeling every curve and toned muscle.

Max leaned in to my right ear while placing his hand by the side of my breast. In a circular movement, his thumb rubbed against it, making me moan. "I've been wanting to do something with you all night." His whispering hot breath sent erotic tingles to every inch of me, making my knees weak.

"To...do...what?" I asked, closing my eyes, enjoying his soft teasing nipping on the side of my neck.

"Invite me in and I'll show you," he dared, sucking my bottom lip, then biting it with his teeth, producing both pleasure and pain.

Somehow my hands found their way to his waist. With one hand behind me, I managed to find the doorknob and clicked it open, and with the other hand, I hooked his jeans belt loop with my finger and pulled him in.

Once inside, Max didn't wait after he locked the door. He lightly slammed me against the wall and crushed my lips into his. His hand lifted my dress and sensually ran up my thigh to my G string behind, where he gripped my buttocks tightly. Then his hand shot up to my breast as he continued to devour my mouth as if I were his dinner.

With a yank, the right side of my bra was exposed. The cowlneck design of the dress made it easy access for him. Tugging my bra to the side, his tongue taunted my nipple, blazing more heat between my legs. When he sucked harder, I could not stand on my own two feet. Max pressed me against the wall with his hardness, and I could feel he was ready for me.

"You want me inside you?" he breathed out of his mouth as he lowered himself to his knee. Lifting my left leg with his hand, my knees were bent and my vagina exposed. As he teased me with his tongue, I couldn't take it anymore. With a hand full of his hair in my fist, I moaned while I covered my mouth with the other hand.

"Max…yes…please," I whispered as my head thrashed from side to side. It was too much. I didn't even know what I was saying at that point. Needing him inside me, I pulled him up and sucked his tongue the way he had done to my clitoris, and started to unbutton his jeans.

The anticipation of him being inside me was driving me crazy. I wanted and needed him, but a part of me was hesitant since we were in his parents' house, and thoughts like "what if someone knocks on the door?" came to mind. But a part of me didn't care. I wanted to do something I hadn't done before, and the urge down there was burning, over powering any of my rational thoughts.

Still holding onto me, he turned on the faucet, letting the water run to cover up the sounds we were making. I took this opportunity to caress the front of his jeans. When Max moaned, it gave me pleasure knowing I could affect him so much just by touching him. As I wondered if we were really doing this in his parents' house, the phone that was attached to his belt loop started to ring. Even after he turned the sound off, it kept vibrating. Irritatingly, the phone would not stop.

"You should get that," I told Max, breathing heavily. "What if it's an emergency?"

With a frustrated groan, Max picked it up. "Hello?" The look in his eyes said it all. His face turned pale and he walked out without a word, leaving me to wonder who was on the phone.

Max seemed distant toward me after the phone conversation, and though he sat next to me and smiled, something felt off. Thinking that I was worrying too much, I brushed it off, but I couldn't help but wonder if Crystal had been on the phone. Using the excuse of being tired, Max and I left first, before the other guests. On the drive to my house, he was quiet too. Perhaps he was really tired, but he hadn't seemed tired in the bathroom.

When he walked me to my apartment door, I couldn't take it anymore. I had to ask the question that was on my mind. Peering up at him, I tried to read what his eyes were expressing. "Max, is everything okay?" I also wanted to ask him about Crystal, but I bit my tongue and shut her out of my mind. It would make me sound jealous, and I didn't want to be that way.

Max didn't answer at first. He looked at me tenderly and brushed my cheeks with his hands. "Everything is fine," he said softly, running his thumb carefully along the line of my bottom lip.

"You can tell me anything, Max. It doesn't seem like everything is fine. Is it work? Your family?" Instead of answering, he kissed me…deeply…passionately…to the point I wanted to rip off his clothes.

When he pulled back, the worried expression was still there, so I tried to lighten the mood. "Becky went home to her parents. Want to come in?" I asked shyly.

Max slowly curved his lips with that smirking expression I loved, then a second later, it was gone. "I'm feeling tired today. I promised to go golfing with Matthew early tomorrow morning. Why don't we meet up Saturday or Sunday?"

I didn't know why his rejection felt hurtful…perhaps because he had never turned me down before, not that I had offered many times…maybe just once.

"Hmm…sure." I tried not to sound disappointed, but knowing something was wrong, I wanted to know what he was thinking and what it was that was bothering him so much.

"I'll call you soon," he said wearily. "Go inside so I know you're safe."

Opening my purse, I took out my key and opened the door. "Max—" I thought I'd try one last time.

Max jumped in before I could say another word. "It's nothing, Jenna. Everything is fine. I'll call you soon."

There was nothing I could say after that. I wasn't going to push more of his buttons and add more to whatever was going on. Since he'd assured me everything was fine, I began to wonder if he was getting tired of me and didn't have the guts to tell me. But he wouldn't have done what we did in the restroom if he felt that way. What troubled me the most was the phone call he'd received. There were many other times he had looked like that when he'd gotten a text, too. What was going on?

Chapter 34

The dark gray clouds spread across the sky, full and thick, getting ready to release more of what was already pouring. Shivering from the sight of lightning from my apartment window and the booming sound of thunder that always followed, I took a sip of my green tea.

"Come sit with us," Becky said. She was sitting on the sofa with Nicole and Kate.

Kate was breast-feeding Kristen, her four-month-old daughter. Bringing her along meant she could stay longer, and we didn't mind. She was a joy to have around. Kristen was a reminder that we were not ready to have children.

Gazing out the window, though not really looking at anything, my mind was on Max. We had spoken on the phone and he had texted every day, but something was not right...or was it just my imagination? After all, I'd only seen Luke once a week. Perhaps I was used to having Max around more since we both worked at the same place. Whatever the reason, I had to stop thinking negative thoughts. It wasn't like he stopped paying attention to me. He was busy with work...or so he'd claimed.

After I placed my mug down on the table, I sat next to Nicole. I couldn't believe she was getting married...not the idea of her getting married, but the fact that it had happened so fast. One minute they were broken up, and the next week they were engaged. For me, it didn't matter if she was with him or not. As long as he treated her well and she was happy, that was all that mattered to me.

"I was thinking after New Years, we can go shopping for bridesmaids dresses," Nicole said, looking at each of us one by one.

"Sure," Kate said, gazing into her daughter's eyes while she was still feeding her. Kristen's tiny hand was wrapped around Kate's index finger. It was the sweetest thing I had ever seen.

"Just let me know," Becky said, holding onto her mug of coffee. "So, do you ladies want to just hang out here all day and watch a movie on demand? I can order pizza. It's pouring outside."

"Let's just do that. I don't want to take Kristen out if I don't have to," Kate replied.

I didn't blame her. The wind was howling, uplifting everything that got in the way. The weather channel said it would be like this all week. Tomorrow was Sunday. Hopefully, it meant till then.

"I'll order the pizza," I offered as I headed for my room to retrieve my phone. It was almost noon and I was starving. Grabbing my phone, I saw a text flash on my screen. One was from Luke, which I ignored. I guessed I should let him know I was officially seeing Max, but I didn't want to talk to him, let alone text him, so I let it go. The other one was from Max. That made me smile...immensely.

Hello, my lady in red and my lunch buddy.

You're too cute.

I know.

I guess you didn't learn the word humble.

Haha...I invented the words arrogant, greatness, awesome, super.

Lol! I got it!

What are you doing?

My friends are over.

What are you wearing? G-string? Bathrobe? My T-shirt? Naked?

My face flushed.

You'll have to come over to find out.
I don't think your friends will like that.
True, and I don't want to share you.
Then come over anytime. You have the key to my heart.
Awww...you're so sweet.
I know.
Humble...be humble...lol!
But I was joking. I liked him just the way he was.
Don't go outside today. It's raining like it's the end of the world.
You too.
I'll let you go. Think of me touching, kissing, licking, and sucking all over your body.
His words were too hot. I felt a rush jolt between my legs as if he was actually there doing it.
Already feeling you!
I'm going to take a cold shower. Kissing you like crazy. TKLS
What's TKLS?
Touching, kissing, licking, sucking.
Got it. Now I'm going to take a cold shower too.
Staring at his text, I knew I had imagined things for sure. I had worried for nothing...I hoped.
"Did you order pizza, Jenna? I'm starving," Kate asked.
"Oh...I'm on it." I snapped out of Max's world and called for pizza.

♥♥

With a good restful sleep, I got up early and decided that I was finally going to use the key Max had given me. He had told me many times before that he didn't want to push me. Perhaps that was one of the reasons why he seemed a bit distant lately. Since it was early Sunday morning and knowing the likelihood of Max still being in bed, I wanted to surprise him.

Leaving a note to let Becky know what I was doing, I slipped out of the apartment quietly. Making sure I had Max's key, I drove to his place. As excitement brewed inside me, my heart pounded at the thought of how surprised Max would be. I knew he would be thrilled, so I was overly excited and could hardly contain myself from the anticipation of what I was doing.

As the elevator sped up to this floor, I held the key in my hand. When the door slid open, I stepped out and turned left. What I saw next dropped my jaw, turning my world upside down. Completely shocked, I froze as blood drained out of my body, and I felt my heart rip out of my chest.

A gorgeous blonde was striding down the hallway toward me...more like toward the elevator...buttoning her blouse. Upon seeing me, her eyes went to the key I held, and she plastered the biggest, satisfied, devious smirk on her face. Standing in front of me, she said, "You have one too. Well, you're right on time. You must be his Sunday. Don't forget the bananas, chocolate, and whipped cream. He really likes that." Then she got on the elevator.

Had there been another penthouse on that floor, I wouldn't have immediately thought she had come out of Max's door. But knowing his was the only dwelling on that floor, I didn't need to question it. Unable to breathe, the walls closed up on me and started to spin. As I gasped for air, I turned and pushed the elevator button with my trembling hand. I needed air. I needed to leave quickly, and get as far away from Max as possible.

Now it all was too clear...the texts and the phone calls. They had to have been from the blonde, and she must be Crystal. Max was...I couldn't even say the word. All I could think at that point was how I wasn't enough for him. Perhaps he needed someone more experienced, someone who could satisfy whatever his needs were.

Angrily pushing on the button, I felt unpleasant heat rush to my face, and I wanted to vomit as acid filled my stomach. Just as the elevator door opened, I heard Max's voice.

"Crystal, you forgot your jacket!"

I think he yelled. I wasn't sure since my body cringed as Max confirmed who she was. All I heard was the voice I no longer cared for. The voice that used to be soothing and calming was sickening me, burning inside me with hatred.

"Jenna?" He sounded shocked.

Blood rushed to my face and my pulse raced beyond control as I panicked. Looking straight ahead, I refused to look at him. I didn't want him to know I had given him my heart by being there and deciding to use the key.

"Jenna...Jenna," he called again.

I wanted to look at my Max, the Max that I had fallen in love with, but I couldn't. I didn't want to see the Max I hated, the Max that had hurt me to the point of no return. We were broken, unfixable. Not only did I not have him, I had lost the job that I loved too. Tomorrow would be my last day. I would give some reasonable excuse and quit. How could he do this to me...to us? Feeling nauseous again, I wanted to throw up.

I heard fast footsteps—or were they running steps?—and my name being called multiple times with desperation, pleading. As I stepped inside the elevator, I dropped the key, but I didn't care. I would never need it anymore. Then I heard a loud thump sound on the elevator door from Max apparently hitting it just as it closed. What was he angry for?

Stepping outside, the harsh wind lifted my hair and coat. I should have felt the freezing air, but I felt nothing, nor did I feel the pounding rain that was soaking me, drenching me as if I was taking a shower with my clothes on. Somehow I managed to take out my key and get in my car. As I pushed the gas pedal, I saw Max run out of the building, barefooted and topless, from the corner of my eyes.

What was the point of running after me? How stupid was he? No, how stupid was I? As I sped faster, trying to get home as soon as possible, the blonde kept invading my mind. All that I saw was his lips on hers, his body and his hands all over her. Things he did to me, he must have done to her. Then everything I'd felt with Max—his touch, his kisses, us making love—felt disgusting. All I wanted to do was go home and wash him away, out of my body, out of my mind, out of my heart.

The phone and the sound of my text kept ringing. Knowing it was Max, I didn't bother to check. After the lightning blinded my eyes, the thunder roared in anger, and the rain poured harder. I wanted them to strike me, to take me away from this unbearable pain. It should have struck me awhile back, to knock some sense into me. Turning on the fastest speed mode of the windshield wiper wasn't fast enough. I wasn't thinking...no, I was thinking, but only of Max and what he had done.

As my trembling hand dialed Becky's number, it hit me hard. Suddenly, the hurt crushed against my chest, squeezing my heart in agony. Max had cheated on me. The words came easily to my mind now that I was out of his place. Having the initial shock wear off put me back into reality, and tears suddenly started to fall, harder by the second, blinding my view.

Sobbing relentlessly, I heaved and gasped for air. I tried to wipe the tears that had drenched my face, but it didn't help as more gushed out, burning my eyes. There was so much pain! It hurt so much that I wanted to rip out my own heart. It was the strangest feeling. I could feel it pumping with misery that was making my muscles weak. My coordination and self-control were diminished, as grief had sickened them. My whole body shuddered and my mind and body were not in sync. Every inch of my body hurt like hell.

The pain was so excruciating, it felt as though a knife were peeling my heart away layer by layer, until now, there was nothing there. A hole occupied the space where my heart should be, and although I should have felt numb, I felt absolute, agonizing pain beyond words.

"Jenna?" I head from the speaker on my cell phone. Not knowing where my blue tooth was, I didn't even bother to look for it.

"Hello, Jenna? Can you hear me?"

"Becky...Max." My lips quivered so much that I could barely get the words out. "He...." Heaving, I was out of breath, and endless tears streamed down my face, strangling my words. Oh God! He lied to me. All those smooth, sweet words he whispered were lies. He was supposed to be my something great. How could he do this? Why? It was my fault. I let him in. I was the fool.

"Jenna, are you okay?" Her tone was concerned and desperate. "Are you crying?"

"Becky...Max...Max...." I couldn't even say the word "cheated." All I could do was continue to gasp for air and choke when I tried to speak, as uncontrollable tears would not stop. "She...blonde...Crystal...Max."

"Jenna, calm down. Are you driving?"

"Yes," I managed to say between loud gasps. My tears were pouring just as hard and fast as the rain, and I couldn't think, and I couldn't see.

"Stop the car! I'll come and get you. You shouldn't be driving in your condition. Tell me where you are."

I only heard half of what Becky said. I was almost home...I thought...though the road didn't look familiar. As I tried to focus and wipe the tears that were never ending, my phone flashed and beeped. It was from Max, and that made the ache and the tears worse. Even seeing his name affected me. I blinked and turned away for only a split second, but that second was crucial.

"Jenna...are you there?" I heard Becky...sort of.

It happened so fast there was no time to react. Breaking as hard as I could upon seeing the red light, my car hydroplaned to the right. The oncoming car, which had the right of way, had nowhere to go as I came toward it, and our cars collided. On impact, I felt the air bag explode in my face, jerking my body back in full force. Feeling the car tumble multiple times, I was sure death would find me as I fell into darkness. At least now I will find peace.

M. Clarke

Chapter 35

Briefly opening my eyes, I noted that I was in a hospital room. Trying to recall what had happened and why I was there, I wanted to reach over to call for the nurse, but my eyelids were so heavy, I had no control as they closed again.

As I floated in and out of consciousness, I could hear conversations, but they sounded muddled, and I could only hear bits here and there. If I was lucky, sometimes I heard full sentences.

"What the hell did you do?" Becky's tone was stern, but she spoke quietly, as if she didn't want to disturb me.

"This is my fault. I should have told her when it happened."

It was Max. He had followed me to the hospital. The place that held my heart was utterly empty, to the point I couldn't feel anything anymore. My heart was gone; my feelings for him were destroyed at his place.

Their voices sounded jumbled and confusing. I wanted to let them know I was okay, but I couldn't move. I couldn't open my eyes. Everything about me was heavy, as if I had sunk into the mattress. Perhaps it was from the drugs they had given me. Or…oh God…please don't let me be paralyzed!

"You could have avoided this. Why didn't you stop her from leaving?" Becky sounded like she was yelling at him, but in a silent way. She was still furious at him. Since I couldn't do it, I was glad she was able to do it for me.

"I tried. But she was already by the elevator door. I tried to tail her, but it was difficult to find her in the rain, and I think she got lost. When I heard the ambulance I just had this bad feeling, and I followed it. Did you call her parents?"

Becky let out a deep sigh. "No. They're in the middle of the ocean somewhere. I can't get ahold of them."

"It's okay. I'll take care of her."

"The hell you are. I'm here. You can leave." There was a long pause. "Sorry. You should've told her. She's a big girl. She's not as fragile as you think. We can take turns staying with her, but I don't want you here when she wakes up. She'll probably fall back into a coma just from the sight of you. Not until after I explain, or you explain to her first, or...I don't know. You weren't on that phone call. You didn't hear her cry. You didn't feel her pain like I did."

Why was she being nice to him? And what did she mean by explaining it to me? Explain what? There was nothing to explain. I thought Becky was crying, and I thought I was crying too...at least on the inside, because I couldn't feel any wetness on my face. In fact, I couldn't feel my body.

Throughout the day, as I drifted in and out of sleep, I knew Nicole, Kate, and even Matthew had visited me. Poor Matthew. I wondered if he and I could still be friends...maybe not. It would probably be too painful. He would remind me of Max and his family...and of how awful this situation was. This indicated even more how I needed to quit my job.

"Max...go home. I'll call you if there are any changes." Becky sounded tired.

"No. I'm staying here. I'm not leaving her. Why don't you go get something to eat? Or you can go home and rest."

"Okay," Becky agreed. "I'll go to the cafeteria and get something for the both of us."

Why was Becky being nice to him? What was wrong with her? Did she not hear what I was trying to tell her over the phone? Then I wondered if Max had fed her lies.

My left hand was lifted off the bed, and the warm feeling indicated Max was holding it. I wanted to yank it away, but I couldn't no matter how hard I tried. I didn't want to be touched by him.

"Jenna," he called softly as he stroked my hair away from my face. "I don't know if you can hear me, but I need you to know. I'm just going to say it, and hope that you are awake in there even though your body isn't responding."

There was a pause and a sigh. "I didn't cheat on you. I promise on my own life that I didn't. The woman you saw was my ex girlfriend. Her name is Crystal. She had the spare key to my penthouse, and when we broke up, I asked for it back. She gave it back, but she had made another copy...I guess. That's the only explanation I could think of. Anyway...she came inside without me knowing, and snuck into bed with me. I thought it was you at first, but when I realized who it was I kicked her out.

"She left her jacket, so I ran after her because I didn't want any of her possessions inside my place, especially since I'm with you. When she found out I was dating you, she kept on texting and calling me. She threatened to break us apart; and not only that, she threatened to charge me with sexual harassment. Knowing her, she would follow through with her words.

"You see Jenna, you replaced her. Mrs. Ward probably told you that the lady before you took a permanent leave of absence. That wasn't the case. Mrs. Ward fired her shortly after we broke up...not because of the break up, of course, but because of her work ethics. I should have told you what was happening from the start, but I wanted to keep you away from all of this. I thought I was protecting you. I didn't know it would turn out like this. I swear nothing happened. Please don't let her win. You and I are meant to be together. I feel this to the depth of my heart and soul. We belong together."

Max paused and gripped my hand tighter to one side of his cheek. "I'll cry...I'll beg...I'll get down on my knees and crawl to you if I must; I'll do all of these and much more, just to show you my love for you. Please...wake up. I need you, Jenna. I've never needed anyone the way I need you." His tone was closer. It sounded like he was right in front of me. "I don't ever pray, but I'm praying now. If God could just give me you, I'll never ask for anything else. Please come back to me. We've only just begun. We can get through this. We're not broken…this can be fixed. I'll fix it for us. I've never felt this strongly for anyone before. I can clearly say with all my heart that I love you. I know this seems too soon, but I can't help the way I feel. I feel like I've known you all my life, and my past lives if reincarnation is real. And I can say with certainty that I've loved you all the life times ago, and never stopped loving you even after death. Every lifetime, I was searching for you…my something great."

Max said he loved me? As I took in all of his words, the hole in my heart started to fill up; fill up with his words, his love for me, and his tears that fell on my cheek. The clarity of all that had happened was like a Band-Aid over my wounds.

My Max was crying. He needed me. I should have stayed and listened, but anyone in my position would have run…I think. The irony of all this was that it could have been avoided, just like when Max took off when Luke kissed me. Misunderstandings and bad timing had definitely gotten in our way a couple of times. We had to stop this. I needed to tell him how I felt, and move forward with our relationship.

He was right. We were not broken. This could be fixed…if only I could just wake up. And the thought of me being paralyzed scared me to death. What if I was? I would have to let Max go. It wouldn't be fair for him…though if the roles were reversed, I would still be with him. I couldn't be…oh please God…give me one more chance. Then something worse came to my thoughts. What if I never woke up? Please God…not now…I want to live. I want to live a full life with Max. My parents, friends, and Max needed me, and I needed them. But I couldn't think anymore, I couldn't hold on any longer. I fell back to sleep, or worse…coma.

I don't know how or why it suddenly happened, and I don't know how long I was out, but my toes and fingers twitched. Max must have felt it while he continued to hold my hand.

"Jenna?" He sounded excited. "Can you hear me?"

I couldn't speak right away, but I managed to squeeze just a little.

"Squeeze me again," he ordered.

With all the strength I could give, I did.

Max let go of my hand, cupped my face, and kissed me on my lips softly and tenderly. "I'm calling the nurse."

By the time the doctor came into my room, I was groggy and weak. Blinking my eyes to open them, my vision slowly became clear. Focusing on the person in front of me, I felt disappointed to see a doctor instead of Max. Where was Max? Was it all just a dream?

"How are you feeling?" the doctor asked, flashing something bright into my eyes, blinding me.

"I think I'm okay." My voice sounded hoarse and hardly audible...at least to my ears.

"Can you move your legs?"

It was difficult to do so, but they moved and I could feel them. What a relief! As the doctor asked more questions, he examined me, and informed me that I was out for two days. From my peripheral vision, I could see Becky smiling at me, her eyes sparkling from the tears pooling in her eyes.

After the doctor left and told me I would be just fine, I breathed a sigh of relief, and Becky did not waste a second to give me the biggest hug, along with some tears.

"You're going to be okay," she assured me. "Nicole and Kate came by. I just called them, so they know you'll be fine. We were all so worried. Why didn't you listen to me? I was on my way to pick your dumb ass up."

"Sorry," I said, looking up at the IV bag. I felt so bad for causing trouble and making everyone worry.

"Anyway, the doctor said he wants to observe you for twenty four hours, and then you can go home. You have a very bad concussion. You were drifting in and out of a coma, and we didn't know if you would come out of it. But you'll be fine. Thank

God…I couldn't even call your parents." Becky took a deep breath.

Seeing the worried look in her eyes disappear, I felt much better and less guilty…sort of. "Becky…where's my car?"

"Jenna…you're gonna need a new car."

"That bad, huh?"

Becky nodded. "You're so lucky your body didn't end up looking like your car. Don't think about that now, okay? You need to rest."

Nodding, I agreed. I also didn't want to think about the cost right now. It would only upset me even more. "Becky…was Max ever here?" I asked timidly. I was wishing with all my heart that it wasn't a dream and all that he had said was real.

"Yes. But I told him not to be in here when you woke up. I didn't want his presence to affect your recovery. I thought if you saw him first, you would purposely slip back into coma," she giggled lightly. "Before you think anything, it wasn't what you thought had happened. Please…just listen to what he has to say."

Hearing Becky's words confirmed that Max had explained his side of the story to Becky. Now I understood why she wasn't mad at him when I was able to hear bits of their conversation. And happily, everything I heard from Max was real.

"Okay…can you tell him I want to see him, and can you give us a moment?"

"Sure. I'll go get him," she smiled, then speedily left the room.

"Hey," Max said softly, standing by the door with one hand inside his pockets, and holding a small brown paper bag with the other, shrugging sheepishly. He looked so tired and worn, just like Becky. His stubbles along the line of his jaws were enough to bring out my sex drive, so I focused elsewhere.

Clearing my throat, I suddenly got really shy. A part of that shyness was due to my stupidity of running away instead of…but what could I have done? "Why are you standing there? Come closer," I said softly.

Seeing Max pace toward me after he closed the door behind him made my heart race, and if the heart monitor was still attached to me, I'm sure it would have warned the nurses. Max's smile was gone when he placed the brown paper bag behind him and placed his bottom on a chair. He sat close to me, but not next to me, as if he was afraid I would hurt him, or maybe that he would hurt me.

Max raked his hair back, folded his hands together as if almost begging, and released a heavy sigh. "Jenna. I need you to listen. Please...don't shut me out. You need to hear everything before you sentence me to death." His words were spoken slowly, cautiously, as he studied my facial expressions.

I raised my brows regarding his last sentence. He was exaggerating of course, but somehow he made it sound cute, coming out of his mouth with that smirking expression on his face at the end.

"Max, before you start, I want you to know that I already know some of the things you're about to tell me. I heard you when I was drifting in and out of sleep." I could have let him shake a little and have him wondering if I would forgive him, but already knowing some parts of the truth, I didn't have the heart to be malicious like that.

His eyes lit up, looking hopeful, and a smile that had disappeared, reappeared. "Okay," he nodded, inching the chair closer to me...scooting...scooting...now next to me. "Let me start from the beginning so you will get the full story. I don't want any misunderstanding between us. My past isn't rosy and full of lollipops like yours. I didn't do anything bad, but I had fun. You're the angel and I'm the devil...I think...sort of...if you want to define the differences between our past, that is."

Max held my hand and explained everything again. We told each other that we were sorry, and that we had to learn to communicate better. It was the key in having a successful relationship. Speaking of which, he told me Matthew helped him take care of changing the lock to his place, and he had also taken care of Crystal...basically, he had paid her off. Max didn't tell me how much, but I didn't want to know. I just wanted the past behind us. And they also hadn't gone golfing that day, they'd had a meeting with a lawyer regarding sexual harassment policy.

He also told me that nobody at work knew about what had happened. He told my team that I was on a special assignment, and that I would be working from home for a week or more. I thought that was very thoughtful of him. That would come in handy, especially since I needed to shop for a car too. Knowing that even his parents didn't know made me feel better, since his dad was the main boss. Though I wasn't happy about any of the situation, I didn't have a choice. I had to let Max take care of it this time.

After he had told me everything he wanted to say, there was a long comfortable silence between us as he held my hand and looked at me as if he hadn't seen me in months. Since all was well, I wanted to be in his arms again. "Max."

"What is it, babe?"

I loved it when he called me that. It somehow made me feel special. "Lay with me."

Max immediately stood up and eyed the bed, most likely thinking how he was going to do it. As I scooted over, he grabbed the brown paper bag and lay sideways next to me. My back touched his front, and the curve of our bodies molded perfectly together. Feeling his arms around me made this all real, and from one loving touch to another, I knew without a doubt we would heal.

"Max?"

"Yes, Jenna."

"What's inside the bag?"

Max chuckled. "It's your favorite. If my words couldn't convince you, I thought maybe the heart-shaped Rice Krispies Treat could."

As I giggled, I heard ruffling sounds. I knew Max was taking it out of the bag. Propping up, he placed it front of me. "Lunch buddies share feelings, stories, and goodies, and unfortunately, sometimes they share tears and heart aches, but they never forget why they were lunch buddies in the first place, and what sharing truly means."

A tear trickled from the corner of my eye as his words tugged my heart in a happy and sad way. To think I'd almost lost what I was feeling and who was holding me at that moment. I sure did something stupid, and I vowed to never to run again.

"Don't cry," Max said softly, wiping the tear with his thumb before it fell to my pillow. "You know how I don't like to see you cry."

"Don't worry, Max. They are happy tears."

"Jenna," Max called softly, laying back down after he placed the Rice Krispies Treat back into the bag.

"Yes, Max."

"I was really happy that you came, but I wasn't happy about what happened."

"I know…me too."

"Don't run next time."

"Next time?"

"I'm joking."

"You—"

"I made you smile."

"No need to crack a joke. Just the sight of you makes me smile."

Max held me tighter. That was his reply, but his reply lingered as he found a way to slide his naughty hand through the open slit of the hospital gown I was wearing. Gasping lightly, I felt his warm hand on my stomach, inching higher and higher, sending shivers everywhere he touched.

"Max?"

"Yes, Jenna."

"What are you doing?" I yawned, trying not to make it obvious that I was. Though I was tired, Max's hand was keeping me wide awake.

"I'm not doing anything, Jenna. It's my hand. Bad hand. Shall I tell it to stop?"

Now his hand was under the base of my breast as his index finger gingerly caressed back and forth, making me moan, making me want him even in my weak condition. I wanted to say no, but he'd stopped.

"Sorry…I couldn't help myself. Every part of me missed you, my heart…my mind…and my body." His tone was somber and sincere that I felt the depth of his sadness. Then his tone changed. "I had a talk with my naughty hand. It didn't want to stop, but I told it there would be another chance."

Giggling, I intertwined my hand in his, feeling the same. I'd missed him more than he could possible know. "Hot, Max," I said wearily, trying to tell him he was making me hot down there.

"I know," he chuckled. And though I couldn't see his expression, I knew he had a smirk on his face. "You can call me that anytime, babe."

Feeling drained from what I had endured, I could feel myself drifting to sleep. But before I did, I needed Max to know. I needed for him to hear it from me. He had expressed how much he cared for me many times before, and though I may have spoken through my actions, which spoke volumes, hearing the words would touch his heart, too.

"Max."

"Yes, Jenna."

"You're my something great, Max."

Feeling his breath release as his chest rose and fell on my back, he squeezed me tenderly but tighter, and that was his reply.

Chapter 36

A day later, I was released from the hospital, and Max picked me up and drove me home. I asked him to stay and he happily agreed. When I opened the front door, I was completely speechless.

"Welcome home," they all said in accord, surprising me. Becky, Nicole, Kate, and even Matthew were waiting for me by the door. Max must have let them know we were on our way. I had seen him texting when we stepped inside the elevator.

My eyes glistened with joy in seeing those people I called my family. Not only that, the familiar scent that I loved filled me up. Multiple vases of red roses were set everywhere I looked. "Max?"

"They're not just from me. Your friends wanted to be included."

"Thank you," I said genuinely, and I wanted to cry.

After the hugs, we all sat around the living room. After an hour, Nicole and Kate left. Nicole had asked for an extended lunch, and Kate needed to go home since her mother-in-law was watching her daughter, and she didn't want to be out too long.

When dinnertime came around, Matthew ordered from a Chinese restaurant that their family ordered from quite often. Though they didn't normally do home delivery, they made a special exception for us.

With a light blanket over me, Max wouldn't let me get up except to use the restroom, and even then he followed me.

Propping me up with pillows behind my back, he placed my plate on my lap.

Sitting next to me, he made sure I was comfortable, and occasionally fed me too. He was so sweet, even though I was perfectly fine to do everything for myself. After dinner, Max and I cuddled on the sofa. Becky and Matthew were sitting on the opposite side, but I could feel the chemistry between them.

Occasionally, while observing them, I would see Becky's eyes shift to Matthew, and when he'd gaze at her, she would quickly focus on something else. There were moments of shy stolen glances, and the conversation was minimal between them.

Max and I looked at each other, and I knew from his expression he saw and felt the same way as me. It wasn't just my imagination. I wasn't sure what Max was thinking at that point, but he lifted me off the sofa.

"Max," I squealed.

"Time for bed."

"What? I'm not tired."

"Let's rest in your room." Max winked and gestured his eyes toward Matthew. Then I understood.

"Thanks for coming, Matthew," I said.

"See you later, Jenna," Matthew smiled.

"Later, Becky," I muttered.

Becky gave me a lost puppy look, and if I could have read her thoughts she would be asking me what she was supposed to do with Matthew. Instead of saving her, I winked at her. She gave me a pouting look that only made me giggle. It was the first time I had seen Becky so nervous. After Max took us into my room, we didn't go to bed. We stood by the door like two mischievous spying children.

"Excuse me," Becky said politely to Matthew, bumping into him. Matthew had stood up just as Becky passed him to clear the paper plates off the coffee table.

"That's okay. You can pretend to bump into me anytime," Matthew said playfully.

With paper plates in her hands, she turned. "What?" Becky's brows arched with confusion. "I didn't pretend," she giggled lightly, and shook her head as if that was the most ridiculous thing she'd heard. Then she headed toward the kitchen. "You wish I did. Maybe you got up purposely to bump into me," she mumbled to herself, but Matthew had heard since he was right behind her.

"Oh...I know you did," Matthew said.

Becky swung around, and I think accidently slammed the used paper plates onto his sweater. Either that or she was a great actress who looked astounded from what had happened. Not only did they smear on his sweater, the left overs dropped to the floor. Thank goodness we had wooden floors.

Matthew just stood there with his eyes wide, not moving a muscle. Instead of apologizing, Becky went straight to the kitchen and came back with paper towels. I guessed she felt bad and only needed a second to cool off. Giving one to Matthew, with the other she got down on her knees to clean up the mess. Standing above her, as Matthew dusted off the leftovers stuck on his sweater with the paper towel, they fell on Becky's hair.

Biting her lips from irritation, she lifted her head, which put his precious jewels right in front of her face. Though I couldn't see Becky's face turning red, I knew she would be blushing because I would have turned beyond red myself.

"Nice view, isn't it?" Matthew chuckled lightly.

Becky's fists were folded as she stood up. Crossing her arms, she looked straight at him. "I've seen better."

"We'll see about that," he said arrogantly, with a hint of challenge in his tone.

"I don't think so," she snarled, leaning on one side of her hips. Unexpectedly, Matthew slipped out of his sweater.

Becky froze, her eyes on his chest, admiring, most likely throbbing between her legs. Matthew's chest was just as firm and sexy looking as Max's. Max was already holding me, but he used his other hand to cover my eyes. "You don't need to see that."

"Max," I whispered so they couldn't hear me as I tugged his hand away. I wasn't interested in seeing Matthew. I wanted to see what Becky would do next. This was like watching a soap opera, though I really didn't watch them. I'd only heard about them.

"Are you going to stand there and undress the rest of me with your eyes, or are you going to help me wash this off? Cause I have a date, and I don't think she'll appreciate me smelling like Chinese food."

Becky peered up again with a heated expression in her eyes. If steam could have come out of her head, it would have. "I'm not going to help you wash your sweater. It was your fault in the first place," she snapped. "Go to the kitchen and wash it off yourself; or better yet, ask your date, who's dumb enough to go out with you." Then she headed to her room.

"Don't be jealous. I can cancel my date and go out with you instead." Matthew's tone was smooth and relaxed. He was enjoying seeing Becky all wired up way too much.

"Jealous?" Becky turned around after she opened her bedroom door. "If you were the last man in the universe, I still wouldn't go out with you." Then she slammed the door.

Shaking his head, he chuckled. "Bye, Max and Jenna. I know you were watching. Invite Becky to our family dinner next time. I'm going out. See you later." Then he was out the door.

Giggling, I turned to Max. "Is your brother this charming to all the girls?"

"Not this much." Max rolled his eyes, and as he held my hand, he led us to my bed. Pulling the blanket aside, he gestured for me to get in first. As we snuggled, we started laughing again.

"Matt hasn't dated seriously in a while," Max started to say. "About two years ago, the girl he fell in love with died from a car accident. Her name was Tessa. They had a fight and she ran off like you in the pouring rain. So you'll have to excuse him for not being there for you. He did stop by, but he couldn't stay. It was just too much for him."

"That's okay, Max. I didn't even expect him to come. So what happened?"

Max laced his fingers through mine and kissed the back of them. "She fell into a coma, and eventually her organs gave up.

Afterward, he was a mess. He drank his sorrows away and bummed around. I don't blame him. I would've done the same if that had happened to you. That was the reason why he was gone for a year. My parents and I thought it was good for him to just get away from life. We were hoping he would heal and find himself again...and I think it did help him. I just didn't expect him to be gone that long. Anyway, before Tessa, Matt was irresponsible, but when he dated her, he was a different person. I really liked her. She was good for him. I know he's still in pain, but I also know he's healing and dealing with it."

Recalling that night of Thanksgiving when Matthew had said a prayer before the meal and got all choked up, I now knew the reason why. He was thinking of her. How difficult it must be for him. I recalled the pain when I thought Max was cheating on me; Matthew's pain must have been a thousand times worse. I couldn't imagine losing Max.

"Thanks for sharing Matthew's story."

"I wouldn't share this with anyone, Jenna. You're not just anyone...you understand?" He tilted my face by placing his index finger underneath my chin and tenderly stroked my lips with his.

"Yes. I understand," I smiled, gliding my hand over the curve of his bicep.

"Don't ever do anything stupid like that again...ever. I thought I'd lost you. Sometimes we'll have obstacles in our path, but that doesn't mean it can't be fixed. Yell, hit, or punch me...just don't get yourself hurt, or I'll never be able to forgive myself. I'm not saying there will be a reason too. Relationships are never perfect, and sometimes we may fight, but we'll always make up...okay?"

"Okay," I nodded. "I'm sorry to put you through all that." And I really was. Now, knowing what Matthew went through, being close to his brother, I was sure Max was right beside him going through the pain. Trying to help him move on must have been difficult too. I could only imagine what he was thinking and how he was feeling when I was in a coma. My poor Max!

"You don't need to apologize. You just need to trust me. I know there are rumors about me, but they're not true. Women threw themselves at me and expected me to love them, but I felt nothing, no connection, and no spark of wanting forever with them…until you came along." He paused to caress my face. "And even when I let them know how I felt, they didn't care, and somehow it's my fault." Then he changed the subject. "What shall we do with Becky and Matt?" Max chuckled. "Clearly there is something there. I've never seen him act like that before…I mean after losing Tessa…unless the trip changed him."

"I don't know, Max. Becky will eat him alive if he's like that around her." I shook my head, already envisioning what their future encounters may be like.

"I'll have to have a little talk with my little brother. Man…I'm not that arrogant, am I?"

"Hmmm…not arrogant, just confident," I replied.

"What does that mean?" He narrowed his eyes at me playfully.

"Nothing…just…hot Max," I said shyly, and stuck my finger in my mouth. I was recalling those times when he got me all heated up, the first time I saw him, the time I ran into him at Café Express, the restroom, and at his office. All those passionate, blazing moments before we even kissed.

Those two words got him excited. "Don't forget that," he said with conviction, and took my finger out of mouth, only to put it into his.

"Bad, Max," I whispered, as tingles shot through me from head to toe. It was intense, producing raw pleasure. After I got all heated up and the urge between my legs burned, he let go. He had done that on purpose. Really bad…bad…bad Max, but he was mine, mine to hold, mine to keep, and mine to love.

Becky was right. I would rather love hard and get hurt, than not really love at all…but in my case, it was different. I got the happy ending. I didn't know what I was missing until Max entered my life, and I was glad he'd found me. When you know you've found the one, your whole life changes. The mind, body, and soul connect and become one. No obstacle is as bad as it seemed, because you know that together you can conquer what life throws at you.

The storm had finally died down and the sun found its way up again. It was never too dark or gloomy in Los Angeles, and just like anything in life, the sun always did come up…sometimes when you least expected it to.

"Get some rest, Jenna. I'll be right here. I'm not going anywhere. When you feel better, I'll take you car shopping."

"Okay," I said, nuzzling into his arms as I thought about how much damage this would do to my bank account.

Oh…." Max reached inside his pocket and took out a key that was hooked to a key chain. "Matt helped me changed the locks. I want you to have it, but I'll understand if you don't want it right away."

"Thanks, Max. I'm ready for it. I don't want to wait," I said as I took it from his hand and traced over the words "Something Great."

Max's eyes expressed happiness, and he gave me the big, irresistible grin he did so well, making my heart and stomach flip like crazy. Then he leaned in and gave me a tender kiss on my forehead.

Holding the keychain inside the palm of my hand, I cuddled closer to him and closed my eyes to welcome sleep. Ever since I'd laid my eyes on him, I'd never touched the ground. All the things my mom had said to me over the phone reminded me of Max. To me, Max was, according to her words, someone I could not live without. Max was without a doubt my something great…and together…we would be…something wonderful.

M. Clarke

Something Wonderful—February 10, 2014

Enjoy—Max's point of view

BONUS PAGE—Max's Point of View

Leaning forward, I rested my elbows on the banister. From the second level, I had a better vision of the attendees below. It was the same party year after year, and the crowd was pretty much the same. I decided to hang out up here alone. Had I been down there with the crowd, I would've been surrounded by models, and I certainly didn't want Jenna to see me as a player. Checking my watch, I searched for Jenna. She should be walking through that door any minute if the traffic was bearable.

Recalling sitting next to her during the fashion show, I'd loved watching her facial expressions. Her eyes gleamed with excitement and that beautiful smile of hers that melted my heart made me blush. I did enjoy the fashion show this time around, but only because I had the most amazing company.

Jenna was different. She was everything I wanted as my partner for life. She was independent, beautiful, and kind hearted. It was rare to find a woman like her in my line of business. Most of them just wanted to get into my pants, use me for status, or wanted my money, but with Jenna, I could feel that it was genuine. Not that she even cared about me that way, but I would change that soon.

Though she would never know, I had sent my secretary an email asking Mrs. Ward, the human resources director, to request Jenna to represent the Knights at the New York Fashion Show. I wanted to make her dreams come true. A remarkable woman like her truly deserved this opportunity, and I was happy to do it…more for my selfish want and need. I even made sure we were on the same flight and stayed at the same hotel. Seeing that my room was bigger, I'd asked the receptionist to switch them when I checked in.

Just when I was starting to get worried, I spotted something red. It was Jenna. Just at that moment my heart flipped and sizzled. The dress shaped her body seductively, and the way her hair was swept up made her look sexy as hell. God, how I wanted to run my hands all over her, but I had to stop thinking with my urge. Chuckling to myself, I continued to admire her.

As she glided across the floor, all eyes were glued to her, taking in her beauty. I couldn't blame them, for I was doing the same. Holding up her dress enough to walk comfortably, she looked so nervous and shy. I could tell she was searching for someone…perhaps me?

Knowing she didn't know anyone besides our group, I should have gone to her right away so she wouldn't feel alone, but I couldn't help myself. I wanted to wait and enjoy my view, and plus…I was in my playful mood.

I texted her.

She looked surprised and reached into her purse.

Hello, lady in red. You look breathtaking. I could just stare at you all night.

Who are you?

She didn't have my number. This was going to be fun. *You don't know? Shame on you!*

Sorry!

You should put your hair up like that more often.

Why?

It would be easier for me to nibble on your ear.

Okay…you either know me well or….

If you want to know, look to your left.

Jenna turned to her left, but I wasn't thinking straight…I should have told her to turn right. Instead of finding me, she found Jake. Growling sound escaped my mouth. I didn't want her to think those texts were from him so I quickly texted her, but she didn't respond. I kept texting.

Jake was gawking at her, smiling a dorky smile. Okay…it wasn't dorky, but I was jealous. Her smile was warm, but she looked surprised. Maybe she was thrown off at the idea that it was from him. Jake reached for her, pressing his body against her. I didn't like that at all. Good thing I wasn't nearby…I would've punched him hard or shoved him out of the way. Great…I'm not the violent type…what was I thinking?

They exchanged words and she even giggled shyly. He must have been complimenting her; well, if he was half a man he should, even though I didn't like what he could be saying to her to make her cheeks red. Feeling irritated, and thinking I should have gone to her instead, I kept texting…and she finally picked up her phone.

Not that left, the other left. And I hope you're not disappointed it wasn't Jake.

I guess I shouldn't have texted that part, but before I even thought about it, I had already pressed send.

Where? Do I even know you?

That's not a nice thing to say. Look up.

She looked confused and upset, but her frowning lips looked too adorable. I just wanted to lick, bite, and suck them. Twisting and shifting her eyes, they finally went to the right direction. Then…bam! Our eyes locked and I gave her the most heartfelt smile. A feeling that I couldn't describe tickled my heart and spread throughout every vein in my body. And she was reeling me in with just one simple look.

There was no denying it…she took my breath away. It was as if she sucked me into a tunnel where only she and I existed, staring into each other's soul…if that was even possible. It felt like I'd known her all my life. There was an undeniable connection, and the most frightening part of it was that she owned me at that moment. Yup…I was a love sick fool and I would do anything for this woman.

My ego got bigger when she couldn't seem to peel her eyes off me. I could see her chest rise and fall just as fast as mine. There was hope that I could charm her to go out with me, though she had turned me down many times before. But I knew deep down inside she wanted to say yes. It was the only reason I was being relentless. Regardless, I would do anything to show her how special she was to me and that we belong together. I would find a way to convince her.

Before she walked away or decided to hang out with Jake, I had to make my move. Still locking my eyes on her so she knew I meant business, I paced toward her, steadily and slowly. With every step I took, her eyes radiated brighter, and she was taking my presence in…just what I was hoping for. I was going after her and nothing was going to stop me. Then…shit! I broke my gaze when someone kept calling my name. Jenna turned away with sadness in her eyes, and my heart did not like that at all.

M. Clarke

Enjoy a teasers from:
Pretty Little Lies by Jennifer Miller
Smash Into You by Shelly Crane
Diary of a One-night Stand by Alexandrea Weiss
Crossroads by Mary Ting (me)

M. Clarke

Sneak Peek
Pretty Little Lies
by Jennifer Miller—Out now
www.facebook.com/JenMillerWrites

"This club is amazing!" I can't keep from looking around, trying to take it all in. "How long did you say it has been open?"

"Not long, maybe a couple weeks now." Pyper speaks loudly into my ear to be heard over the loud thump of the bass, "There was an article in the social section of the Tribune talking about the opening I guess, but I didn't see it. A restaurant that closed down a while ago was here and the owner did a complete renovation, it seems. Caroline was talking about it at the spa the other day."

"Well I'm really impressed, it's fabulous. I'm glad we came."

The bartender hands us our drinks and Pyper pulls bills out of her bra and slaps them on the counter. The bartender grins slyly at her, but Pyper turns and we start making our way to look for seats. With perfect timing, a few girls have just vacated a couch, so we snag their places before someone else beats us to it.

Pyper turns to me, takes a sip of her drink and then asks, "What article are you working on right now?"

"Funny you should ask, because I thought I would ask for your help on this one. I'm working on an article for *Martini* magazine. Each month, their magazine is comprised of a lot of sex related articles, along with the usual fashion fluff and celebrity interview." I take a sip of my drink and continue, "The article I'm working on is *Things You Should Never Say to a Guy.* Want to weigh in?"

M. Clarke

Pyper immediately smiles devilishly at me, "Absolutely. What do you have so far?"

"Well of course the worst thing you can say to a guy is, 'Is it in yet?'"

Pyper laughs loudly, almost spitting out her drink in the process, "Yes! Definitely not a good thing to say! You may as well kill him instead. Less painful!"

Her reaction has me laughing too, "True. That would certainly be more humane! I don't think I could ever do that to a poor guy! Next is the ever popular, 'It's not you, it's me.'"

Pyper laughs and then admits, "I may or may not have used that line once or twice myself."

"Why does this not surprise me, Pyper?"

"Hi ladies, excuse the interruption, but can I get you another drink?" A very petite blonde-haired waitress asks us, interrupting our conversation. Pyper answers, "That would be great! We are drinking vodka cranberries. Thanks!"

"Sure. Be right back."

"Okay Olivia, what else have you got?"

"How about 'Does this make me look fat?'"

"Oh! There are sixteen thousand possible answers to that question and any one a guy would mutter would be incorrect."

"Exactly!" I laugh.

"How about 'Size really *does* matter!'" Pyper suggests.

I snort at that one! "Yes, that or, 'That's it?'"

Pyper and I laugh so hard we can barely breathe!

While we are trying to catch our breath, a couple of guys walk up and stand in front of us. We look up into their smiling faces to see one guy has blonde hair and blue eyes, while the other has brown hair and brown eyes. They aren't bad looking and they seem friendly. "Hi ladies, my name is Dylan and this is my buddy Ken. We couldn't help but see you two laughing over here and we thought we would come over to see if we could be let in on the joke," says blondie.

"Yeah. What are you two hot girls laughing so hard about?" says Ken. I really want to ask him where Barbie is. That would be rude though, and cheesy.

Pyper looks at me with a smirk. "Actually, I bet you boys would be able to contribute to our conversation. My friend Olivia here is writing an article for *Martini* magazine about the things a woman should never say to a guy. Care to weigh in?"

They both take seats, a little too closely, one on either side of us and we proudly tell them the answers we already have.

"Well you forgot, 'You remind me of my Dad,'" Dylan suggests.

"Ewww! Don't tell me you've actually heard that before!" Pyper gasps while wrinkling her nose in disgust.

Dylan just shrugs in answer, and Pyper and I giggle in response.

Ken says, "Oh my personal favorite, 'Oh my God, thank you for the drink! I can't believe the bouncer fell for my fake ID.'"

We all break into hysterics. I can't help but ask, "Oh my gosh! What did you do?"

Ken looks at me like that is a crazy question, "Well I ran, of course."

We all laugh harder, the alcohol we've consumed adding to the humor.

"Good contributions guys, thanks for being such good sports." I definitely have some good material for my article.

While we've been chatting, the waitress returned with our replacement drinks we ordered, plus Ken and Dylan bought an additional round as well, slippery nipple shots for all of us. I'm definitely starting to feel more than just a buzz. I'm slightly nauseated and realize I haven't eaten anything since we had a light lunch of a salad at the spa. Not good.

"So tell us ladies, how good of friends are you?" Ken asks raising his brows at us.

"We are best friends, pretty much sisters," Pyper says. "Why do you ask?"

Ken looks at Dylan and the look they exchange makes me feel uneasy. "We were just wondering if maybe we could interest you in a foursome. You are both gorgeous, and with the way you two were laughing and talking with us, I know you find us attractive too, so what do you say the four of us get out of here and go make some fun of our own?" Dylan asks.

Pyper and I look at each other, totally grossed out and speechless.

"Hell to the no." I tell them.

Before they can utter a response, Pyper tugs on my arm, "Come on, let's go get our dance on!"

I smile and nod at her, words seem beyond my ability at the moment.

Pyper grabs my hand, tows me to the dance floor, and keeps going until we are in the middle of the moving mass of bodies, safely escaping the two creepers we left sitting on the couch. The speakers are blaring techno music and it feels like it's echoing inside and outside my head. I close my eyes, trying to center myself and end up losing myself to the music. I raise my arms above my head and move my body to the beat. Pyper links her fingers with mine so we can make sure we stay together and not get pushed apart. I squeeze her hands gently and keep dancing.

I feel a body come up behind me, pressing flush against mine and it startles me. I open my eyes just in time to see Pyper being pushed flush against the front of my body because Ken is behind her pressing himself against her, which means the asshole at my back is Dylan. "What the hell?" Pyper asks.

"Dance with me baby," Dylan slurs into my ear.

Dylan grabs my hips and slams his pelvis into my ass. I can feel his erection against me, and I am immediately uncomfortable and pissed off. "Pyper...let's go."

"Guys, we don't want to dance, we are going to head home," Pyper tries reasoning with them.

"I don't think so," says Ken. "You ladies have been teasing us all night, we know you want us, now let's dance." Ken smashes his hips into Pyper's ass, making her slam against me again. Her head smacks into my mouth and I taste blood almost immediately. I cry out and cup my mouth with my hand. I can feel the inside of my mouth where my tooth just cut it starting to swell.

"Oh God, Olivia, I'm so sorry! BACK OFF YOU FUCKING ASSHOLES," I hear Pyper start screaming, trying to get us away from Dylan and Ken, but they just won't listen. People around us start to realize there's a problem and finally, I see someone pull Ken away from Pyper. He's a big guy and I hope he is a bouncer. I'm still struggling to get away from Dylan when I hear, "Get the fuck off her."

I freeze.

I can't move.

I know that voice.

It haunts my dreams and my memories.

I am still cupping my mouth and I look over at Pyper, eyes wide to see her eyes matching my own while she's looking at the person standing behind me.

I feel Dylan get pulled away from me and the voice I could never forget says, "Ian, escort both of them the hell out of here. They are not to return again, ever."

I very slowly begin to turn around and look right into the eyes of Luke Easton. The first boy I ever truly loved. The first boy that ever broke my heart. My high school sweetheart. The boy that I've never been able to forget. The boy that was supposed to love me forever.

That boy is now a man and he takes my breath away, his blue eyes as mesmerizing as I remember.

I sucked in a breath. I feel sick.

"Hello, Olivia."

I remove my hand from my mouth, open it to respond…

And throw up on his feet.

M. Clarke

Something Great

Sneak Peek
Smash Into You
by Shelly Crane—Summer 2013

<u>ONE</u>
It was a case of mistaken identity.
The kind that ended with appalled, parted lips and evil glares.
The worst kind.
The girl was cute enough. Cute wasn't the problem nor the solution for me. I needed to blend and be invisible in the most plain-as-day way and girls like this, girls who just walked up to guys because they had hope somewhere deep inside them that I would fall for that pretty face were the opposite of plain-as-day. Those kinds of girls got guys killed. At least the kind that were on the run.
She had mistaken me for a normal guy.
And this girl who approached, who could see that I was already surrounded by two, which was more girls than I knew what to do with, must've thought I had a hankering for something sweet. Because when she spoke, her words were soft and almost made me want to get to know her instead of send her packing. But I couldn't stay in this town. It was better to hurt her now when she wasn't invested than it would be to leave one day without a trace.
The girls who were currently soaking up my attention - that they thought they had - they'd move on to their next prey and forget I ever existed. But sweet girls got attached and asked questions.
Don't stop running...

I swallowed and stared bored at her as she finally made her way to me from across the hall. She tucked her hair behind her ear gently and smiled a little. "Hi, uh, can I just-"

Showtime. "Honey, that's real sweet, but I'm not interested." I slid my arm around one of my groupies. I didn't even know her name, but they were always within arm's reach. "As you can see I have my hands full already, but thanks for offering."

She scoffed and looked completely shocked. I took her in, head to foot. She *was* cute. She had a great little body on her and her face was almond shaped. He lips looked…sweet. She was not the kind I wanted within ten feet of me. She was still standing there. I had to send her packing.

I grinned as evilly as I could muster and felt a small twinge of guilt at the vulnerable look of her. I looked away quickly. I didn't even want to remember her face. "Run along, sweetheart. Go find a tuba player, I'm sure he's more your speed. Like I said, I'm not interested."

She didn't glare, and that was a first. Most of the girls who approached a guy were confident, I mean that was the reason they thought they had a chance, right? But she looked a little…destroyed. When her lips parted, it was in shock, it was to catch her breath. I continued my bored stance, though at this point, it pained me in my chest.

But I was doing the best thing for this and any other girl. People who got involved with me were collateral damage when Biloxi came around. He was a ruthless bastard and if he found me and knew someone cared about me, or worse, that I cared about someone, he'd be all over them.

So when she turned without a word and swiftly made her way down the hall, I was thankful. I probably saved her life, though she had no idea. She thought I was an ass, but I was really looking out for her. That's what I told myself as I watched her go. That I had hurt her feelings for a reason, and that she'd get over it.

A slender hand crawled over my collar.

"What's this from?" she asked in a purr and slid her thumb over the long scar from my ear all the way to my chin. "Mmm, it's so sexy."

It followed my jaw line and it was not sexy. Unfortunately, it wasn't the first time some girl had said as much and it pissed me off to no end that they thought that, let alone said it out loud.

It was my reminder of what happened when I let my guard down and it was anything but sexy.

I bit down on my retort and sent her a small smile that showed her I was listening, but she had to work for my attention. "Is that right?"

"Mmhmm," she said and kissed my jaw. "I have a little scar, too." She pointed to the place between her breasts. "Right here. Wanna see it?"

I managed a chuckle. "Is there really a scar there?"

"Pick me up tonight and you can find out," she purred, making her friend giggle.

"Don't think so. Busy."

"Ahhh, boo." She pouted and let her other hand hook a finger into my waistband. "Well here's something to keep you company tonight."

And then she pulled me down by my collar and kissed me. I tried not to cringe away, but her lip gloss was sticky and sweet. When she tried to open my mouth with her tongue, I pushed her away gently with my hands wrapped around her bony arms.

"Let's keep this PG, honey. Settle down."

She giggled. I knew she would.

It was the last week of school. It was my last week to pretend that I was still *in* high school. The next time I made a move to evade Biloxi, I'd enroll in college because I was getting too old to be a high schooler. I didn't know where I was going. I would have graduated from high school already, but at the rate I was going, I didn't know if I would have *actually* graduated or not. School was not a place of learning for me, it was a cover, a place to blend in and be normal until Biloxi found me and then I'd be gone to the next place.

This was my life. No time or want for girls, no parties, no movies, no parents.

This was my life, but it wasn't a life at all.

Six months and one lonely birthday later…

College towns sucked.

The big one.

I had only been here for a couple of weeks. It was part of my cover. I practically chanted those words in my mind as I trudged everywhere I went and worked my butt off. But one thing remained the same. Desperate girls ran rampant and I still wasn't interested. Every once in a while, they were good for a distraction if need be, but mostly…not interested. There was this one chick, Kate, who would not take no for a answer. She'd 'found' me over the summer when I was apartment hunting and hadn't 'lost' me yet, no matter how hard I tried. To get her to go away one time, I'd even given her my phone number. I was going to ditch it in a couple weeks anyway when I undoubtedly had to move again, so it didn't matter, right?

Wrong.

The girl was as annoying as a Chihuahua all hopped up 'cause there's a knock at the door. The texting and come-hithers were nonstop.

And now, as I stared out into the dark rain to see a POS car sideways in the road, I knew the world hated me, had to, because someone had just smashed her car into my truck.

I got out and braced myself. It wasn't easy to pay cash for new cars every time I needed to skip town. It was hard living when you couldn't be who you really were. Finding people to pay you under the table was almost impossible these days.

I groaned and glared at the beauty standing at the end of my truck. "Look at that!"

"I'm so sorry," she began. I could tell she really was, but I was beyond pissed. "I'll call my insurance company right now."

That stopped me. "No!" I shouted and she jolted at the verbal assault. "No insurance."

"Well," she pondered, "what do you mean? I have good insurance."

"But I don't."

She turned her head a bit in thought and then her mouth fell open as she realized what I was saying. "You don't have *any* insurance, do you?"

"No," I answered. "Look. Whatever, we'll just call this even-steven, because you did hit *me*."

"Even-steven my butt!" she yelled and scurried to jump in front of me, blocking my way.

"And what a cute butt it is."

Even through the noise of water hitting metal, I heard her intake of breath. The rain pelted us in the dark. I hoped no one came around the corner. It would be hard for them to see us here in the middle of the road. She might get hurt. Then I wondered why I cared.

"Look, buddy," she replied and crossed her arms. It drew my eyes to her shirt. My eyes bulged 'cause that shirt…well, it was see-through now. She caught on and jerked her crossed arms higher. "How dare you! You're on a roll in the jerkface department, you know that!"

"My specialty," I said and saluted as I climbed in my truck. "Get your pretty butt in your car and let's pretend this never happened, shall we?"

Because if cops and insurance were brought into this, I'd be on the run sooner than I thought.

She huffed. "Excuse me-"

"Darling. Car. Now." She glared. "Like right now."

She threw her hands up in the air and yelled, "I knew chivalry was dead!" before climbing in her car and driving away. She didn't know it, but I was being as chivalrous as they come. I made sure she got out of the rain and back into her car, even though she didn't like the way I did it, and I got her as far away from me as I could.

In my book, I deserved a freaking medal for being so chivalrous. Because people that stuck with me didn't live long.

M. Clarke

Just ask my mom.

Oh, wait, you can't. She died long, long years ago saving my life. I refused to bring anyone onto this sinking ship with me. If it finally did go down, I was going down alone.

I made my way back to my place and parked in the lot. I took the stairs two at a time to my crappy apartment and plopped myself on my bed, feeling a sudden exhaustion settle over me. The facade, the lies, the daily life of me wore down on me like rubber sneakers on pavement. I felt raw and ground up. I wondered how long I could actually live like this before I collapsed in on myself.

The tune of *Bohemian Rhapsody* alerted me that I had a message. I jerked it from my front pocket and looked at the text from Zander. He was the school's resident party boy and he was definitely the kind of guy that I always found when I went to a new town. Because a guy that threw parties on the fly could *get things*, and for a guy on the run, I needed someone like that. I texted him back that, yeah, I'd come to the anti-frat party he was throwing tomorrow night. I had no classes. I only took one elective night class, that was only in session two nights a week, just so I could say that I was a college student there, but I really wasn't. And the class? Freaking Spanish. Odio españoles.

x

I showed up to work with exactly thirty-seven seconds to spare. I blamed gorgeous-crash-into-me-girl. I swore my truck was acting funny and I had no cash to fix it.

I nodded to Pepe, the owner, and winked at Mesha, the wife of the owner. She giggled behind her hand, and so our day began just like every other day. Pepe owned a feed store and the guy had muscles the size of tangerines. So, that was my job description. In fact, on occasion, he even called me that instead of-

"Hey, we need muscle up here!"

I shook my head. "Yep!"

I trotted up front to help the dude in duds load thirteen bags of chicken feed. It wasn't a glamorous job by any means, and the pay was *caca*, but it kept me fit and busy. That was what I needed. If I had to up and leave, I wouldn't be leaving the guy in a jam because guys like me were a dime a dozen.

The day wore on and at punch-out time, I felt a familiar hand reach across my back. Slither was more like it. "Hey, Jude."

"Mesha," I mumbled back without turning and rolled my annoyed eyes. Were all women the same? They never wanted me for anything but a good time and then see ya later. Which was great for my life, but dang did it get old. Especially since the tune never changed.

"Pepe's playing cards tonight." The insinuation hissed from her lips in what I'm sure she thought was a sexy whisper. It made my skin crawl.

"That's great for him." I grabbed my metal lunchbox and turned the other way, the long way around the back, but it was worth it to evade her.

"That's it?" she practically yelled. "I thought you'd jump on it?"

I stopped. Dang. She just caught me on a wrong day. I turned. "Why? Because of what you've got between your legs? Honey, there's a hundred girls on speed dial. Sorry. I'm a busy guy."

And wait for it..."You're such an ass, Jude! I was just testing you anyway!"

I waved above my head and kept going. Women. Typical.

I threw my lunchbox through the open truck window and prayed the truck would start as I climbed in. She sputtered, but held out, I'll give her that. I tapped and rubbed the dash. "Come on, girl. Come on."

She cranked and I drove straight to the auto parts place. I popped the hood and waved away the heated smoke. I sighed and closed my eyes. Mother...this was going to cost a paycheck to fix, which I didn't have to spare. I went inside and priced a radiator. I almost punched the man in his teeth when he told me the price. "Are they made with titanium now and I'm just out of the loop?"

"Economy's bad for everyone, son."

I held the counter with both hands and hung my head. "Well...dang."

"Look, uh, I might need a little help here tomorrow. If you come help me for the day, I'll take half off the radiator, all right?"

I looked up, unable to stop the incredulous look. People didn't do good deeds for nothing. It just wasn't the world we lived in any longer. But I looked up into the older man's eyes and saw that he was serious. There was a story there. A son, maybe, a nephew, he was trying to make up for. I didn't want to know. I didn't want to get attached.

"You serious?"

"Dead," he countered.

I spoke slowly, "OK. I can be here at around two when I get off from my job. That all right?"

"Yep. I need some help stocking the shelves, so that's perfect. I'll work you a full eight hours," he warned.

"It's worth it." I swallowed and hesitated. "Thank you."

"Sure thing, son."

I nodded and turned to head back to my busted truck, not real sure what to think. But for now, I'd take it.

As soon as I got home, I showered and threw on some clean jeans with my boots and a button-up. The party was going strong by the time I arrived. Zander met me in a flourish at the door, the non-stop host. He offered me smokes and dopes and every kind of liquor under the sun. I waved him off and took a soda from the fridge. I never had been a drinker, and taking things to make me disoriented and off my game wasn't smart for someone who needed his head on straight at all times. I hopped up on the counter and nodded my head to some of the guys that always hung around Zander. "Hey, man."

"Jude! Didn't think you'd make it," he yelled over the music and bumped my fist. "Dude, the honeys are in full force tonight." He grinned this calculated little grin. "Zetas are here, dude. Zetas."

I laughed. "I thought this was an anti-frat party?"

"Fraternity, no. Sorority, yes!"

I shook my head as he took off laughing. "Idiot," I muttered under my breath with a laugh.

"Who, me?" I heard the sugary voice and dreaded looking up. I didn't even know why I came out. I didn't think I had the energy to play this game tonight.

I lifted my face to find one of the party circle regulars. She wasn't one of those awful girls who slept with anything that hit on her and purred all over you. She was a harmless flirt and a pretty sweet girl. Which was why I always tried to steer clear. Sweet and harmless meant I'd just hurt them instead. I couldn't do it. "Hey, Lila. How's it going?"

She sipped her red Solo cup and shook her head in a cute noncommittal way. "Ehh. There's way too many girls here tonight." She peeked back and laughed at Zander trying to keep up with someone on the dance floor. "See? How can I compete with *that*?"

We both watched as the clearly intoxicated girl fell all over the place in her gyrations. "Yeah," I agreed. "All right. See you later."

"Wanna dance later, maybe?" I hated the hopefulness in her voice.

"Nah, not tonight." I hopped down and left without a backwards glance, calling over my shoulder. "See you around, OK?"

They were playing Eminem and I was so over it. This whole scene...just over it. Maybe it was time to start looking for a new identity. Instead of college towns, maybe I could try a farm town or something. I was young, but been forced to grow up too much, too fast, too soon. I just wanted quiet and peace, even if for just a small amount of time.

On my way out, I waved to Zander so he would know I was gone. Just as I turned back, lightning struck up my spine. Daggum....it was her.

The girl who crashed into me.

My feet made up their mind before my head did and I was walking her way. She was leaning against the hall wall by the stairs and was currently being cornered by a guy with two red cups in his hands. She was trying to politely wave him off while simultaneously looking for someone in the crowd. Or maybe that was just a decoy move to make this guy go away.

Before I could think, I found myself helping her with that problem. "Beat it."

END OF PREVIEW
You can find information on Shelly and her books at her website
http://shellycrane.blogspot.com/

Sneak Peek
Diary of a One-Night Stand
by Alexandrea Weiss—out now.
www.facebook.com/pages/To-My-Senses

"You're here," a deep voice said in front of her.

Kara opened her eyes and beheld Scott Ellsworth's handsome face. He was wearing a long-sleeved white shirt and a pair of gray slacks. His dark, wavy hair looked a bit disheveled, as if he too had been anxiously weighing the pros and cons of their meeting. His deep-set gray eyes gazed up and down her slim figure.

"I wasn't sure you would come," he admitted as he stood back from the door.

"I told you on the phone I would be here."

Kara walked into the suite and took in the finely decorated living area. To her right she spied a gold sofa, coffee table, and two matching gold and mahogany chairs. Beyond the living room there was a small bar with a sink and mini refrigerator. Placed atop the bar were two crystal flutes, with a silver ice bucket sitting between them. In the bucket was an open bottle of Veuve Clicquot La Grande Dame.

She turned back to Scott. "Champagne?" She raised one blond eyebrow. "That's rather cheesy, don't you think?"

Scott closed the door. "I figured it would help get you in the mood."

Kara tossed her black purse onto the couch. "In the mood?" Kara arched one eyebrow as she walked up to him. "That's what foreplay is for, isn't it?"

Scott put his arm about her slim waist. "So, am I to skip all of my well-planned seduction material and just get right to it then? That's rather a lot of pressure to put on a man, Kara."

Kara gracefully ran her hands up his white shirt. "I thought you were the kind of man who worked better under pressure."

Scott grinned. "Yes, I am."

He placed his other arm about her and pulled her close. His eyes drank in the aristocratic curve of her chin, dainty nose, exquisite cheekbones, and round, red mouth.

"We've waited long enough," he mumbled, and then he lowered his lips to hers.

Sneak Peek
Crossroads Saga, book 1 by Mary Ting (Free on kindle and nook)
(Crossroads, Between, Beyond, Eternity, Halo City)
www.facebook.com/crossroadsbook

I started walking in circles around him, engrossed by his wings. His shirt was torn on the back. From where the wings protruded out, there were long slits to form an upside-down V. He was beautiful, his wings were beautiful, and I was even more in awe of him.

Perhaps my reaction embarrassed him, as he quickly closed them. It was amazing how they completely disappeared without a trace of their existence remaining. Even his shirt showed no sign that it had been torn to allow such a phenomenon.

"May I please take a look again? For me, please?" I pleaded.

"You're not freaked out?" He looked utterly astonished.

"Should I be?" I wondered why he felt embarrassed about his precious gift.

"I thought it might freak you out. Something not by human standards."

I leaned closer and placed my hands on his shoulders. "I'm not freaked out. I think you are amazing just the way you are. I wouldn't want you to be any other way," I said tenderly, trying to sound convincing with my words and through my body language.

His eyes were still steady on the ground. I needed to try harder to make him understand that there was nothing freakishly wrong with him, and that his wings were just as incredible as he was.

"Michael, please, open for me," I pleaded again, with my hands still resting on his shoulders. Then I gave him the biggest smile, hoping he couldn't resist, and he would do as I asked.

He opened gracefully, slowly expanding, not to rush the excitement of what I wanted to see again. I placed both of my hands gently on this mysterious gift and stroked them like they were gold. I was amazed by the many delicate layers of feathers, soft as cashmere and smooth as silk, but equally taken aback by the power and strength they exuded.

The same wondrous feeling had rushed through my senses when I was wrapped inside them after the fall, just before I had panicked. Had I known then that they were Michael's wings, I would have stayed there for eternity.

Slowly I turned my back toward him and tried to wrap myself inside his wings again. I wanted to be back in the arms of an angel, back to the feeling of peace that was so desired. He fidgeted away from me, mumbling, "This is too dangerous. I won't be able to control myself." His voice was worried and low.

I didn't heed his warning. When I pulled him closer, he ultimately gave in, and held me gently with both of his arms and wings this time. All I needed was his touch, for him to hold me that way; it made all the difference in the world. I was safe again. Without thought, I turned toward him.

The look in his eyes was so tempting, telling me that he wanted me too. I knew it was impossible for him to want and need me the same way, but his eyes told me something else. The depth of my yearning and what I wanted to do at that moment were undeniable.

I leaned toward him and tenderly placed a kiss on his supple lips to thank him. It was an innocent kiss. What was the harm in just one small kiss? I was extremely surprised that he didn't push me away. I was even more surprised at myself, since I was never the type to make the first move.

"Thank you for saving me," I whispered, looking straight into his soulful eyes, as something came over me. He was right. It was dangerous, but it was me who couldn't control myself. His eyes gave me permission to continue, so I gave him another kiss, but slower and longer this time. His lips were warm and sweet like honeysuckle, just how I imagined they would be. When he kissed me back it was hesitant, but it was enough to spread heat through my body like a blazing fire.

Still holding me, he pulled me away with a sudden jerk as his eyes pierced into mine with anger. His left hand was tightly wrung around my hair and the other gripped my shirt so I could feel the tightness from it. Panting, wanting more of him, I forgot how to breathe, and so did he.

His eyes, still fierce with anger, gripped me even tighter as he slightly pushed and pulled me, fighting and uncertain of what he wanted to do. Feeling petrified, I had to prepare myself for the consequence of my actions, for I knew I had crossed the line.

I was waiting for him to release me and push me away. I also anticipated the lecture he would preach about how humans and angels couldn't have any physical contact. Recalling the last time, he suddenly stopped as we almost kissed. Then, he drew me even closer, and kissed me hungrily. Passion that I never knew could be possible claimed both of us. My toes curled, feeling immense pleasure that tingled to the very depth of my being as my fingers tugged lightly on his muscular shoulders. Then his wings were totally wrapped around us.

We were in the dark, just Michael and me inside the cocoon of his wings. I couldn't believe what was happening...our first real kiss. Pressing his whole body against mine, I could feel his heart racing just as fast as mine was. We both lost control, and every part of me quivered with intense pleasure I had never felt before.

M. Clarke

About the Author

Mary Ting resides in Southern California with her husband and two children. She enjoys oil painting and making jewelry. Writing her first novel, Crossroads Saga, happened by chance. It was a way to grieve the death of her beloved grandmother, and inspired by a dream she once had as a young girl. When she started reading new adult novels, she fell in love with the genre. It was the reason she had to write one-Something Great. Why the pen name, M Clarke? She tours with Magic Johnson Foundation to promote literacy and her children's chapter book-No Bullies Allowed

Blog: www.marytingbooks.blogspot.com
Facebook: www.facebook.com/authormclarke
Facebook: www.facebook.com/crossroadsbook
Tweet: @MaryTing
Goodreads:
http://www.goodreads.com/author/show/4388953.Mary_Ting
Book   Trailer:
http://www.youtube.com/watch?v=z1Z9xLucouc&feature=em-upload_owner